THE ATOM CURTAIN

By
NICK BODDIE WILLIAMS

I0541395

ARMCHAIR FICTION
PO Box 4369, Medford, Oregon 97504

*For more information about Armchair Books and products, visit our
website at…*

www.armchairfiction.com

Or email us at…

armchairfiction@yahoo.com

HE BROKE THE BARRIER
TO A CONTINENT IN EXILE!

For two hundred and seventy years America had been totally cut off from the rest of the world by an impenetrable wall of raging atomic fury. To the frightened countries of the Old World, what had once been the greatest of all powers was now the most fearful of all mysteries.

No man ached to know what lay behind that frightful barrier more than Emmett O'Hara, restless air-sentinel of the International Patrol—whose American ancestors had been stranded in Britain the day the Atom Curtain was raised.

Then, on December 20, in the year 2230, while on routine patrol, O'Hara did the impossible. He broke through the barrier—and lived! But the full story of O'Hara's discoveries and adventures in Atomic America is so utterly breath-taking that readers are sure to rate it a classic of modern science-fiction.

FOR A COMPLETE SECOND NOVEL, TURN TO PAGE 153

CAST OF CHARACTERS

EMMETT O'HARA
He was an ace pilot for the International Patrol, but when a storm pushed him into the Curtain, it was by sheer luck he survived.

ARTHUR BLAIR
As a reporter he meant to tell O'Hara's story. Unfortunately there was someone who didn't want the people to hear it.

ANSTRUTHER
He was one of the best pilots around, but after meeting "Father" and "the Degraded," he became hungry for power—fearfully so.

NEDRA
This warrior bride would rather be dead than be taken by the Degraded. The question was…could O'Hara win her back—alive?

STEPHEN "FATHER" BRYCE
This ancient scientist was in an unenviable position; he alone controlled all the lands and sky under the Atom Curtain.

THE ELDER
The wisest and oldest man of Nedra's cave-dwelling clan; he had a fondness for Colts, and other technology.

THE TWELVE OLD MEN OF GENEVA
To these old rulers change was dangerous…and they weren't above using any means necessary to keep things as they were.

PART ONE

Now at last I must make this accusation and disclose the truth.

I make it with the hard realization of the dangers that are inherent for us all. I make it knowing that these risks have terrified those whom we chose to govern us, and I make it only because their terror has paralyzed their minds. And you and I—the world as we know it—cannot wait any longer.

We must not underestimate these risks. We take the chance of losing everything that mankind has accomplished in the tens of thousands of years since our first ancestor shed his tail and rose erect and walked in the full consciousness that he, alone of all God's creatures, had a soul.

But it is a risk we must take. We must take it now, while there is still time, or we condemn our world—the countless billions of Europe and Asia and Africa—forever to our chronic agonies of hunger and disease, which I now know are needless.

Between what we stand to lose and what it is possible to achieve, if we act wisely and in time, there is a middle course which means freedom from starvation and pestilence. The truth is that we need fear only our greed. If we can content ourselves with enough, and not insist upon too much, if we act with iron resolution in this immediate future, we can revivify our static history. The facts as I know them convince me of this, and more to the point, they have convinced far abler minds, although not those of the World Council of Nations, which in the final analysis means the Twelve Old Men of Geneva. It is their minds which you and I must now convince. Or we must set the Twelve Old Men aside.

And so I am compelled before the bar of public opinion to accuse these Twelve Old Men. It was they alone, acting in secrecy, who ordered that the sensational O'Hara Report be buried deep within the archives of the International Patrol at Geneva, never— they thought—to be made public. They have buried the Report and they have attempted to blot out even the vague rumor that it did exist. Those few who actually read it, the officials at Croydon

Airport here in London who first received it and sent it sealed upon its way to Geneva, have been transferred to the more remote corners of the earth, never two of them together and none of them knowing where the other is. Not more than a fraction of the upper hierarchy in government has even heard of the Report and that fraction has gone and will continue to go to extreme lengths to prevent inquiries concerning it. It is the greatest hush-hush document of all time.

But within hours of its receipt at Croydon, I, Arthur Blair, obtained a first-hand summary of the Report. For reasons which will become obvious I was ordered by my paper, the *Observer*, to obtain the text of it, and for reasons which were even more imperative to me I sought to do it. I went at once to Croydon, where I was rewarded only by blank and noncommittal stares, as if I were inquiring after the secrets of the fourth dimension or the precise geographical location of the lost continent of Mu.

I did not resent that attitude. I had expected it. But what I did not anticipate was the reaction of the Twelve Old Men. I was in Paris, on my way to Geneva, before I realized how far they meant to go to silence me. The warning was delivered by a small, clean-shaven little man in a business suit who called while I was absent from my hotel room. When I returned, he smilingly assured me that he had no interest in me—the condition of my luggage proved him a liar—and in the next breath told me that my chance of leaving Paris alive, if my direction was Geneva, was less than zero.

The little man in the business suit impressed me. A more oblique approach and possibly some short cuts were indicated. In consequence I went from Paris quite openly to the resort of Trieste. I spent three weeks there, as obviously "resorting" as I could, until the night I chose for departing aboard a chartered fishing boat that landed me eventually at Salonika.

An old acquaintance of mine at Salonika, an incurable romantic, suspecting me of extraordinary journalism—a missing blonde, perhaps—provided me with what I asked, a private plane for the Prefecture of Turkey.

That plane was shot down two minutes after leaving Salonika. I happened not to be aboard it, although my labeled luggage was. I had the satisfaction of reading an account of my accidental death in the Istanbul press when I arrived there two days later.

I felt certain that I had thrown off any pursuit and that I could now proceed safely direct to Geneva. You may imagine my concern when my host in Istanbul, who knew me only by a pen name I had used obscurely years before, offered me my morning coffee and then sipped his own, and immediately keeled over.

A charge of murdering my host was subsequently filed against me. That charge is outstanding today. I do not doubt the evidence is there to convict me, manufactured evidence, were I located and returned to the Prefecture, of Turkey.

But I have no intention of being located until the world knows what I have to tell. I had no such intention from the moment I saw my host's complexion changing to that ugly blue that goes with cyanic poisoning. And before the spittle upon his writhing lips was dry—it was intended that they should have been my lips—I had disappeared again.

All this scrambling is a personal matter, an adventure I suppose, of no importance save to those who befriended me. Some of them are dead and beyond the dangerously long arm of the World Council's Bureau of Security. Some of them are not dead or aware that they ran the risk of death, for I did not share the purpose of my frantic journey home. Yet I cannot—I dare not—trace any further the slow zigzagging pattern by which I returned to London.

My journey was a failure. I did not get the text of the O'Hara Report. I am never going to get it, for the august authority which decreed my persecution has consigned it to oblivion. That authority was unquestionably the Twelve Old Men.

Yes, theirs must be this terrible responsibility. Theirs alone must be the blame if future generations of our world are doomed so needlessly to subhuman levels. It is they who have decided—unless we can break through the lethargy of hypercautious minds—that in this year of A.D. 2230, more than two hundred and eighty-five years after the first splitting of the atom, the Sahara must still remain the Sahara a vast wasteland capable of feeding all our starving and multiplying billions were only water made available. It is they who decree by their conspiracy of silence that the deserts of Australia and Arabia and China are as parched today, and the tundras of Siberia as utterly fruitless, as they were in the years before the miracle of Los Alamos. It is they, these dread-chilled Twelve Old Men, who are insisting that the Western Hemisphere, which at one time seemed destined to redeem us all from want, must remain for further centuries a whispered mystery behind its impenetrable Atomic Curtain.

Why are they doing this to us? Why were they so determined that I must be silenced? Are they brutal men, incapable of understanding how our billions suffer? No, the answers are not so simple. Their minds grope vague through the twilight world of doubt and fear, for they do not trust us—by their very natures they cannot trust us—to guide ourselves according to the facts laid down in the O'Hara Report.

But I insist that the people must know these facts. The people must get the truth—as I got the truth—from Emmett O'Hara himself.

Yes, I got the truth from Emmett O'Hara himself, soon after he filed at Croydon the text of his astonishing Report. That is why my life is at forfeit—not that the Twelve Old Men are sure I know, but they suspect it. They are capable at least of decision in one respect, they will do anything to preserve the status quo. But they are panicked at the possibilities that Emmett O'Hara has brought back to us. They cannot bring themselves, these doubting old men, to believe that he is acting in the interests of both our world and that which lies behind the Atomic Curtain, the fabled Western Hemisphere. And they will never accept, unless we force them—and there is almost no time left to do it now—the offer that O'Hara brought to us.

That offer will come to us formally, and we will have to act on it at once, at any moment in these next few days. And I pledge you this, that if we accept, our world begins to live again. And theirs.

I wish for your peace of mind that I could tell you precisely what has happened to O'Hara and that magnificent creature whom he introduced to me as his wife. And she was his wife, I think. Certainly she was his woman, bound to him by all the custom of that strange society from which she came. And if O'Hara had the time, in the brief interval between the filing of his Report and his abrupt and traceless disappearance, I would like to think that he further complied with the laws under which he was born and reared, although I know it would not have mattered to anyone except myself—O'Hara would not have cared. And she would not have given a snap of her exquisite and completely capable fingers. What could possibly have seemed of value in our conventions to those two? When you know what they knew—or at least what O'Hara knew—when you have experienced the nadir of disillusion and the zenith of human living, what could seem of essential value except the savor of the next moment's breath?

As I say, O'Hara vanished. He filed this Report of his in London at four o'clock on the afternoon of his return, which was the day after Christmas. He immediately went to his old flat in Bloomsbury from which he telephoned to me at the *Observer*, and at six o'clock I dined with him. By eight o'clock I had heard from him the substance of his Report. It was then that I met his wife, if wife she was.

At eight-fifteen I left them, and went immediately to the *Observer*, where for two hours I was in conference with the Editorial Director, Edgar Soames, who told me that the story could not be published without the complete documentation of the text. The *Observer*, as Soames pointed out, had its reputation as a journal of fact to remember and not even the paramount importance of my story could be permitted to override that.

Very well, documentation. I returned to O'Hara's flat in Bloomsbury by eleven o'clock. O'Hara was not there, nor was that splendid red-haired creature who—well, they were gone, and their few belongings were gone, and the flat itself, so I was told repeatedly by the manager of the properties, had not been occupied at all for the past three years. Surely I was mistaken—O'Hara? Never heard of an Emmet O'Hara!

No, the manager had never heard of an Emmett O'Hara. And neither, I soon discovered, had anyone else. He seemed to be a delusion I had suffered. I had spent those two hours listening to his amazing Report, and there had never been such an O'Hara in the International Patrol and the letters that I had earlier received from him had never been written. Or they were forgeries, perhaps—yellow journalism!

Someone had moved very swiftly. But whether it was O'Hara himself, or whether it was the Bureau of Security, I could not determine. It is essential for me—and the rest of us—in this hour of imminent crisis to rely upon faith in his indomitable skill and courage, and to believe he managed his escape. Although he had had his luck twice over.

That was a phrase that O'Hara used himself. "I have had my luck twice over," he told me, and then he laughed, that deep roar of mirth that I remembered from our school days together.

"Twice over?" I answered. "A thousand times, I should say."

"I don't mean this business I've been telling you," O'Hara said. "Or rather, not the hazard of death. Although," he smiled, "there is the hazard of death in this part of it too. Will you come into the next room? I want you to see Nedra."

"Nedra?"

"Yes," he said. "Nedra. You didn't think I'd leave her there?"

I stared at him. "Is this in your Report?"

"Certainly not. It is a private matter. But the boys at Croydon saw her when we landed there. I remember their surprise—more surprised even, I suppose, than when I wirelessed that I was coming in, and that knocked them flat. Are you coming with me?"

"Yes."

"Then get behind me," he cautioned. "And hand me that gadget."

It was a length of intricately carved wood, about four feet long, tapering toward one end and worn smooth by the palms of many hands. O'Hara took it, tossed it into the air and caught it expertly by the smaller end, a trick that must have taken practice. "Very useful," he said, "if living is important—though I'm not too sure that it is. We live too long, most of us, and at last we begin to think that living is an end in itself. And so we want it easier and easier, with never a thought that it can become too easy."

"You haven't found it easy lately, have you, O'Hara?"

"Not until I landed at Croydon," he replied. "But that was four hours ago and it's gotten boring." He gripped the club of carved wood tightly. "Now, open that door—"

So it had gotten boring, had it? Within three hours O'Hara had vanished, both he and Nedra, as if they had never existed. I should have known that I was not going to get documentation for any such articles in the *Observer*. I must have been bemused by my real joy at seeing O'Hara again after supposing that he was lost forever. Then, too, the impact of what he had told me had blunted my sense of the realities of life. For the moment I saw it all only as a tremendous story—a story particularly tremendous to O'Hara and myself because of our mutual origin.

For we were children together, went to school together, were inseparable until he chose for his career the thankless if adventurous life of a pilot in the International Patrol. I cannot say that I chose my own career—I drifted into it, as so many journalists do, trying my hand first at this and that and gradually retreating into the job of writing about what others, with more spirit or greater advantage, were doing in this world.

Yet it never occurred to me in those early days that the biggest job that I would undertake would be writing about O'Hara. Nor to him, I am sure. Adventure—yes, he had expected adventure, but not of the sort to interest anyone except himself and possibly his surviving relatives. The doubtful thrills of supersonic speed, the sensation of flirting with death from atomic poisoning, the constant prospect of plunging through the polar icecap at better than two thousand miles an hour—these, perhaps, O'Hara anticipated as the ultimate possibilities of his career in the Patrol. And then, always, he would be closest to the riddle that since his childhood had absorbed him, flying his charted course along the outer fringes of that dense wall of radiation that enclosed like the half of a glass globe the Western Hemisphere—the Atomic Curtain.

Neither of these were careers a native of the Prefecture of Britain would have selected, but the truth is that they were among the best open to us. Our two families had come together to England in that great migration from North America which immediately preceded the establishment of the Atomic Curtain. I remember O'Hara, then not quite eighteen years old, questioning his father one night when I was visiting him, as I often did, for he was my idol in those days, much bigger than I and much bolder. I had never dared to ask these things.

"Why did our people leave America?" he asked. "It was their country, wasn't it?"

"Yes, their country," his father answered solemnly, for that word—*country*—still had a peculiarly religious sound to it, however outmoded it had now become. "But they—your ancestor and those who agreed with him—believed that what America was going to do was wrong."

"Excuse me, sir, I don't see why it was," O'Hara said. "If the Americans—the Yanks"—and how he loved that word—"didn't like the rest of the world, why shouldn't they have cut themselves off from it?"

"I'm sorry, Emmett, you're too immature to understand," his father answered.

"Isn't that the answer that men give when they themselves do not understand?" O'Hara persisted, and I held my breath.

But his father considered that, as he always considered anything O'Hara said—they were people of logic, people of the exploring turn of mind. At last he said, "Yes, that is true. I've never really understood why they did it. When I was your age, I asked my father these same questions. It seemed unfair that we should have given up what I had so often heard was a considerable position in that world—in North America—to come to this crowded hemisphere as emigrants, as a suspected people, second class by birth and law, and solely in obedience to the dictates of an ideal. But your grandfather himself was a little vague upon these points— after all, he did not remember the trip, he had only heard of it, how his people had been forced to give up all possessions, to begin life anew in a country already too poor to support its own citizens."

"You mention an ideal, sir," O'Hara said. "What is it?"

"It was that this was one world, or should have been one world, not irrevocably halved by the Atomic Curtain. It was that if Providence had wished them separate worlds. It would have made them so."

"Then it was a mistaken ideal," O'Hara said, "for if Providence had intended this to be one world, it would be now."

His father smiled. "That's enough, my young philosopher. To bed with you!"

And so we went to bed, but not to sleep, for O'Hara was excited by the conversation. He lay flat upon the counterane, his cheekbones pressed against the butts of his palms and his dark eyes restless, seeming lighted by the intense curiosity of his young mind, talking on and on for hours, long after I was drowsy.

"It's always been like that," he told me. "Down through the countless centuries of time—when a people have made a bad decision and have lost everything by it, they have described their motive as obedience to an ideal. Remember your American history?"

"How could I remember it?" I asked. "Nobody teaches that."

"They used to teach it. And they still have the books at Oxford. Great reading, too—the Revolution, the Civil War, the three World Wars. You'd be astonished how often that theme recurs in them—obedience to an ideal. Yes, I suppose it's true, those of us who left the Western Hemisphere before the Atomic Curtain blamed it on an ideal. And I'd bet it's equally true that those who stayed, knowing that they would forever be isolated from the world that you and I know, invoked the same apology— an ideal guided them. Eternal peace, freedom from want and from fear—"

A clock was striking somewhere in the house. It was one o'clock. I shivered without knowing why.

"And did they find it, I wonder?" O'Hara's voice resumed. "What has happened to the Americans in these two hundred and seventy years since they launched the Atomic Curtain? And what would have happened to the rest of us—to Europe and Asia and Africa—if they had not launched it? For they were a wonderful people, wonderful improvisers, wonderfully inventive. Oh, I don't mean the little things that we have here, electric lights, the radio— but the big things; the sublime things that changed history—or seemed about to change it. The atomic bomb of Los Alamos, the hydrogen bomb of Bikini and the tests at Yucca Flats, those alone were leading the world into new, strange paths, glorious paths for the scientific mind, and all the world was following them swiftly. All of us were to have the blessings along with the horrors of atomic fission, until—"

"I know that much," I said. "Until the Third World War."

O'Hara smiled queerly. "So you do read some?"

"I read a great deal," I retorted. "Contemporary things, the important things, not long-forgotten books of useless American history."

"But you remember, don't you, why the Third World War stopped?"

"Oh, yes. It was thorium."

"Thorium," he whispered. "Yes, that was it—thorium. The greatest of their improvisations! For when they devised the techniques for the fission of thorium, so infinitely more plentiful in supply than uranium, no combination of powers that lacked the formulae could longer challenge them. They wrote the peace that they wanted with those formulae. And that peace forbade atomic fission for the rest of the world. No nation dared touch it, no scientist anywhere, except in America, dared to experiment with it, knowing that the slightest radiation detectable by Washington's scintillometers might bring within the next half hour obliteration, complete obliteration.

"And actually, that was the conquest of the world. Yet they chose instead of ruling their conquered world to erect around and above the Western Hemisphere that vast umbrella of radioactivity, the Atomic Curtain. And the two continents of North and South America were lost behind it as utterly as if they had been swallowed in the seas that girt their shores."

"Even with their thorium, they must have been afraid," I said.

O'Hara scoffed at me. "Of what? Maybe of themselves, maybe of their own power, but certainly of nothing else. They could have destroyed the other nations of the world, and the others were so well aware of it that they have not since risked the science of fission, still dreading the rain of warheads that might come screeching through the Atomic Curtain. Even today, although a century and a half has passed, we're still so obsessed with that dread that we maintain the International Patrol, ceaselessly flying the outer fringe of radiation in the stupid hope that if that rain of warheads comes, we shall have a warning of it. But what good would a warning do? A few minutes prayer, perhaps. For there's no defense and so it is a stupid, useless dread, made terrible because beyond the Curtain all is mystery to us, something that we no longer understand—"

"And cannot help," I pointed out.

But O'Hara did not hear me. "That's it," he cried. "The Mystery! The greatest of all powers, unknown to us, a terra incognita. I'm surprised that we, dreading them so much and knowing nothing of their mind, do not worship them, for dread and ignorance and mystery are the requisites for a god. A race of gods!"

"They may be all of that," I said. "I rather like the notion that I am descended from a race of gods. Inflates my ego, which can bear a little of it. Can't I go to sleep now?"

"Not even a race of gods could possibly keep you from that," O'Hara said, and he put out the light.

It was a fixation. What he had said was true enough—for later on I did get around to those long-forgotten useless books that gathered cobwebs in a cluttered Oxford subcellar—but for most of us, scrabbling like insects to earn a living for ourselves, the two lost continents of the Western Hemisphere were not much more important than the rings of Saturn—a phenomenon that did not drastically affect the price of eggs. We knew, of course, that the World Council kept its International Patrol circling as near the Atomic Curtain as its aircraft dared to go, but that was a problem for the Twelve Old Men of Geneva, much as the gradually extending icecaps of the two poles were their problem. Theirs and O'Hara's—and the Sunday supplements.

The point is, we had lived with the vague knowledge of the Atomic Curtain all our lives, and the whole thing was too fantastic either to understand or to matter to the average run of us. It was like the toadstools of our forests—they were quite poisonous, but so long as we did not have to touch them, we ignored them. I remember a passage from one of those books I finally unearthed at Oxford—a curious thing, possibly a fake, and yet dressed out in the most pompous language, purporting to be the considered opinion of some distinguished man of science at what apparently was a famous university, a place called Harvard, and confirming a suspicion that life was possible on Mars. Yet nowhere in the American histories of that year, nor in any of the contemporary

American publications, could I find any evidence of general alarm about it. So there was life on Mars. Presumably no one bought extra ammunition for his gun, nor hoarded food, nor drank himself to death, nor went to church more arduously because of any such remote impracticality. Who was going to Mars? And who—to bring this analogy down into our times—except the pilots of the International Patrol meant to venture toward the well-defined and fortunately distant zones contaminated by the Atomic Curtain?

Yet I must admit that something of O'Hara's fascination for it crept contagiously into the letters that came back to me from those far-flung and frigid bases out of which he flew for the Patrol. There was news in them, too, although I did not always recognize it.

The first of these letters reached me within a month after I squeaked onto the staff of the *Observer*. O'Hara had by then completed his basic indoctrination with the International Patrol and was serving his initial hitch in the least desirable of the Patrol's assignments, with nothing behind him but the Antarctic seas and the vast polar cap, not a city worth the name closer than Hobart, in Tasmania, completely across the Antarctic Circle from his base.

It must have been dull work, flying from the Falkland Islands to South Shetland, deafened by roaring jets and blinded by the frightful gales that swirled around Cape Horn, and for variety he had the constant ticking of his scintillometer telling him how closely he was approaching the southern boundary of the Atomic Curtain, quite narrow there, encompassing the Cap itself and the wild seas immediately beyond.

Dull work? I remember O'Hara's first letter: "The black sky meets the blacker water upon a horizon even more intensely black, a horizon that is a ribbon of mourning constantly below the level of my eyesight, as if these were dead seas and dead heavens. But the coloration is deceptive, for they are not dead. The howling violence that must have been the planet's birthing wail still echoes here, the raging winds that must have screeched throughout infinity when Earth ripped loose from the Sun—and beyond, ten miles ahead of me, perhaps, the Wall of Death invisibly stands shimmering.

"One second's miscalculation at the speed I fly and I'd be into it. Freezing one instant, roasted to the bone the next. How thick is that wall? The guess that we credit oftenest is twelve miles. A scant twelve miles of radioactivity, and I could fly that far in the time it would take you to snap shut the fingers of your hand—perhaps my craft on its momentum would plunge through. I think it would. I think I could aim it for the southern tip of South America, and by the time that you could walk across the editorial room there at the *Observer* in London, I would have smashed across the Atomic Curtain and landed on that coast that once was Patagonia. Isn't that a challenge? A terrific challenge to be the first within two hundred and seventy years to reach the two lost continents! But it has the undeniable drawback that I would be dead, and so could not gloat like stout Balboa on a peak in Darien.

"I saw the Curtain doing its merry routine one day last week. I was flying quite low, not a hundred feet above the surface of the sea, making a customary check upon the water's radioactivity. We do this every flight, to check upon the contamination of the water, which usually is quite constant, flowing out from below the Curtain a distance of fifty miles but decreasing in activity with an almost mathematical precision. Yet when there is a really powerful gale blowing southward or westward from the Curtain, from the tip of what once was called Chile or Argentina, both now encompassed by the Curtain, the surface currents sometimes are reversed from the Cape—the fabled Cape Horn of early mariners—and the contamination flows much further toward the Antarctic before it diffuses.

"Of course our base in the Falklands is mildly contaminated, all these fringe areas are, and all of us have a touch of the atomic sickness, just as those living in the tropics have malaria. You know what it's like—nausea sometimes, and always diarrhea, a tendency toward bleeding gums and conjunctivitis and—well, yes, dammit, falling hair, baldness. I shall resemble the egg of the great auk in another ten years of this. Sounds terrible. Actually, though, these are only tendencies, for we do not expose ourselves beyond the lowest background counts upon our scintillometers. We're taking no chances—this is a Patrol, not a combat unit, for there's nothing to combat. Nothing, nothing but that invisible curtain, at a fixed latitude and a fixed longitude for every foot of its tens of thousands of miles, with only the variances of the surface contamination that I mentioned. Which brings me back to what I meant to tell you.

"I was patrolling one hundred feet above the ocean's surface when I saw ahead of me, not quite to that black ribbon of a horizon I have described, a strange dark object apparently floating on the sea. Immediately I changed course toward it, but when I had reached the absolute limit of radioactivity that we are permitted the dark object was still ten or more miles ahead of me.

"It must have been, at that instant, extremely close to the Curtain itself. If it was not within it! Yet it was plowing toward me through heavy seas, the first moving object I had ever seen in this sector.

"I was forced to turn back. Within the fraction of a second I had lost it. But barring a gale, I had sufficient fuel for some minutes' cruising. I made a tight arc and approached again. The object was still there, and still approaching.

"I'm sure that had my squadron commander been spying upon me, he would have grounded me for life. For in the next ten minutes I flew perhaps a hundred oval patterns, approaching the object, retreating from contamination, then reapproaching, again and again, trying to keep in contact with it until it got close enough for inspection. By that time my fuel could not be further safely expended, and I wirelessed back to our Falklands base with my report, then continued on to South Shetland.

"A snowstorm screamed down on me minutes before I landed and I came in blind. Had I spent another five minutes at those oval patterns I would not have made it. Frightened me a little. I suppose I can become too damned enamored of that mystery out there.

"But delay your literary fancies a minute. There is a sequel—for we flew double patrols throughout the following week. The dark object was not sighted again upon the surface of the sea—the blizzard, I presume, obscured its week of passage. Then just yesterday a Patrol craft over South Orkney Island picked up a disturbing buzz upon its scintillometer. There should have been no such extreme contamination that far south and west of the Curtain. We threw a dozen craft into the sector within half an hour, and finally, wrecked on the craggy shores of Coronation Island, we found our dark object.

"It was hot, very hot—too dangerous to examine closely. We put an amphibian down alongside Coronation and they worked for several hours with telescopic cameras. The pictures have just been developed here. And I really did have something!

"What we've got, as nearly as we can determine from rather grainy prints, is a kind of ship, fashioned of undressed logs, a very crude and unseaworthy vessel I am sure, but also with the virtue of being unsinkable. There is a cabin of sorts admidships of it with some sheets of a shining material, similar to asbestos, tacked onto it. And close to that, extremely blurred upon our prints, are three black objects that we have decided must be men. That is, they must have been men once, before they drifted into the Atomic Curtain. They are charcoal now, but the pattern of arms and legs, however distorted in their horrible death shows distinctly. Three men upon a boat of logs from where?

"The Sandwich Islands, possibly. It would represent a tremendous voyage, thousands of miles through the worst of weather, but where else could men come from in these desolate seas?

"Unless you want to go along with me in the most improbable of fantasies—unless they came from behind the Atomic Curtain! From the Western Hemisphere from the Lost Continents! Too absurd, of course. We know the level that their civilization had achieved. They would not now be using boats so crudely built of logs, and most assuredly, if they did build it, they would not sail it into their Atomic Curtain. No—purely fantasy, and yet I like it. I would give my next promotion to go aboard that vessel! But I am not yet prepared to give my life, which it would cost me. Ten years from now, possibly, when the contamination has abated, if it does abate—jot that down, remember it—ten years from now, on Coronation Island in the Antarctic there still may be the wreckage of a boat that can reveal to us what Man behind the Atomic Curtain nowadays is like!

"Ah, well—"

Yes, there was news in that letter, but I mistook it instead for a bit of a feature, and did quite nicely with it in a little piece that must have given old Jules Verne a turn or two within his grave. Improbabilia—the pseudoscientific flare. Good reading for small boys on rainy Saturday!

O'Hara was back in London two years later, on his way to Stockholm for reassignment. I picked him up at his flat in Bloomsbury. He wore by then the three gold bars and half-globe of a lieutenancy, and in his brilliant blue uniform he seemed more than ever to me a man set apart, for not many Patrol pilots and none like O'Hara were walking the streets of London, so far removed from their duty routes. He had put on weight, a good deal of it, yet he had managed somehow to absorb it compactly— six feet three and a good two hundred and thirty pounds, his dark face burned and weathered, only less dark than a Polynesian, and his thick, clustered hair jet black—for his prediction had not come true, he was no auk's egg.

"What happened?" I asked him. "The atomic sickness?"

We were lunching together at Swall's, where the roast is excellent, and O'Hara finished his before he answered me. "I'd forgotten that," he said at last. "You get over it. I suppose you build up a tolerance for it. The first year is a little rough—you can spot a cadet immediately by his red-rimmed eyes and the unhealthy color that comes through windburn pallidly, like an underglow of yellow. And this although they're never bucking more than .165 milliroentgens an hour. Then all at once, within a month's time, you're over the hump and it goes away and you're safe enough at .225—you're safe enough, that is, for short periods of time, and unless you're a damned fool and ram yourself into the Curtain. You don't tolerate that—though you never realize it. For you don't have time. You're cinders rather instantly."

"You lose cadets?"

"A percentage—a definite percentage—three out of ten. They simply cannot seem to learn that all of this has been estimated exactly and that there is no margin for error. The Curtain is constant, and the pattern of your flight must be constant, barring the variations caused by gales, for which there is a single rule—get the hell down south before your craft is slammed into the Curtain. We had a new man last summer, though—"

He paused, his shoulders hunching forward and his eyes seeing beyond me, beyond Swall's, back into the Antarctic. His fingers tapped three times, slowly, upon the table.

"Yes?" I said.

O'Hara jumped. It seemed incredible, but he did exactly that, he jumped, as if I had screamed out at him.

"Excuse me," he said, and laughed quickly, "Lost myself for a moment. Because we've never known precisely what it was. A mistake in his readings, certainly. He must have been confused, which can and does occur when inexperienced men are making those long overwater hops. Perhaps their vision blurs. And possibly—well, we ought not to get that type, they should screen them out, but there's considerable pressure for replacements, losing 30 percent. If a candidate can pass the twenty-twenty test he's taken, but there should be a sharp downgrading on fatigue and on emotional reaction."

"Surely they get emotion ratings?"

"Yes—up to a point. But it's still not selective enough. It wasn't in Anstruther's case."

"The new man you mentioned?"

"Yes. He was in my squadron basing on the Falklands. Nice lad, well set up, an angel face—blond with blue eyes. Well educated, too, and rather religious. He had intended going into the ministry until this Patrol bug got him. I liked the boy—reminded me a great deal of myself when I first got out there. You know—eager, imaginative. I think that was the trouble—too imaginative. On that last flight of his, a pattern he'd flown a dozen times by then, down to South Shetland, it happened that I was catching his calls at our wireless hut. That's no part of my job but I was disturbed about him. Only a hunch, or was it more than that? I suspect that I knew, out of my own experience. I knew, how he felt about those hops and I should have cashiered him. But I didn't do it—you hate to do it, you've got no reason that makes sense, you'd look hysterical putting it into a report, for the boys in medical had given him the go ahead. And so I was listening to his calls, that feeling of my guilt just dormant, just across the border line from actually wirelessing him to swing away from the Curtain while he could—to turn back."

O'Hara's fingers made those three rapid taps upon the table once more. Then he continued:

"It was all so routine, I keep insisting to myself that I had no warning whatever—it was all completely routine. A series of latitude and longitude readings, the constant repetition of his milliroentgen count, quite safe. He was keeping his distance from the Curtain and had worked his way to the latitude of the Cape, the point beyond which there's no extraordinary danger, for the Curtain ends about there and the rest of it is simply overwater flying to the South Shetland base. I was beginning to relax. I was telling myself that men with premonitions are the spiritual cousins of water dousers and the little gents who peer myopically at crystal balls. And then all at once the droning of Anstruther's voice broke off.

"That could happen any time. And yet the silence slapped me. It was like that exactly, a cold slap in my face. Not over four seconds of complete silence. Then Anstruther's voice came back again and it was a scream.

"But not terror, I want to emphasize that it was not terror. The boy simply cracked. Excitement. But a shocking excitement to me, jubilation. As if he were cheering his crew to victory—a shattering vibration in the wireless and these words: 'It's gone! It's gone! There's no count. I can't find it—it's gone—the Curtain—'

"And then nothing. Never another word. Never a trace of him or the craft."

"And you think—?"

"No, we don't," O'Hara said. "We speculate, but there is no basis for thinking anything. Not the slightest clue, not the shred of a fact. Flying at better than a thousand miles an hour he could have done anything, once he'd lost control of himself like that. The bottom of the sea."

"Or rammed against the Curtain?"

"Yes. Quite probably."

"And through it?"

"You're remembering one of those silly letters I wrote you when I first got out there. I don't know—there's no evidence. But I should think his craft would atomize, I don't think he'd get through it. Whatever it was, Anstruther simply lost his bearings—

his readings definitely establish that he was not near the Curtain when he cracked, his last actual reading in milliroentgens was well within his safety limit—and then, when his mind blew up, he misinterpreted what his instruments were showing. And that killed him. Somehow, and it doesn't really matter how, that killed him. Have we time for pudding? I'm off for Stockholm at three-ten."

I did not go to Croydon to see him off. They are not keen on that in the Patrol. Farewells, I imagine, are depressing, although it would not have depressed O'Hara. Nothing was very likely to depress him for long, even Anstruther's fate. Cadets came and went, and if their officers took to heart too much that unfortunate 30 percent there were always the sanitary rules of the Twelve Old Men of Geneva, who had conceived out of their latent if stupid fear the organization of the globular operations of the Patrol. Those who became morose simply were pensioned off. Utilized, as they expressed it—they were utilized, used up, discarded. But in style and comfort, like old race horses.

A year passed before O'Hara wrote that he had got his captaincy. He was based then on Wrangell Island, one hundred miles from where the Curtain swerves toward the outmost top of Siberia, crossing the Anadyr Mountains to enclose the lost passage to the Indies, Bering Strait.

"Think how they searched for it," he wrote, speaking of the Strait. "The ancient Norse king, Bloodyaxe, hunting whale and walrus through the moving ice as far toward the east as Novaya Zembla on this Siberian coast, Sebastian Cabot in the time of Henry VIII seeking the northern sealane to Cathay—or have you dug this far yet in your histories? And John Rut of Plymouth and Hugh Willoughby who perished with his men on the Kola Peninsula, and old Barents the invincible, and Henrik Hudson driven back westward by the polar ice and so forced to explore the continent that's long since lost again, Hudson Bay and Hudson River, and dying with his young son finally while drifting in a small boat in the seas that he had opened up; until in 1728 old Vitus Bering working for the great Czar Peter pushed eastward from Okhotsk and ascertained at last the Strait—yes, history, my boy, the grand epic of the Northeast Passage, hundreds dying valiantly, and now their work forever lost, their passage closed by the impenetrable Curtain.

"Time telescopes up here. Within a day I can be above the Anadyr Gulf, the eastern reaches of the Bering Sea and not six hundred miles from where our ancestors launched rockets to obliterate the port of Vladivostok in the Third World War—the great base that was in Alaska, at Nome—I can be over the Anadyr Gulf at dawn, cross the Anadyr Mountains to our base at Wrangell and before my fuel's gone land at Bear Island, guarding the Kolyma River that flows northeast from Siberia. Refueling, I can hit New Siberia Island or our Lena River operations base as Barkin, take off with more fuel for the Yenisei, touch at Franz Josef Land, tag up in Ice Fjord in the Spitzbergens, drop down to Stockholm and be with you for roast beef at Swall's by night—provided ground crews nowhere along the line are dogging it. From the stamping grounds of Vitus Bering, year 1728, to Swall's in London, year 2230—within a day's flying. And so, what's time?

"But that's a fat route I've outlined for you—that's the easy stuff, the points we'd like to be flying between. For actually after the Curtain passes the longitude of Wrangell it curves much closer to where we presume we'd find the North American continent, south of the pole on the far side from us, crossing the vast seaborne ice sheets in its path toward the northern tip of Greenland. And for anything like an effective patrol we must fly deep isoscleles triangles toward it from our land bases strung across the top of Europe and Asia. We cannot fly for long close to the Curtain in the Arctic—we must fly toward it and then back, a series of exploratory fingers extended out to it, which is tougher than our Antarctic patrols. Over water—which means ice—and out of sight of land almost entirely. Navigation problems. Adds to the strain—there now, the nasty word! Must not say that.

"But I've seen more of Northern Europe and Siberia in the last twelve months than all the expeditions of the czars and Muscovite Bolsheviks explored in their thousand years. The debris of their two cultures lies scattered across the top of this vast Eurasian land mass, with immense glassy pockets where their cities once stood, the scars of the Third World War. And through the air that we are flying that first cloud of rockets came from the continent of North

America, leveling all Russia down to the latitude of Moscow before the ultimatum and the surrender. A creeping barrage of rockets, and I've seen the evidence that it spared nothing, neither cities nor forests nor ice floes nor the barren tundras. It's all down there below us when we're flying, the record of that last war, the really Great war that shattered the political pattern of Europe and Asia and forced the eventual formation of the World Council of Nations and the division of the earth outside the Curtain into its system of prefects, bearing their old and now quite meaningless national names.

"Yes, here in the frozen north was the Earth remolded into the system we now know, before the Western Hemisphere retreated finally behind the Curtain.

"And so to us of the Patrol time seems to telescope. The past is with us. We are, in truth, the guardians of the past, for if there is a future—which means change—it lies beyond the Curtain, among the peoples of the Western Hemisphere, who alone now possess the knowledge that could rear and maintain this Wall of Death. Or is it actually, for them, a Wall of Life? What are they doing there in those lost continents? What wonders have they now achieved in their two hundred and seventy years of isolated and unimpeded progress? And what remains as the grand adventure for the rest of us unless it is the penetration—?

"Ah, you see, I am very close to utilized. And that nasty word creeps through my mind again, the word we must not whisper among ourselves in the Patrol—strain! Soon, I do not doubt, I shall be back forever in London, washed up much as poor Anstruther was washed up, a victim of proximity to the Curtain. Prepare a pleasant little snuggery for me."

But O'Hara was not coming back to London as soon as he pretended to anticipate. I have included these letters from him here only to indicate the acuteness of his mind, how very close he often was to the scientific truths while he rambled on in his most extravagant mood. But this is not a scientific paper—my aim is political, and in particular it is economic, if anyone nowadays distinguishes between the two. My aim is Truth and the revelation of it, as I got it from Emmett O'Hara on that evening of his return, a few days more than one year after he disappeared while flying on patrol out of his base on Wrangell Island.

Two days before Christmas, December 23, 2228, I heard that O'Hara had vanished. His father telephoned me as soon as they got the cable, asking if it were possible for me, through the *Observer*, to obtain further information. I was able to learn a few details, but there wasn't much to learn.

O'Hara had left the International Patrol's base at Wrangell on a routine long-distance flight toward the Curtain at 12:15 P.M., December 20th. His flight pattern called for him to proceed to the seventieth degree of latitude and to fly along it until his scintillometer recorded .250 milliroentgens an hour, which was the maximum permissible even for a veteran. He was then to pivot westward, proceeding for three hundred miles along the Curtain's fringe, then turn back toward Wrangell and arrive by 1 P.M., the slow time because he would be taking readings constantly and must keep his craft well throttled to do it. He took off with an excessive fuel load, for his rank as a captain permitted him to make any necessary extensions of his flight, subject to confirmation of the change by wireless.

O'Hara did reach the seventieth degree of latitude and did reach the Curtain fringe. That much he reported in radio casts made at intervals of three minutes. Then, soon after he began the 300-mile leg of his flight along the Curtain, according to Colonel Alfred Tournant, base commander at Wrangell, O'Hara reported a sudden gale, with violent southward winds and electrical disturbance, but nothing that his craft should not have been able to penetrate. Then, at 12:34, according to Colonel Tournant, O'Hara's voice came in:

"O'Hara, Flight Twelve, Latitude 74, Longitude 163, Milliroentgens, 255—a little close to it, eh? Miles per hour 897 and retarding—there's a gigantic thunderhead piling up and I— Tournant? You listening? I don't like this—lightning's too thick— Tournant? Request permission to change course instantly! Milliroentgens .268—I'm heading north toward the Pole. Miles per hour 1004—but I'm not—getting away—"

A blast of static drowned his voice.

And that was all.

That was really all the details there were about O'Hara's vanishing. Within a dozen words he was talking jestingly and then calling Tournant in sudden alarm. And changing course. And then those final words: "—but I'm not—getting away—"

On the tenth of March Colonel Tournant arrived unexpectedly in London and the *Observer* sent me to interview him. He'd had a splendid record with the Patrol and was considered the coming man in it, quite probably its next Vice Marshal. The *Observer* did not need to send me—nothing in London except the Bureau of Security itself could have kept me from seeing him. He received me in his rooms at Claridge's, and after we shook hands, he indicated a well-laden liquor cabinet.

"You should find something there you like," he said. "Let me help you. You—ah—you knew Captain O'Hara?"

"From childhood," I replied. "My best and perhaps my only friend."

Colonel Tournant smiled quickly. He was a small and dapper man—what I should have considered the raw material for a martinet—thickly mustached, brown-eyed, and with the dark tan of most men in the Patrol, a very nervous brittle manner, a pacer. "Yes, you'd think that," he said: "O'Hara gave everyone that impression, I can tell from the way you speak, though—you're also an emigre, aren't you? Descended from O'Hara's Yanks? Some of the words you and he use, some of the inflections. He was my best friend too though not from childhood. How old do you suppose I am?"

The question startled me. There seemed to be no connection. "Forty-five," I guessed.

He flicked his fingers through his hair. "Gray enough for it," he said, his smile a little forced. "It happens that I'm thirty-two, six years older than O'Hara was. And here I am in London for my terminal—I'm utilized."

"You're utilized! But we supposed—"

"I know," he snapped. "You supposed that you were interviewing the next Vice Marshal of the Patrol. The truth is I'm finished. At thirty-two, I'm finished."

"That's news with an upper-case N," I pointed out. "Am I permitted to disclose it?"

"Why not? It's no disgrace." He shrugged. "I asked for it. I've lost my stomach for the work. If it got O'Hara, I know damn well I'm too old for it. For if ever there was a pilot whom I considered superior, who would not—well disintegrate—it was O'Hara. He had everything to qualify him for the work, coolness and brains, resourcefulness, an utter lack of fear. Yet the Curtain got him."

"The Curtain? Excuse me, Colonel, I understood it was that thunderhead. He said in that last radio cast of his that he could not get away—"

"Don't be an ass," Tournant snapped. "O'Hara knew weather. Besides, I personally flew one hundred hours in the sector of his final call and there was no wreckage. I flew that much! And I sent four squadrons into it. We'd have found the feather of an albatross had it been there. Thunderhead be damned. The Curtain got O'Hara—do you recall the sequence of readings in his final radiocast? Milliroentgens .255 and then again in seconds milliroentgens .268—notice that jump? In seconds, mind you! And within those seconds he believed that he was turning toward the Pole, which meant away from the Curtain. Do you want to know what took place? His mind disintegrated. The best of minds—the most stable of minds, and O'Hara certainly had that—can take so much of that constant strain and then without warning it happens." He stared at me pugnaciously, then he snapped his fingers. "Like that, my scribbling friend, the mind blinks out and that's an end of your pilot. No, thanks I've had enough. I shall cultivate roses—tea roses. And when I die, they'll not need to handle my body with tongs. Have another drink?"

I considered my empty glass a moment and then I said, "Yes, for a toast. To O'Hara."

We drank it together.

And that drink set the stage, I like to think, as completely as it could be set for the day after Christmas, December 26th, 2229. For what nicer thing can a man do for a lost friend than to embalm his memory in the best of Scotch? Yes, the stage was set, but it so happened that on the twenty-sixth of December I was writing about quite another stage—I was doing my annual squib on the glories of Peter Pan, the timeless pageant of the season, and how

Jill Ferguson best typified the centuries-old tradition of the ageless boy. I had got as far as the second paragraph, and was beginning to feel the spirit of the thing, when the telephone on my desk at the *Observer* began ringing. I picked it up.

"Caught in the purple prose again," a voice came over the wire. "You're writing about the pageants, aren't you?"

"Is it any of your business?" I snapped.

"I'm making it my business."

"Are you, indeed? Just who the devil are you?"

"My name is O'Hara, Emmett O'Hara."

"That's a very rotten joke."

"Yes, isn't it? But I do want to see you. I've just gotten in from Cairo after four days' flying and I need a drink and Nedra doesn't drink and I hate to drink alone. I've opened up my flat in Bloomsbury. How fast can you make it?"

I pressed my face within my hands. Then, listening for the sound of the voice, I said, "O'Hara?"

"Do you realize you're wasting time and I haven't much to waste?" he said. "I want to see you. Now shake it up, old boy, I've poured for you—"

"O'Hara, is it really you?"

"Can you make it by six?"

"But it's—"

"I know—impossible. But can you do it?"

When I knocked, he opened the door. He stood there casually, grinning at me as if I had just come back from an errand to the corner grocer's. The collar of his brilliant blue uniform was open at the throat. The three bars and half-globe were missing. His jet-black hair was touseled carelessly.

"Well, come in," he said and pulled me into the sitting room of the flat. "I've got us something for supper. Here drink this up."

"O'Hara!" I cried.

And he laughed, "I'm glad to see you, too." He gripped my shoulder and then thrust a glass into my hand. "Drink it up. That's good. The principle of the funnel."

"But where—? Colonel Tournant told me—"

"Now, here's another, though you may nurse it longer if you wish," O'Hara said, and filled my glass. "The supper will keep, it's tinned stuff anyway. Colonel Tournant told you, eh? I'll give him the shock of his life. Aren't you going to sit down?"

"Not until you tell me where you've been?"

"Really," he said, you'd better sit down. Because it so happens that I am going to tell you. That's the chair for you. Attend to your drink. And while you're doing that, I'll take you back for a moment to the 74th degree of latitude and the 163rd degree of longitude, one year ago plus four days."

He raised his glass. When he put it down it was empty.

"If you saw Tournant, you know that much," he said. "But I don't think he could have told you what I found there."

"The sudden gale?" I asked. "The thunderhead—"

A cry came from the room beyond us. A strange, low cry, mournful, somehow distressing, very sad, as if someone were lonely beyond the point of bearing, and I confess I leaped up and turned toward O'Hara.

"Now, that's a deceiving noise," he said, perfectly calm. "You think it sounds heartbroken, don't you? I assure you, it isn't, I'll get around to that in time, but not if you keep fidgeting. Yes, it was that sudden gale—"

I managed to remember where we'd been, O'Hara was talking very rapidly.

"Remember that I wrote you our Wrangell base is not too far from where the continents of Asia and North America once joined, where Bering Strait broke through. It's a weather factory, storms are put together there. Winds often swirl well beyond hurricane force, howling in all that icy desolation as if there were the slightest sense to it, for there's nothing at all to terrify." He was leaning forward now, recalling it. "On that day I wasn't terrified. I didn't like it but I'd beaten winds as bad as that. So I kept on the course laid out for my patrol that day, holding my speed around nine hundred miles an hour and sticking to an arc that gave me milliroentgen readings of .250 an hour. Not too close to the Curtain for an old hand at it."

He paused to fill his glass. He glanced just once toward the room beyond, then back to me. "You know, I'd never taken chances with the Curtain. I'd seen its effect, and I'd never really gotten over losing Anstruther, I want to make it clear that I was not taking chances—I was flying it safely, accurately, giving myself the full margin. The gale was bothersome but the flight was going perfectly. Nothing unusual. Around 12:30 I began plowing through an electrical field, sheet lightning, vast livid flashes, but it wasn't until two minutes later, 12:32 P.M., that I first saw the thunderhead.

"One glance was all I had—time to report it on my radiocast— and instantly the thing was blowing up. It seemed to erupt, caught in an updraft, and belched blackly high above me in enormous toppling billows, the Arctic's unleased fury roaring with a thousand forked, flaming tongues.

"My scintillometer's buzzing caught my ear. It was up to .268. I was veering straight for the Curtain. I swung at once, heading toward the Pole, due north away from the Curtain, and shot my speed above one thousand miles an hour, but the thunderhead seemed now to be collapsing on me and I could not accelerate swiftly enough to get from underneath. I could not break loose, I knew that within an instant I was going to be in the vortex of that swirling mass of wind and shrieking fire. Then it exploded.

"I remember that distinctly—it exploded into flame. And it blacked me out.

"I came out of concussion slowly—seconds, probably, but I seemed to be dragging myself back into consciousness. My craft was 500 feet above the ice. And there was no thunderhead. The wind was strong, around 120 miles an hour, but my speed was stabilized at 1125 miles per hour, and my milliroentgen count was 320. Very dangerous. And worse, my craft was headed south again. I swung it back toward the Pole.

"That should have cut my MR count. But within seconds the scintillometer was jumping up to .325, then .350. I was approaching the Curtain, and while headed due north!

"I turned back south. The MR count was dropping instantly. It didn't make sense. It was not possible, because I'd been between the Pole and the Curtain when I had blacked out. It was then that I made an automatic check on my position. Latitude 73—I'd gotten far off course during the time I'd been blacked out. Longitude 136—I checked that again. But that was it. The longitude was 136 degrees."

O'Hara knew exactly where that position placed him. But he did precisely what any laboratory technician would have done—he repeated his experiment, trying to find an error in his calculations. There was none and he knew it. He knew, even before that final check, that he had got through the Atomic Curtain.

Somehow, he had got past the wall of death that had cut off the Western Hemisphere for almost two hundred and seventy years. He now was flying above the ice field that abutted the upper reaches of the North American continen.

He glanced at his fuel gauge, and then turning south he set his motors at their maximum cruising speed. If he was trapped within the Western Hemisphere, the terra incognita that had fascinated him since he was old enough to read, he knew that he must fly as far below the desolation of the Arctic as his craft would go. And then—

"Then we shall see," O'Hara told himself. "Yes, we shall see—at last."

PART TWO

WHEN he at last convinced himself that he had got through the Atomic Curtain, O'Hara said, his first feeling was a wild and utterly unreasoning elation.

"I've done it!" he kept repeating to himself, much as if he had booted home a twenty-to-one shot at the races at Aintree. "I've actually done it—the first man in two hundred and seventy years to smash through. Now we shall see!"

But that exuberance did not long continue. For here he was, presumably in the Western Hemisphere, the cradle of the future, a terra incognita since that Third World War, and it seemed no different from the polar regions that he had been flying for the International Patrol. No different at all—the limitless gray reaches of the sky, the same vast twisted sheets of polar ice pierced only at great intervals by craggy, barren peaks—the islands of the Beaufort Sea, above the northern coast of Canada.

O'Hara was cruising at two thousand miles an hour. His fuel gauges indicated that he might keep going for three thousand miles, depending on his altitude. It was necessary, he knew to get above forty thousand feet and to stay there for his best distance, and he had to have distance toward the south—for the storms of December would have driven snow deep along the lost continent of North America. He was not equipped for any lengthy existence in snow. His craft had the Patrol's usual paraphernalia—an inflatable boat, a signal pistol, a .38 automatic with six clips of ammunition, emergency water supply, emergency rations, the items considered indispensable when a rescue team could be expected to begin search soon after he failed to report to his base at Wrangell Island. But now, south of the Curtain, no rescue team was coming. None could get through. In consequence his life depended on getting below the wasteland or the Arctic.

These things, O'Hara said, ticked automatically through his mind in those first few minutes after he realized that he had got through the Curtain—these, and the overwhelming importance of the fact itself, that the Curtain could be pierced. He had, of course, no idea how the thing had been achieved. It had happened while he was unconscious, but as he reasoned it, his craft must have spun from north to south and then rammed through. Nor had he any data on the milliroentgen count of the Curtain itself—he had no idea of the contamination to which he had been exposed. He realized that at this moment he should have been a charred mass of carbon, like the bodies of those men on Coronation Island, in the Antarctic, after their vessel of logs had drifted into the Curtain.

But the indisputable fact remained that he was not carbonized. He could only accept it and take whatever precautions seemed most likely to keep him alive, which now, at this moment, seemed to call for flying south.

Within minutes he was crossing a coastline, and following the bed of a frozen river that pointed roughly south. Far toward his right—the west—the saw-toothed stubs of mountains poked their glittering ice-sheathed peaks up from the continent, and O'Hara was remembering the maps he'd studied as a boy. That way, the west, must be Alaska. Again he checked his position in latitude and longitude, then deciding that the river course below him must be the Mackenzie, reaching down past Great Bear Lake in Canada toward Great Slave Lake. And somewhere distant past the snow-packed tundras toward the east would be the landlocked gulf of Hudson Bay.

"Remember," O'Hara said, "I wrote that time telescopes in the Patrol? It was telescoping for me now—I was back again with old Hendrik Hudson, though thank God not in quite the same kind of boat. I was opening up the West again, seeing the amazing continent, the wonders that I'd seen before only as dotted lines and red-and-blue ink sworls on long-forgotten maps. And in five minutes—the five since I had passed the Curtain—I was exploring more of this tremendous northland than old Hendrik ever dreamed of."

Wonders, yes—but wonders unfortunately very like those of the land mass of Siberia, and so no different from what he'd known before he smashed through the Curtain. O'Hara felt somehow as if the myths of the Lost Continent had let him down. Until he noticed the recording of his scintillometer.

It had dropped only to .305 milliroentgens an hour. That was high—dangerously high according to the flying regulations of the Patrol, yet it had been much higher further north, toward the Curtain. He could only hope that with his progress south the count would gradually decline. Then it occurred to him that radioactive water might be running underneath the ice of the Mackenzie, draining southward from the Curtain, and he swerved hard toward the east leaving the river bed some hundred miles behind before he made another reading. The milliroentgen count rather than dropping, had risen to .325 an hour. And simultaneously OHara's memory dredged up a curious fact—the Mackenzie flowed toward the north. It could not possibly be contaminated from the Curtain.

O'Hara now turned again toward the west, crossing the Mackenzie and heading for a tremendous region of icecapped peaks, their vast flanks swathed with the silver sheen of the greatest glaciers he had ever seen—the northern reaches of the Rockies, he concluded, the neckbones of the spinal column of the continent.

In this race westward, his milliroentgen count was sliding steadily, until, above the mountain chain itself the count seemed stabilized at last at .285. Yet when he pushed beyond, toward the western coast—the Pacific—the count immediately began to jump again. He made the indicated correction in his flight, adhering to the southeast curvature of the mountain chain, and concluding that he had discovered a corridor of lesser contamination, its base upon the Curtain in the north, and its two flanks on the eastern and western sides of the mountains, strongly radioactive.

He had now been below the Curtain—below that is the northern ellipse of the Curtain, for it was known to enclose the Atlantic and Pacific coasts as well—for thirty minutes, boring steadily south despite the zigzag pattern of his exploration, and the character of the terrain was changing, not less mountainous but with some indications of a seasonal variation in the snow pack, for oftener now the bare rock precipices and peaks showed through, and beyond the upraised spine of the Rockies, toward the distant shimmering deep blue of the Pacific, the snow itself had taken on a stippled appearance—immense forests, O'Hara concluded, blanketed but shaping the white contours upon them. And farther still, merging into the rim of the ocean's curve, lay a varying band of dark brown and black and vivid green, presumably a thickly forested shore, completely free of snow. O'Hara made a quick calculation based on his known altitude and an approximation of the distance to the horizon. The result astonished him. The forest belt extended inland for three hundred miles.

Yet the flight was becoming monotonous to the point of lulling him. The letdown that followed his discovery that the upper reaches of the continent were so remarkably similar to Siberia had increased, and with the passage of time he felt his eyelids inexorably closing. There was nothing to it. The dreaded continent was a fable made mysterious only by distorted memories of its history. It was, after all, a hoax—an empty shell, and he was penetrating deep—

His next thought jerked him erect in the cockpit of his craft. Suppose it was in fact an empty shell? Suppose there was nothing in this immensity behind the Curtain, the land which had been his fathers' fathers, but these ice-choked rivers and frozen tundras and forests and these tortured and interlocking mountain chains? Suppose it was dead—without life?

And it well might be. O'Hara himself had been exposed steadily now for the better part of an hour to a degree of contamination that the International Patrol considered beyond dangerous, and in his flights to the east and west he had plunged through belts exceeding .300 milliroentgens an hour. Was it not probably that these Americans in establishing their Atomic Curtain had simultaneously contaminated their two continents beyond endurance? The suicide of a race?

In an instant of panic, O'Hara swung in a tight arc to the north. He had, he felt, only the one chance to escape—a dash at maximum speed back to the Curtain and through it.

But, as instantly, he discarded that. Whatever it was that had got him through the Curtain in the first place could not be expected to work twice. He was convinced that it had been a kind of providential accident, something to do with that splitting blast of electrical power in the thunderhead, and he was here, within this Western Hemisphere, inescapably cut off.

His reason, too, came quickly to his rescue. These mountains and the far slope toward the Pacific Coast were smothered in their forests. And trees were life—biological life. If there was plant life there would be germination, bacteria—surely animal bacteria, surely animal life at however low a scale. Though perhaps not men.

Perhaps not men! Then this was indeed the grand adventure. He headed south again.

All these speculations and the resultant skittering about, as O'Hara said, had eaten into his flying time and he had not made the progress that he had anticipated, yet it was not quite two o'clock, not ninety minutes after he had crashed through the Curtain, when O'Hara saw a compelling flash of light upon his right. It was the first time that he had been conscious of the increasing clarity of the sun, no longer so obscured by clouds or ice fogs. O'Hara spiraled down toward a wide plateau, ringed with a lesser inner range of mountains.

The flash, he discovered, was reflected from a rectangular object, rather like a huge jewel, set into the face of a tall pile of masonry that reached some thirty stories high, a single needle rising from the snow-clad plain. Losing altitude fast, very nearly making of it a power dive, O'Hara pulled out of it level with the tower— for that was what it proved to be, a giant tower of stone and metal, expertly fashioned, a glittering and soaring pinnacle unlike anything that he had ever seen.

The flash was a reflection from the gem-like surface, which apparently was glass. The upper story seemed to be a kind of solarium, with six facets so arranged that they caught the sun constantly. The stories below it lacked openings of any sort, and O'Hara concluded that if in fact the tower had once been used for offices or dwellings those who lived there had relied entirely upon indirect lighting.

He was convinced that it was deserted now. There was a complete deadness to it, a stone and metal tower rising abruptly from a snow-blanketed plain, long abandoned, long forgotten. And descending lower, he could make out the geometric patterns of low structures and broad avenues, but with a skeletal emptiness about them, the roofs collapsed, the walls themselves in many places having toppled into the general ruin. A dead city, certainly, yet once it must have been a metropolis, culminating in its strange, massive tower before it died.

"Forgotten names from forgotten histories came back to me," he said. "The northwest coast—not Vancouver? Not Seattle? No, for both of them had been upon the coast itself. Spokane, then? Or possibly some city that had flourished after the establishment of the Curtain? But it did not matter, the place was dead, with the anonymity of the dead. A graveyard of a civilization that had been the mightiest on Earth. Yet the proof that this civilization actually had existed—that it was no myth—was enormously stimulating to me. It was my second big moment."

The tower and the ruined city had taken his attention from the business of flying. Now suddenly he was startled by the rapid-fire of his scintillometer. It was recording .400 milliroentgens an hour—unendurable!

"The dead," said O'Hara, "were reaching out for me. They wanted me, an alien probing through the skies above their tomb. And I felt their hostility, as if a shower of warheads had come roaring up. The contamination was as murderous as any warheads would have been."

The tautness of his steep climb skyward and sharp swerve back toward the spinal cord of the continent precluded any further observations. He was now acutely alarmed. He expected at any moment to discover upon his body the raw violence of radioactive burns, he anticipated bleeding and there was at the hinges of his jaws a definite sensation of nausea. Yet moments passed without development of these symptoms. The nausea abated. He was not stricken yet, or if he was, the effects were not yet obvious. And this raised possibilities of conditioning to the contamination that had never been explored—that no one, in the world he knew, had dared to explore. It might yet prove to be that man could exist in these extremes of radioactivity.

Large mottled patches now were appearing between the pale blue-white stretches of endless snow. The mountain peaks and the high plateaus still presented their heavily drifted appearance, but in the deeper valleys an occasional ice-free river twisted, seeking its outlet either toward the east or west—the east, O'Hara remembered, would lead to the intricate arterial system that would at last merge into the Mississippi River, the continental sewer that dumped its burden of silt and debris into the swampland delta of—what was it? Louisiana? The whole once-familiar pattern of maps he had intensely studied as a child now was coming back vividly—the two mountain systems, Appalachian and Rockies, the great valley of the Mississippi, the Atlantic and Pacific coastlands, the spider web of fabulous cities, names like New York and Washington, Chicago and Kansas City, Los Angeles and San Francisco, and somewhere in these Rockies which he was now following were—or had been—Salt Lake City and Denver.

There was a definite excitement in these names that for O'Hara rolled back the drab present to that glittering past, when the word tomorrow had meant more than a repetition of today.

O'Hara felt positive now that he had established a second major fact. For almost two hours he had been flying these forbidden skies, yet no patrol—save the atomic radiation of the dead city—had so far challenged him. It was inconceivable that any important civilization could exist upon the northernmost of the two Lost Continents without patrolling its skies, and consequently, if a civilization did exist, it must have shifted to the south, leaving these wastes. But for some minutes past, he had observed a peculiar series of geometric designs, resembling the drawings of ancient

Cretan labyrinths, far below him on the frozen surface. He now was approaching another of these, extending for miles upon the floor of a wide valley, and very cautiously, with his eyes constantly flicking back to his scintillometer, he began to descend toward it, diving.

As rapidly, his milliroentgen count began to climb, reaching .290 within the first five thousand feet of descent, then to .300 when his altitude was down to 30,000 and jumping very sharply at 24,000 feet to .325. The strange labyrinth was much too hot for inspection. But the regularity of its form seemed proof that it was man-made, and that decided O'Hara. He continued down until his altimeter registered 5,000 feet.

The labyrinth's pattern was precise. It was composed of an almost infinite number of thick parallel lines, joined at the ends, so that it actually resembled an endless pipe, though various segments of it were colored in a multiplicity of pastel shades—a vast farm of pipes, reaching for miles across the valley's floor, its purpose not apparent to O'Hara. His milliroentgen count now was approaching .400, and again he made that steep climb back to 40,000 feet.

These pipe farms soon were visible in every major valley, and further toward the east, upon the great slope of the plains toward the Mississippi, they were everywhere like the squares of a continental checkerboard, in some places partly obscured by snow drifts and in others lying exposed to the sun's brilliance.

For 130 minutes of continuous flying through this long corridor south of the Atomic Curtain the milliroentgen count had remained almost steady at .295, but at 2:30 P.M., and without an obvious physical reason for it, the count suddenly made an abrupt rise even at the 40,000-foot level at which he was flying. O'Hara tried swerving both to the east and west, also changing altitudes, but the contamination continued rising above .400 with every second's flying time. Here was a new phenomenon—a density of radiation that indicated some intense new barrier, and moments later O'Hara saw a strange, enormous white oblong reaching from east to west, not quite to the horizons but effectively spanning the area that he had determined composed the North-South corridor of least contamination. And such was the milliroentgen count that O'Hara felt it must in some way be a source—or excessive consumer—of atomic power, O'Hara's latitude calculation fixed his position as the southern part of the state of Colorado. The long corridor was in truth a closed rectangle, a box—a coffin without escape. He could only turn north again into it.

But the arc of his explorations had swung him well toward the east, and in these seconds he passed once more above the ruined debris of an empty city, the same pattern of collapsed roofs and time-dessicated walls extending for miles around a single sky-piercing tower of stone and metal with that glass-encased solarium at its summit. And this time, although it was gone in an instant, a place name fixed itself in O'Hara's mind, corroborated by his memory of latitude and longitude—the sky-high city of Denver.

His milliroentgen count was dropping back toward the .285 level he had anticipated, but all at once his motors cut out on him. His fuel was exhausted.

"There are such things as heroes," said O'Hara and paused, tilting back in the comfortable easy chair of his Bloomsbury flat, a fresh drink in his hand. He took a long pull at the glass, reflectively. And for a moment it was as if we were stepping back across the Atomic Curtain, both of us, back from the Lost Continent, taking within a second's time a giant stride from unreality into the stodginess of present-day London. O'Hara smiled crookedly. "Yes," he continued, there are such things as heroes—Tournant is rather close to it, I think. He has the courage to do what he can do, and to reject what he cannot. That's a hero in my book. But I'm not and never was, and when I heard the last unhappy cough from my motors and realized quite definitely that I was in for it, my knees were wax. No, not that crusty—they were jelly. When I understood that I was going down and that my craft, which until then had given me some sense of decision, was nothing now, dead metal under me—well, fear does crazy things to you. I screamed. It's true, I bellowed like a gored ox, striking both fists at my altimeter, shattering it. Until at last the needle, broken, jammed."

After that, he said, he was much too busy for theatricals. The peaks were coming up toward the belly of the plane like sharks' snouts in an open sea. He stalled to cut his landing speed, and at the last second pancaked on a meadow free of trees, cushioned by deep snow.

His craft was not damaged. With fuel, and without the waist-deep snow, he could have taken off again. These were the things a flyer automatically would check, the normal things. He was out of the craft, checking the terrain, when the third thing came to him and he stood there, cursing in the four languages that he knew best. He had forgotten his wireless. As instantly as he had gotten through the Curtain, whether help was or was not possible, he should have messaged his Wrangell base, for the only factor of this personal disaster that had actual significance was that the Curtain could be pierced—not once in ten thousand times, perhaps, but it could be done. And that information should have been relayed at once to Wrangell.

For the next half hour O'Hara worked furiously for contact, with only the nasty mocking whine of space coming back to him. He had flown too far. They could not hear him.

"It closed my record in the logs of the Patrol. Like Anstruther, I'd vanished, leaving nothing but hysterical last words, as valueless to science and my people as the twitterings of starlings on a summer evening."

Night deepened his gloom. He shut himself inside his craft, placing his automatic on the seat beside him, a loneliness that was like coma sapping him.

"Old Hendrik Hudson—drifting in an open boat among the floes. I think I really understood at last. For time had ceased to telescope for me. Time, too, had frozen. As it must in death."

But once, awakened in the night by a sudden howling that was shriller than the wind would be, he gripped his automatic, peering out, watching a ball of fire not far above the surface of the ground that vanished suddenly, as if puffed out. It did not come again. Or if it did, he was asleep, his will a victim of exhaustion and despondency.

When he awoke, the sun was high above the surrounding peaks, O'Hara broke out his emergency rations, afterward climbing from the craft to scoop up and swallow a handful of snow.

"What am I waiting for?" he wondered.

Yet he hated to leave the craft. It was his fortress, both physical and mental, his one link with the world beyond the Atomic Curtain—though a useless link now, he knew. It was futile to stay with it and, so far as he could foresee, futile to leave it. At last the very pressure of idleness drove him to action and he took his automatic, loaded it and strapped it beneath his flyer's jacket, then with his ice ax chopped down a score of small confers and arranged them around and above his craft in a crude camouflage. He turned toward the forest that encircled the meadow and began trudging through the snow. But just beyond the first line of trees he stopped.

The snow there was trampled as if through the night a Rugby team had had a go of it, and lying there, used up, blackened with smudge, was a flambeau of sorts—a length of wood with charred brush lashed to it, O'Hara ran his finger through the soot. It left a smear of oil.

Petroleum! Life for the motors of his craft. And somewhere near—his search had purpose now.

"I don't know what the devil I really thought I'd do with fuel," said O'Hara. "Fly around in that infernal corridor, I suppose, like a bullfinch in an aviary, free as all getout until I wanted to go somewhere beyond it. The truth is, all that seemed to matter was the chance of taking off again. That's what the Patrol does to you—puts pinfeathers on your brains, I wanted that fuel. And bad."

The trail led backward through the forest, a series of lines converging as if the individuals of a herd had searched in scattered formation toward this one meadow on the top of this one mountain, yet a preponderance of feet had trampled south by east, and O'Hara followed that line, keeping his jacket open for quick access to his automatic and using his ice ax when he needed it to chop through underbrush.

"You've seen a gull walk, haven't you? He's out of his natural element and he waddles—fine enough flying, and very good in the water, but he walks—well, like a gull. That was how I felt on foot, scrabbling through that forest," said O'Hara. "Most of it was downhill work, which helped, and presently the brush thinned out and the trees got larger and fewer and I was doing a passing fair job of it, following that trail until it was well after noonday, when I leaned against a ledge of granite for a breath."

But he did not quite get it.

"I gulped at it—and then I gave it up entirely. For crouching on the ledge above was an enormous cat. When I say enormous, don't imagine a lion. The king of beasts is a stinking coward, but this creature stalking me was making a little game of it, a kind of homicidal little game. Its eyes pale yellow with insanity and its two fangs a greenish yellow and larger than the tusks of a walrus. Had it leaped, I would not have known it, not for more than the instant it takes, a severed jugular to spurt your life's blood out. As I say, I did not get that breath—I fired, quite sillily without aiming, but the bullet splattered through one of those yellow eyes into its brain."

And while it threshed, O'Hara walked less like a gull.

But he was not altogether getting away from the creature. The sight of those tusk-like fangs kept coming back to him, insistently, hammering away at some obscure little wrinkle of his memory, until at last the two words formed and were upon his lips, "Saber-tooth!"

It was absurd. It could not possibly be that. And yet it was—the cat had been a saber-tooth, or surely like the skeletons of those long-vanished, blood-imbibing killers of the North American continent.

O'Hara could not bring himself to put his automatic inside his jacket after that. He stuck to the trail of trampled snow, following it down the slopes of the mountain. Gradually the tracks seemed fresher, the snow less melted after it had been disturbed. He began to move more cautiously.

He was passing through a defile, toward an opening in the rock beyond, when he first realized that he was being watched. How long this had been going on he could not guess, for the indication was not conclusive—a shower of loose rock slid down from above. When O'Hara looked up, he thought he saw a head disappearing into the overhanging brush. He halted instantly but there was no sound, nor did the head reappear. After a few seconds he realized the stupidity of remaining exposed in this narrow passage, a clay pigeon for whatever might be hiding on the ledges above him, and he began running.

Once more small rocks came cascading down toward him and this strange barrage continued, always just behind him driving him along the trail of trampled snow through the defile. Whoever had preceded him had managed to get through, and O'Hara kept at it, breaking finally into the open—a sort of natural amphitheater. And there the trail ended. The footprints now diverged toward the walls of sheer rock, on which there was no snow to preserve them.

"I was trapped," said O'Hara. "They had driven me into it as you might drive a hare. It was possible, of course, to get out of that bowl—for they had got out of it!—by climbing up those walls, thirty or more feet, but for that I'd want an Alpine guide, preferably with the rope to pull me up. I turned back instantly toward the defile and made a run for it."

This time, when rock came down, it came in slabs. Nor was he able this time to detect any movement in the brush above.

"I might have got through," said O'Hara. "They might have missed me. But they seemed a little too expert and I preferred to wait, well back from the sides of the bowl, with my automatic ready."

They let him wait until after dusk. Then, very deliberately, a lighted flambeau was thrust out from behind a boulder high above him, definitely a test to see what he would do. He stayed where he was and did nothing.

Other flambeaux now began appearing, neither advancing nor wavering, but fixing him in the center of their glare for a purpose not yet obvious. It was a game they played, O'Hara felt, a childish hanky-panky. But there had been nothing childish in those slabs of rock.

A wild shout from the rocks above now startled him, and through the defile, with ceremonial lack of haste, a lone adversary was advancing, armed only with a tapering wooden club and wearing a garment made of skins that reminded O'Hara of Scottish Highland kilts, the feet and lower legs thickly encased in furs bound with spiraling rawhide thongs, a heavy parka covering the head and face—expert work, all of it. The intruder, although of lesser stature, moved forward with such confidence that O'Hara's automatic felt ridiculous to him.

"Unsportsmanlike," he said. "You just don't shoot a man whose only weapon is a piece of carved wood, particularly not when you know that perhaps a hundred of his crowd are hiding in the rocks above you. I shoved the automatic inside my jacket. As you know, I used to wrestle, and while I measured him at possibly one hundred eighty pounds, I thought I could manage, if they'd keep those slabs off me."

As they turned, facing each other in the dark, O'Hara was conscious that the number of flambeaux above him had increased and were inching forward, and very dimly now he could detect the outlines of their parka-covered heads. The game was approaching a climax.

It came with a rush. His opponent leaped suddenly, swinging the carved club straight for O'Hara's head, a blow that would have crushed his skull had it struck home, but he ducked beneath its arc, coming up under the descending arm. He grabbed it, whirled and threw his heavy shoulder up, sending his opponent flying through the air.

O'Hara picked up the club. His opponent, recovering quickly, now scrambled up and charged again, and O'Hara, his mind concerned most with the throng above made his second decision—he dropped the club and stood there waiting. The next instant he was knocked from his feet by the ferocity of the charge, but in falling he locked his arms around his opponent's neck, attempting again a variation of the trick he'd used before, but momentum broke his hold and he fell backward. Instantly he saw the warclub rising.

The blow crashed into the muscles of his shoulder. He rolled beneath it, got onto his knees just as a second blow splashed blood into his eyes, then plunged again. His groping fingers found the club and wrenched it loose and this time he forgot it was a game—in close, he struck. His opponent toppled backward and lay still.

"I felt," said O'Hara, "rather like reciting a few lines from Horatio at the bridge. Or Spartacus. For my head was splitting. But the flambeaux were moving closer. I could see who carried them now—big fellows, perching up there in the box seats as if they might start throwing pennies to me. I waved the club to them. At the moment I think I would have fought the pack of them, for I was boiling—I'd been roughed up and I never had liked that. And then something touched my foot."

His adversary had crawled across the snow and was reaching out, hand supplicant. The parka had fallen back. It was a woman.

"She held on to my knees and looked up at my face, a mass of waist-long auburn hair now loose upon her back. And she was beautiful—her hair reflecting firelight from flambeaux, deeply auburn, her eyes the blue of glacier ice—a classic face, exquisite, but no tenderness as we know it. Only passion.

"Quickly she got to her feet, her arms locking me close against her splendid breasts, an Amazon who worshiped only strength, which I was glad I had, for those above us now were coming down the sheer walls of the amphitheater like so many chamois, bringing their flambeaux with them. Let me repeat—big fellows! Six-six on the average, and running upward of two-thirty, chests like bulls. And so damned agile! To see them scamper down that precipice toward me, depending on the quickness of their feet where I would certainly have found my hands not adequate, depressed me. I had the warclub and of course my .38, but if they meant to take me, neither was enough."

Instead, they lined up on both sides of him, then waiting while the woman motioned him to follow her, and began to lead the way. So at last they moved off in that strange procession, guided by flambeaux through the night, much as a bridal couple might move underneath an arch of swords.

"The simple act of splitting her noggin seemed to have inflamed—be damned if I'll tell it. Most natural thing in the world, I suppose, when it's the local custom. Yet it was embarrassing. And the studied indifference of our escort made it worse. How does one make love on the march, surrounded by a hundred men? For hours!"

Gradually they were descending the mountain, coming finally beneath an overhanging cliff into a narrow chasm, and there around immense bonfires, a swarm of women and chililien waited—had waited, O'Hara now felt certain, throughout the long absence of their men, for all at once, silent but busier than ants, they began dragging great haunches of meat from a series of caves which were eroded deep into the stone face of the cliff, arranging them upon the fires to roast, O'Hara's woman indicated that they were to sit and the men now ground out in the sand their smoking flambeaux and squatted beside them, silent impassive, waiting.

Primeval said O'Hara. There could have been nothing like it since—what were those ancient caves in France? Cro-Magnon man? The old boys who drew perfect little sketches of buffalo on the stone walls of caves? These silent giants, these women with their thick, abundant hair, the cliff and the caverns, the smell of roasting flesh, the constant scampering of fur-swaddled babies in the sand—primeval, certainly. The tribe—the clan!

Someone was chanting. It was the oldest of the men, using words that were no language that O'Hara knew, yet vaguely familiar. And as others joined in, the men's voices rich in a monotonous refrain, the women's working out a hymn-like counterpoint, O'Hara's woman arose and took him by the hands.

The chant changed now, a lament in it, a grieving for lost things, the women's voices dominating, keening, almost crystalline in iciness, like music locked within the chill stone of cathedral towers, O'Hara's woman led him toward one of the caverns, moving slowly, somberly erect. Within, deep in the gloom, a log fire smoldered. Smoke made fantastic shadows leaping on the living rock. She turned at last and stood there rigid, facing him.

Outside, the chant was changing now, a jubilating chorus of men's voices, gaining tempo until suddenly they ceased, and from the breathless silence finally a voice incredibly high, seeming incredibly remote, sang adoration.

O'Hara's woman freed his hand, then loosening a thong across her shoulders, shook herself, and stood there in the firelight nude. And the next instant she leaped at him, her hands like claws, tearing at his face and throat, driving him backward toward the entrance of the cave, back toward the clan. It was repetition of the struggle in the natural amphitheater, savage, passionate, and with O'Hara understanding now that he must master her or die. He swung his wooden club.

"She fell," he said. "I was getting expert at it—she fell, and that was it. Brutal, you think? Perhaps, I will not argue that. What mattered was that Nedra did not think of it that way. That was her name, Nedra—I learned that, as I was to learn so many things within the next few days."

But that learning came swiftly only after he understood their language. It was a decadent English, elided and bastardized and purified of abstracts, a working language for mountain people, verbs and nouns, only the simplest adjectives. The trick of understanding it was not to attempt to get it word for word—the words themselves no longer had their English identity—but by complete sentences, for three syllables might express an idea which in the original of his school days would have required ten or more words. Much of it depended of course on inflections, whether a question or a command or a statement of fact. And yet, slurred in his mind's ear, repeated rapidly, it suggested the more complex English structure, always excepting the abstract. Or ideas born since the establishment of the Atomic Curtain. It was not difficult, once O'Hara had grasped the basic sounds.

His key to it, his teacher, was Nedra. For two days and nights, by custom of the clan, O'Hara was not permitted to leave the nuptial cave, Nedra herself going only to procure what was necessary in food and water, returning then at once and always with that mating ferocity of her people.

"Violence," said O'Hara, "but not the implied violence of our corrupted European customs, not the ring and the finger, not the bridal veil—actual violence, the club and the ripping hands, and finally submission to the master sex, was implicit in their rituals as it was in their lives constantly. The original combat in that snow-packed amphitheater actually was our marriage by their custom, later consecrated in the chants outside the cavern. Neither a ceremony taken lightly—and not one forgotten readily. Not a blurred memory of dress uniforms and flowers but as sacred, I think. And vastly more impressive. As for courtship, as we know it, what is it but a rather futile attempt at premarital adjustment? Nedra had watched me kill the saber-tooth, and while I claim no valiance in it she had thought it admirable. She'd wanted me. I'd proved myself sufficiently before her people in the amphitheater. It was that simple.

"But with passion and loyalty and respect—which she demanded that I earn—did not come tenderness. Not then or ever. I had to learn that lesson, Nedra was not for the meek. And weakness would have sickened her. It was, I confess, disturbing to learn that I must always be on guard, that between us there could be no gentleness, that the carved wooden club, the symbol of marriage, must ever be ready to strike, but once I had got over my namby-pamby notions, I found myself—well, smug about it, I too could rule my cave."

Yes, a cave-dwelling people, said O'Hara, but not quite so primitive as he had supposed. It was on his third day with the clan, after he and Nedra had at last emerged from the nuptial cavern—O'Hara could follow the language by now, usually getting it the second or third time that something was said to him—that he discovered a facet of their culture that amazed him. He had gone with the gray-haired leader of the ceremonial chant, called simply the Eldermen's names, he was to learn, were functional, last names inconsequential—just beyond the chasm of the caves along a mountain trail with a group of children who were hauling fallen timber, when from a bank of dense ferns a giant bear reared up, a bear resembling the Kodiak that O'Hara had known in Siberia, beyond the Atomic Curtain, but vastly larger, an immense shaggy beast, awing, the rumble of the thunder in its throat.

The children froze. And before O'Hara could get out the .38 strapped inside his jacket, the Elder stepped forward, leveled his fist and fired—the spurt of smoke and flame and the sharp clack of firearms—then continuing boldly to advance, pouring shot after shot into the massive animal until it toppled.

O'Hara's surprise was intense. "I did not know you had these weapons," he said, and the Elder smiled. It was a .45 revolver, the butt of it worn smooth through countless decades of use, a type of gun that O'Hara had never seen.

"Weapon?" said the Elder. "It is called Colt, not weapon. We have always had them. Our people brought them when they came into these mountains."

"Then you were not always here?"

It was the Elder's turn to be amazed. "Always? No—it was not the best place to be always. We came here only to escape the sickness, in the time of my fathers' fathers. Long ago."

"The sickness?"

"You are one of us, you are of our people," said the Elder. "We know that because you use gunpowder, for we saw you kill the saber-tooth. If you had used an atomic gun we would have fled, for they are stronger than Colt—Colt cannot fight the atomic gun. But you are one of us, you must know these things."

"I don't know them," said O'Hara. The children were by now busily cutting up the giant bear, preparing it to take back to the caves. "I came from beyond the Curtain—"

"What does this mean, beyond the Curtain?"

"Beyond the Atomic Curtain, which shields this continent from that other world, my world, the Eastern Hemisphere. Beyond the oceans, Europe, Asia, Africa."

"These sounds mean nothing to us—Europe, Asia, Africa. Are they other mountains, perhaps along the Coast? We have not been there—it is too far and the risk of death is too great."

"You never go down from these mountains?"

"None of us. It would be death from the sickness—or worse than death, were we caught. Below the mountains is taboo for us. Were I to go, one of my people would fire Colt at me. It is our law."

"But you permit others of your people to come here?"

"That is permitted, yet it has never happened until you came. We saw you far above us, in that great flying thing you rode. We had never seen that thing before, but there are stories—myths the older people told when I was young—of the flying thing that men could ride across the skies in, as the condor does. Did you come in it from another mountain, beyond the regions of the Degraded?"

"From the north," said O'Hara. "Beyond the ice and the Curtain. But what are the Degraded?"

"The atomic people, if you can call them people. Those who live in the lowlands below the mountains."

"A different people?"

The Elder looked incredulous. "You must know these things. It is impossible not to know these things."

"But I do not know them," said O'Hara. "Beyond the Curtain we know nothing. Who are these atomic people and how are they different from you? And the sickness you mention. Tell me—"

But it could not come all at once, not while there remained the chore of cutting up the giant bear and gathering wood for the clan's fires burning on the floor of the chasm. The Elder talked as he worked, instructing the children—they were, O'Hara learned, considered the clan's children, not the children of individual couples, for the idea of the family had been expanded to include the entire clan. One family, with the Elder heading it, two hundred of them living communally, owning nothing. Even their weapons—Colts—were property of the clan, handed down from generation to generation. They worked as a unit, directed by the Elder, with strange little islands of technology in their otherwise crude culture. For instance, they knew about ores—they smelted metals and were expert in fashioning them, making the utensils of their working lives, the bowls and pots and knives they used, and the cartridges for Colt. Their mountains were rich in both copper and iron, and when later O'Hara saw their diggings, the evidence was there of long usage and a more advanced technology, much of which the clansmen no longer understood. Among the Elder's most treasured possessions was a large glass retort, once part of a rather extensive chemical laboratory that now lay in ruins, its purpose no longer known to the clansmen, who did not know the manufacture of glass. The Elder considered his retort a sacred vessel—sacred through antiquity alone, however.

"Our fathers who came here from the lowlands understood these things," he explained. "It was a magic, perhaps, that they needed there—perhaps it saved them from the sickness. But we have not needed them and their use is forgotten. We no longer know the ceremonies for them."

"This clan is the only one to escape the sickness of the lowlands?"

"No, there are others. Many of us came together from the lowlands, fleeing together—some of us came here, others went to other ranges there, and beyond there," said the Elder, pointing. "And beyond there—many clans, but not so many as those who stayed in the lowlands and were lost.

"You see these clans?"

They never saw them. They were related peoples, but without any political or blood ties, for the constant incursion of the atomic peoples—the Degraded—made any close association of these mountain clans impossible. Always, the Elder said, the thousands of the Degraded swarmed up through the valleys, searching for the mountain people, hunting them.

"For them, the Degraded, there is never any work—they do not need wood for fires or animals for food or copper for their utensils," said the Elder. "There is no risk in their lives other than the risk of hunting us. They do not want to destroy us—they want only to take us to replenish their blood to halt the sickness. But we wish death to mating with them. They are animals. Surely you know?"

"I do not know."

"They were like us once," said the Elder. "That is the story of my fathers' fathers—they were like us once, when all of us lived in the lowlands, the great plains toward the rivers. But that was in the first years."

"What do you mean by the first years?"

The Elder tried to answer. "It was a time of great things and great triumphs. No one was hungry and no one needed to hunt for food. Have you seen from the flying thing the vast glistening colored objects lying in the valleys? That is a part of it—that was left from the first years. People lived in piles of stones and the sun provided them with everything they needed. But it was long ago. It has no meaning now, no real meaning that I understand. For something happened that had to do with the sickness and our people fled from it. I had heard the old men of the clan, when I was a child, thirty years ago, attempt to explain what they remember their fathers telling them and they could not make it clear to me."

"Thirty years ago. You were a child then?"

"Yes, thirty years ago. That is an old age, older than most.

"These children—?"

"Two and three—with us they mature slowly. Among the Degraded they are old at twenty, older at twenty than I am at thirty."

"Tell me," asked O'Hara, "what is Nedra's age?"

"She has lived nine winters. This is the tenth of them." O'Hara felt as if the earth had shuddered under his feet.

Nedra was ten—for a moment he thought that possibly they reckoned time differently, but the Elder's own words refuted that reasoning—nine winters! She was in her tenth year, mature—in many ways much more mature than women of his own world at the mating age, certainly without the protective claptrap of sentimentality and romantic misconceptions. Was it, then, strange that the degenerated emotions of old age were absent from these people? Passion and ferocity, which were the attributes of youth, but not malice and tenderness. When the life span was cut so short there was not time for these. Returning later to his cavern, he entered with a sense of active guilt, of shame, but the intricately carved wooden club was lying on the floor, significantly, and Nedra was waiting with that look of adoration that he now recognized as the adoration of a child's mind, but she was not a child—she was magnificently dangerous, splendidly strong and quick, knowing what she wanted, and without absurd squeamishness about it.

"I am waiting for you, O'Hara."

"Yes—I see you are. But never mind that club. We'll get along without it—"

"How?" She asked it simply. She could not conceive of placid submission, nor, after that, could O'Hara. It was another turning point.

What the Elder had meant by the first years was never made clearer, but O'Hara, remembering the long-forgotten books of those musty Oxford cellars—the books that had so fascinated him in school—concluded that the first years meant the decades immediately after the establishment of the Atomic Curtain, an historic milestone that these mountain clansmen no longer understood, now lost to them after the rapid succession of many generations, one each ten years. But concerning the sickness of the lowlands, the Elder was better informed. For it was a continuing thing, present among the atomic peoples even now, and the constant dread and loathing of the clansmen.

"What they eat," said the Elder, "is abomination. It grows in the lowlands in those immense systems of colored objects that are like pipes—if you did not see them from your flying thing I will take you to a peak from which you can see them. And these pipes are contaminated, making their food a poisonous stuff—yet they no longer have any other way to feed. Nor do they wish to feed in any other way. For everything is done for them by atomic power—

"Who does these things by this power for them?"

"These things are fixed. No one needs to do them."

"They are automatic?"

"We do not know your word, but no one needs to do things for the atomic peoples. Everything is done. They have contrivances to work for them—the colored pipes to grow their food, and the water that they drink and that flows in these pipes they draw from the ocean that is said to be beyond the mountains toward the west, but the water also is contaminated. The earth itself—the soil of the lowlands—is contaminated, soaked with atomic wastes. Their cities—"

"What about their cities?"

"None of us has seen them, but we have heard that they exist. Our fathers' fathers told these things—once they built places out of stones and metals, like mountains with many caves, but they fled from them in the first years. That was before our people left. They were driven by the sickness—"

"How does the sickness injure them?"

"It is in their get."

"Only in their get?"

"Only in their get—it does not injure those already born, but their get become different. Each generation they become more and more like animals. Undeniably animals though once they were like us. Now their arms are much longer than ours and their feet are different, their jaws are thrust out, their heads are shaped oddly, sloping back above the brows of their eyes—"

"Like apes?"

"Apes?" asked the Elder, puzzled.

"Never mind. You say this sickness comes from what they eat and drink and the cities that they live in?"

From everything that is about their lives. The Tubes, the Sun Beneath the Earth—"

"What are these?"

"We do not know. We have never seen them. They were devised after the first years, when our fathers' fathers fled. But the legends are that the Tubes run everywhere beneath the crust of the earth, as the trails lie across the mountains, and that somewhere among these Tubes there is a Sun that glows, giving heat and light and power—and something else that we do not understand, a strange protection, not against us, but against a great evil—"

"The Curtain!"

"You know what this evil is?"

"Perhaps. And I'll learn more. But tell me one thing now— why did your people flee this sickness?"

The Elder's dignity was impressive. "I've told you that what happens to their get. It is better to fight and to struggle for your life. Man was not meant to exist, as a worm does, pallid and content beneath a log."

And that was as close to an expression of religious belief as O'Hara was to hear among these mountain clansmen. Security was evil in itself.

Considering this, O'Hara decided that in those first years these clansmen who had fled the fat and effortless life of the atomic regions had discovered that security had an inevitable price, and it had been a price that they would not pay. They had turned their backs upon it, fleeing from it, escaping the greatest of all scientific wonders because of the greatest of all scientific mistakes—an unforeseeable error that they grasped only by seeing its result, without understanding of the cause. Yet they must have known it once.

O'Hara knew it.

Atomic contamination, never quite deadly, low enough to be tolerated, nonetheless had wrought its havoc in the genes of the race.

It had reversed the process of evolution.

The people of the lowlands, the atomic peoples, were reverting, returning toward the ape, and at a pace incredibly speeded up by some mutation within the reproductive genes that forced maturity at ten years of age, a generation every decade, ten to a century— twenty-seven since the establishment of the Atomic Curtain! But the rate of retrogression was immeasurably swifter than had been the slow climb upward since the dawn of time. For with the reversal of the process of evolution, an atomic disaster within the genes, had also come the reversal of the law that only the fittest could survive—the perfect atomic state, with security for all, was preserving and multiplying the predominant strain, those who were unfit!

Even these mountain clans who had fled, they too had taken that first short stride back toward the dawn. They had got back to the simplicity of life and the magnificent stature of Cro-Magnon times. For even here, remote from the pipe farms and the reservoirs of distilled and contaminated sea water, the radioactive food and drink of the lowlands, the dangerously hot power plants—even here there was always a degree of radiation. O'Hara's scintillometer had shown .285 milliroentgens an hour just before his craft had crashed—not dangerous, as veterans of the International Patrol reckoned danger, but over a period of time a factor never fully evaluated.

Adults at ten! Old men at thirty! And, as the Elder said, even sooner in the lowlands.

The Elder had described the atomic peoples as animals—as apes—but O'Hara was puzzled by these accounts of scientific achievement, the atomic weapons, the vast pipe farms which were the sources of food, the distillation of oceans, and the Curtain itself. Surely these were not the product of inferior minds, and as surely there must be somewhere in the lowlands another people, a superior people who had conceived and who directed the operation of these superb contrivances. But if there was such a people, the Elder did not know of them.

"The people of the mountains and the Degraded—there are no others," he insisted. "There cannot possibly be others, for if they lived there, they too would have the sickness."

O'Hara could not believe this. Yet he confessed it did not seem to be a greater contradiction of the possible than that a cave-dwelling race should employ gunpowder and understand the lightning properties of petroleum.

The petroleum remained for him a goal to be attained.

The Elder was evasive, and Nedra, who would have told him anything she knew, considered it a mystery she neither comprehended nor cared about.

"Why talk of their torches?" she demanded. "If we need them, they will give them to us. Am I not enough to amuse you?"

"Yes Nedra but I want to know—"

"Are you really one of us, O'Hara? You ask questions that could interest only an old man of thirty, yet you cannot be more than twelve. You are restless, you are unhappy with me. I am not beautiful to you."

"No woman anywhere is quite as beautiful."

"There is something that you want. Is it babies, O'Hara? Soon we will have them."

"For the clan, I suppose?"

"For the clan, of course. Would you like to take them with us and leave the clan, go to another mountain? Is that what you want? But the Degraded would catch us. Would you want your sons and daughter to breed with the Degraded? No, we must stay with the clan and our babies must be for the clan."

"Our babies," he said, for he had forgotten that. There would be babies. And before he was an old man they would be older men. And Nedra—Nedra would be gone.

"In the place that you came from in the flying thing, O'Hara," Nedra was saying, "are the people there like me?"

"Not like you, Nedra. But they would admire you."

"As you admire me?"

"Yes."

Then, peremptorily, "Admire me, O'Hara, and let us begin to have our babies."

The eternal antidote! Wherever women were, they had this cure for restlessness. And there was something to it. He was not going to find, on either side of the Curtain, a life more idyllic than this. They had drawn a screen of skins across the mouth of the cavern and their log fire gave sufficient light and warmth; they had eaten together and now they were lying together on a heavy pad of furs, Nedra luxuriating in the tigrish grace of her naked body. Was there more than this?

"Nedra," he said at last, "I've got to know about the torches."

"The Elder knows these things. Ask him."

"Where does he get the petroleum?"

"That is a secret word. I do not know it."

"The oil—the stuff that burns in them. The black water."

"Why do you need to know about the black water?"

"For my—for the flying thing."

"That makes it fly?"

"Yes, Nedra."

"You want to fly away again?"

"I want to fly, though perhaps not far away. Perhaps that can't be done—not far."

"You wish to fly above the lands of the Degraded?"

"Perhaps."

"Then I will kill you."

"No," he said, "you won't. You must understand this, Nedra. As it is your nature to love, it is my nature to fly."

"Then I have not been a strong mate for you, I have been too weak, but I—"

"Leave the club where it is," O'Hara laughed. "And I'll talk no more to you of torches."

But with the Elder he was finally more successful. It came about through the Elder's reverence for the weapon he called Colt. The mechanics of it had an almost ecstatic fascination for him. He would take hours to explain the workings of each part, diagramming it in the sand before the caves, stopping from time to time to recite some victory he had won with it, a giant bear, a saber-tooth, a monster ground sloth that had come wandering from the lowlands.

"And do you know what makes it eternal?" he asked O'Hara. "It is the black water of our torches."

"I understand about the black water," said O'Hara instantly, determined now to trade on the Elder's reverence. "For that is what takes my flying thing into the air, like a bird."

"The black water does that?"

"When certain things have first been done to the black water. Would you like to see it?"

The Elder drew himself erect, a gaunt six feet eight, his face turned upward to the sky. "I would like to see the flying thing go up."

"Then I must have the black water."

"We will go to the place tomorrow."

"And we must boil it. We must build a machine, something like the machines you use for smelting copper. Come into the cavern, I will draw the parts for it in secret for you. I will show you on the walls of the cavern how it must be done."

"We can make this machine?"

"It will take time. But if you can make the cartridges for Colt, you can make this machine. We will do it together."

Using a pointed splinter of obsidian, O'Hara tediously worked out the design for a rudimentary still, sufficient, he was certain, for refracting kerosene. "This part must be copper," he explained to the Elder. "A retort to contain the black water."

"I see it, O'Hara."

"And here we must have pipes. Like a hollow reed, like the barrel of Colt. Can you do this?"

"It can be done. We will make a rod of clay and dip it into molten copper. When it cools we will wash out the clay."

"That will do it. You must have a very hot fire here—I think that if we spray black water on a bed of coals—with perhaps a bellows here—"

"You must draw that."

"Here it is. And we will need these coils—we will bend the copper pipes for this—"

O'Hara rapidly continued drawing. The sketches were making some kind of sense to the Elder.

"They are like the bright clear metal that I showed you in the old place," he suggested, and O'Hara nodded—like the glass retorts in the abandoned laboratory.

"This is the machine," he said. "The black water will become colorless, and with it, then, the flying thing will soar into the sky. But first we must have black water."

"We will go for it in the morning," said the Elder. "It will take two days to reach the lake that has it. I must go now—your woman is angry. Women do not like these secret things."

When the Elder left, Nedra seized O'Hara's arm. "It was evil of you to make these drawings," she burst out, angry. "They are like the drawings of women who design new pots. They are unmanly."

"You think I am unmanly, Nedra?"

"When you draw these things, yes."

"You think so, Nedra?" He moved backward quickly, seizing the carved club and then walking very slowly toward her.

When at last it was over, and she turned sleepily on the bearskin at his side, her voice, for once, seemed almost gentle. "We have begun our babies, O'Hara. And I will never leave you now."

With dawn, the Elder marshaled his caravan for the journey to the lake that had the black water—a natural pool of petroleum, O'Hara felt certain. And Nedra, alone of all the women, was going. The Elder had his say upon that issue—a scornful speech, addressed to O'Hara, concerning the proper management of women. But Nedra ignored it. Her arms were taut around O'Hara's neck, her face obstinately buried against the brilliant blue of his jacket.

"She will delay us," the Elder insisted. "And we must travel swiftly a great distance. We must cross the valley below us, and if there is trouble we cannot wait for a woman to keep pace."

O'Hara smoothed Nedra's hair. "Nonetheless, she is going."

"Then she is your burden."

"Yes, my burden. I understand."

The Elder lashed out the order of the march, and the youngest clansmen fanned out in front as scouts, a hundred yards apart, with those who followed moving now in groups of two at intervals of five minutes, dispersal against a firepower far more deadly than the guns O'Hara knew. The Elder stationed O'Hara and Nedra as the second of these so that their pace would be determined by the scouts out front. In this order, and proceeding at a dogtrot the party swiftly descended the flank of the mountain toward the small valley intervening before, the next range.

They were soon down upon the valley floor, moving steadily through head-high grass broken now and then by densely wooded groves of aspen, and by noon they were crossing the ice of a narrow stream, heading toward a thicket. The Elder, pressing up from behind, now urged O'Hara to increase his speed—the scouts, he warned, having crossed the stream, were running for the lower slopes of the mountain across the valley."

"They are almost beyond danger," he explained, "and you cannot blame them. This is the point of risk, when they are not scouting carefully."

But Nedra needed no urging. They were climbing now, the grade curving sharply upward, exhausting, the icy wind of December cutting into the tissue of their lungs as if they were breathing acid. They reached the first shaggy line of snow-clad conifers and were pausing there, trying to determine where the route now led, when far ahead of them up the slope, a great burst of sound came roaring and a thin column of ocherish fuming matter shot up toward the sky, flattened at the top, changed coloration rapidly toward mottled red, then seemed to sag, drifting down toward the earth again.

Nedra seized O'Hara's hand.

Then down below them, just beyond the stream they'd crossed another blast of sound came simultaneously with that tortured, soaring column of dark yellow matter, pustulant, and like a pustule bursting at the top, fuming into a blackish red, the color of dried blood. Obscene, O'Hara thought—it was obscene. A fire of filth.

Nedra was pulling at his arm. "Get down," she whispered. "Crawl—they do not see well and if we stay down, going from rock to rock, it may be that they'll miss us—"

"They?"

"It is the Degraded. Down below us in the valley."

O'Hara took out his .38, kneeling by Nedra and watching for movement on the slope below. "Nedra," he whispered, "is that it, that fuming matter—the atomic weapon?"

She did not answer. He reached out, touching her, and slowly turned. She was staring straight ahead.

And standing there beside a mass of crumbled granite, gray like the stone itself, his hulking body naked, neither clad nor furred, incredibly long arms now swinging as his weak eyes focused under bone-ridged brows, a man—though not a man—was raising in his ugly hand a shining tube-like object.

"Fire now, O'Hara," Nedra was saying. "Make them destroy us. They are around us now. They want to take us, not to kill. You see, that one—and that—"

"Nedra, I want you to run. When I fire—"

"It is too late. Kill me, O'Hara."

"No, Nedra," he said, but he pressed the .38 against her side. "We can always die, and if they try to separate us, I will do it. But it's you they want—if they see I'll kill you, they'll spare both of us. Can you tell him that?"

"She does not need to tell me that," said the Degraded.

"You live while she lives. Now, come—the Father waits for you in Washington."

PART THREE

"SUPPOSE," O'Hara said to me, leaning forward suddenly, his empty glass in his hand, "you were to fly tomorrow to the Prefecture of Switzerland—leave London, say, at noon, and arrive there twenty minutes later and alight at the Bern airstrip and then start walking, away from the town into the countryside—into the mountains. You'd have the feeling of London clinging to you. At any moment, you'd think, you could return to the airstrip and be again in London—in Bloomsbury, here—within twenty minutes, if you wished.

"Now, suppose further, that while you're walking through those Swiss mountains, you come upon a magnificent woman, larger than most women of Europe and more beautiful by far, auburn-haired, blue-eyed, dressed strangely in furs in a costume very like a Highlander's. And within a half hour's time she has attempted to knock out your brains and you, in defending yourself, have instead been forced to flatten her, and then have found that this was exactly what she'd hoped you would be able to do, and that henceforward she is your woman—not your slave but your mate— the mother of children who will be yours but who will not call you their father.

"And still further, suppose that suddenly from these same Swiss Alps, not twenty minutes from where we're sitting this moment, drinking ourselves into a mild sort of bender, a horde of man-like creatures, uglier than apes because they are men and not apes, surrounds you and destroys the illusion of an ancient time— destroys it with atomic weapons and the evidences of atomic-powered industry—ah, you see?

"We have not telescoped only the time involved since the establishment of the Atomic Curtain around the two Lost Continents of the Western Hemisphere. We have also telescoped time as far back as one hundred thousand years ago—we have got back to the Java Man, and yet we're also far ahead of where Europe and Asia are today, all within the present moment. For you're only twenty minutes from London!"

"It would take more than twenty minutes to get from here to the Rockies of North America," I pointed out.

O'Hara laughed. "It would take," he said, "two hours of straight flying time. And the Twelve Old Men of Geneva are now aware of that. Two hours—imagine it—from where we sweat and scrabble for our daily bread, and we could live forever without so much as wiggling our smallest toes. The abundant life, old man—food for the taking, shelter and absolute peace and freedom, and only those who are bored with that engage in anything resembling human struggle as we know it. And we can have that. All of us. Have it there in North America—or here, if we wish—for by now the Twelve Old Men must be reading my report, sent on from Croydon after I landed just awhile ago. What do you think they'll do about it?"

"I don't know, O'Hara. You have not finished."

"No," he said, and filled our glasses. "I haven't finished have I?" He drank, his eyes intently watching me. "You want the full picture, don't you? Well, you shall have it. Let your mind step back into that plane I mentioned, and take that two hours' flight across to the Rockies, to southern Colorado beyond the Atomic Curtain. We're in a mountain valley, remember—? Nedra, and I, facing a gentleman who speaks that strangely bastardized English I've described for you—and speaks it with a certain dignity, as if used to command. And in his ugly hand he holds that shining tube-like object that creates those hideous explosions that destroy—and without trace—his enemies. The atomic gun.

"I have described him. Ape-like yet hairless, stooped and hulking, his skin as gray as the granite of that mountain a revolting thing, though I've seen men in London's streets quite as revolting. What perplexed me—amazed me—was the paradox of his speech, for as I say, it had a certain dignity that could come only from a mind that had been schooled. But the others of his patrol who now were coming around the rocks toward us, moving quite slowly as their weak eyes constantly kept watching for the scattered mountain clansmen, were, I was to learn, by far his inferiors. They were the horde, the masses if you please, while he—and by sheer accident of birth, for in that society of which he was a member, to be born with intelligence is indeed an accident—belonged to that most tyrannic of all aristocracies, the oligarchy of brains. They called him the Son."

Nedra, O'Hara said, was pressing tremblingly against the muzzle of the .38 he was holding at her side, watching the Son with an expression of absolute loathing, nor did she then or ever see the Son as any different from the members of, the horde—the difference in intellect being meaningless to her. "A blow," said O'Hara, "to the bright boys of this Earth, had they seen her face as I was seeing it. But I do not think it was a blow to the Son. He expected only loathing from Nedra, and if he could have had her, physically, her loathing would not have mattered to him. He knew—that is, he had been taught—that women of her kind were desirable for breeding purposes, as a means of retarding the reverse process of evolution, desirable from the standpoint of the race, but he was utterly lacking in aesthetics—a lovely woman or an ugly one, the flower or the weed, he did not and could not differentiate. And not through lack of intelligence, for he had something resembling that—but because, I think, the essence of romance and the appreciation of beauty is escape. And from what was he escaping, he and his kind? They had everything—everything, including the sickness. That alone perhaps they wished to escape, and that was a simple matter of biology."

"The real truth is," said O'Hara, "they wished to escape the sickness only because the thought of escaping it had been thumped into their brains from the moment when it was first realized that they had brains—so few of them had. It was no inherent wish. Actually the masses were quite content to go along as they were going, back toward the ape, the lizard, the fish, the primal scum. The, masses of North America—both the Americas—are quite content. It is that thought that must be terrifying at this instant the Twelve Old Men of Geneva. For the masses anywhere always are striving toward contentment, and now—well, they can achieve it! Our masses, too. The Twelve Old Men know that now. And yet they also know—as Nedra knew instinctively—the price of it."

"The Son," said O'Hara, "indicates the route we're to follow." He pointed down the valley.

"We must go at once," he announced, "for the cold of night will come swiftly. You-who-fly," he said, his eyes meeting O'Hara's, "are responsible for the woman's life. Remember, if she dies by the metal rod that you are holding against her, you will die instantly. Now, march."

For two hours they proceeded, but with nothing of the cautious and skillful precision that the mountain clansmen had effected before the attack, for although the Son remained just behind them, constantly ready to prevent their escape, the rest of the horde, three hundred when assembled, shambled aimlessly along in groups of two or ten or fifty, pausing now and then to explore an unusual rock formation or to feel the bark of trees, to tear an insect's tiny body to pieces, or simply to stop, having for the moment apparently forgotten where they were going, or why. Only a sharp command from the Son made them resume the march, always apathetically, neither resentful nor willingly, as a troop of small rhesus monkeys might proceed through a particularly interesting part of the forest.

"You called me 'you who fly,' " said O'Hara, speaking to the Son. "How did you know?"

"You were watched," said the Son. "When you came through the Curtain. The Father knew of it at once. The Father knows everything that happens."

"And you are taking us to him?"

"Yes. In Washington."

"Does he know you've captured us?"

The Son looked puzzled, the skin above his bony eye sockets wrinkling up. He seemed uncertain of his answer for a moment, but then his scowl relaxed. "The Father knows everything," he said, as if that bit of catechism demolished any doubts. "He thinks of everything. He sent us here into the mountains to return with you."

There was some interest in this game, watching the Son's mind struggling with unscheduled questions. "Suppose," O'Hara asked, "we had not come down into this valley today? How would you have captured us?"

"It would have been done."

"I see—the Father would have thought of something else?"

"Yes."

"But what?"

"Whatever would have been the best thing possible. If he wished, the Father could have destroyed these mountains. All of them."

"Why doesn't he? The mountain people are your enemies."

"Oh no we have no enemies." The Son was speaking now with greater surety, for these were obviously lessons he'd been taught. "The mountain people are instead a medicine. As the Father cultivates some medicines in test tubes, so he cultivates the mountain people in the medium in which they thrive."

"He permits them to exist?"

"He encourages them to exist," the Son replied. "He stimulates them."

"How?"

"By sending us to fight with them."

"But that destroys them."

"Only some of them. And that stimulates those who survive. Also, it rids their stock of those unfit to multiply.

"An admirable arrangement," said O'Hara. "As you say, the Father thinks of everything. I am beginning to want to meet him."

"You will," the Son said. "You will meet him soon."

They were coming out now into the thickly forested valley that opened eastward toward a rolling plain, then abruptly, sheered off, either by blast or fire, the forest ceased and before them lay one of those vast and multihued fanns of pipes which O'Hara had seen earlier from the air. Each section of pipe was roughly four feet in diameter, its surface slick and with a temperature that O'Hara by touch estimated at eighty degrees, the ends joined as he had observed so that it was in fact an endless coil, extending for miles.

"You must climb over these," the Son explained.

"What are they?"

"Photosynthetrons for western Kansas, although not all of their produce is used here—the solar rays in this region are more favorable for this particular food, much of which is needed in the cities of the Atlantic East. We send it there in the Tube."

"The Tube?"

"We are nearing its local terminal." The Son was pointing toward the approximate center of the pipe farm, from which now a sudden new eruption of these hairless man-like animals—despite their speech, O'Hara could not think of them as men—came clambering, their faces stamped with that unthinking emptiness of the masses, herded along toward the approaching party by another of their kind who like the Son, bore in his hand the shining tube-like weapon that O'Hara was to learn was both the symbol and enforcer of authority. "These are," the Son explained, "Emporians—their City is a very ancient one, although its site was often transferred in the old times, before the deluges began. The Son you see among them tells me that they expect another deluge soon to remedy their serious overpopulation. You will go with him."

"Another Son?"

"Oh, yes. The Father does not lack for Sons. I leave you now—my assignment is the valleys of this mountain range."

And while he turned, the two masses were commingling, so that the task of separating them was like the task of shepherd dogs with sheep—a division of the herd, not by specific individuals, but numerically, the two Sons shouting as they cleaved the shambling and always apathetic horde apart. To O'Hara it seemed an astonishing performance, the docility of the masses, for surely behind their dim eyes must be some semblance of a brain—surely they must know that those who went toward the mountains were to be used for combat purposes, exposed at least to the minor risk from the Colts of the mountain clansmen, yet apparently it did not matter to them, whether war or the placid test-tube existence of a city like Emporia, the sole difficulty that the Sons encountered arising from the inability of the masses to grasp the fact that they must be separated, that before the tumult could cease some of them must direct themselves toward the mountains and some return to the city. It was like the insensate division of an amoeba—a division directed perhaps by a sublime intelligence but without either the acquiescence or comprehension of the masses.

More and more, observing the Degraded—the only less than bestial stupidity of the horde and the derived intelligence or trained reflexes of the Sons—O'Hara was conscious of feeling that it was indeed a sublime intelligence that guided them, something they accepted without challenge as infallible, which in the inevitable pattern of such conceptions that spoke of as the Father but which more probably was a cabal of the more superior of the Sons, a ruling organism probably not unlike the Twelve Old Men of Geneva.

But to Nedra such reflections were not only senseless, they were silly. The masses of the Degraded, the Sons and even the Father were only varying terms for describing a loathsome people—worms, the clansmen called them. And only his curiosity kept O'Hara from tending to agree with that.

"You see?" said Nedra. "You should have killed me earlier, in the mountains, for this is the way it goes when you deal with the Degraded—you are passed from band to band, always deeper into the contamination in which they live, always with less and less chance of escaping them. They will be taking us now down into this city of theirs, Emporia, and how then, O'Hara, do you propose that we shall ever get away?"

There was truth in this. But O'Hara could not see that they were really worse off than before. "Let me coin a phrase or two," he said ironically. "While there's life, there's hope, and we can only die once."

"Those are the worst of lies," Nedra answered, her chin set stubbornly. "You can die a thousand times, each time more horribly than the times before, and while there is life it sometimes happens that it's only life to die again. Are you afraid to die, O'Hara?"

"Not afraid, but reluctant."

"Why? Are better nights coming in our lives than those we passed together in our cavern?"

"Not better, Nedra—but as interesting, perhaps, and certainly I would not wish to cancel out that possibility. A man who is dying of thirst in the middle of the desert does not seek death because the water that he may reach will not be sweeter than the water that he once had drunk. But it's more than that—more than the carrot dangled always just beyond the donkey's nose. In my world, beyond the Curtain, we cling to the belief that life itself is sacred and that always, finally, we may achieve redemption."

"What is redemption?"

"Life after death—a finer life than we have lived."

"You think only of yourselves," said Nedra, "and thinking only of yourselves, that notion may be true. But what of the clan? Have you forgotten, O'Hara, what the sickness does? We have got it now, you and I, as the Degraded have always had it—and what it has made of them it will make of the child that I am carrying."

"That you—?" he said, and gave it up, for there was no answer. None at all in logic, and Nedra had no concept of religion. Instead, he touched his lips against her face a quick caress before she spoke again.

For the horde was separated at last, and those who were to go into the mountain valleys were already clambering back across the endless colored coiling of the photosynthetron, while the second of the Sons, his atom gun held cautiously, was now approaching them.

"We must go down into Emporia at once," he warned.

"The Deluge is coming soon, and you should be safely in the Tube before it happens. The Father does not wish you to be drowned."

O'Hara tightened his arm around Nedra's waist, to avoid any surprise, and keeping his .38 beneath her ribs began to follow the horde further into the maze of pipes.

Six hundred yards deeper, between two pipes of an intense vermilion color, a square of some forty feet of opaque glass or metal or plastic now began to tilt upward as they approached, revealing beneath it a platform of what apparently was magnesium, and onto this platform the Son led O'Hara and Nedra and as many of the Degraded as it would accommodate. The platform now began to sink rapidly, without sound, down a shaft immaculately tooled from a similar glistening metal, descending for what O'Hara estimated to be two hundred feet before it reached bottom. A wall of the enclosing shaft now slid up, and they left the platform, which as instantly began to rise again toward the surface, while the panel closed automatically behind them. They were in the underground city of Emporia.

O'Hara, describing this, could not conceal, even in prosaic Bloomsbury, the intense excitement that he'd felt upon first seeing this fantastic culmination of an epoch. "The atomic epoch," he continued, "the world that Europe might have become except for that Third World War. If you were standing now, as I stood then, in the exact center of that strange and yet contemporary subterranean metropolis, I doubt you'd ever write another bit of pseudoscientific nonsense for those Youth League fans of yours. Because you are an amateur, old man—what your picked old brains consider rather weird, and hence commendable from the standpoint of a fiction writer, is in truth nearer facts—though there was more of weirdness in Emporia than you ever dreamed of. More astonishing probably than the Curtain itself, weirder than the Degraded, and vastly further into the domain of the inconceivable than a clan of Cro-Magnon people walking magnificently through the caverns of the Rockies, not two hours' flying time from where we're sitting now, I should have known—I am mildly psychic, a throwback possibly to some wild Boston Irishman of the twentieth century or a gandy dancer for the Santa Fe. These names confuse you, gandy dancer, Boston Irishman? I read them, later, in the incalculably tremendous library that the Father keeps in Washington, the archives of a dead democracy. Yes, there's Celtic blood in me, thinned out but quite sufficient to be psychic in such matters, and I should have known, when I heard Anstruther scream the day he vanished off the coast of Patagonia, that there were stranger things on Earth than an impenetrable wall.

"You've seen the Roman catacombs? Marveled at them, that men can burrow into the earth like that? Then faintly, though very faintly, you understand how I felt standing there, with Nedra pressed close against me, shuddering—the glistening magnesium walls and avenues of subterranean Emporia extending in all directions from the shaft that pierced the city's roof, the lone communication with the surface of the Earth.

"The shaft rose from a sort of plaza, a wide space, rectangular, with avenues dug through the living stone and lined with metal, top and bottom as well as both sides, and with the various compartments that would correspond to our buildings honeycombed out from each avenue, so that there really was no feeling of a city as we know it—only of immense tunnels, intersecting, none of the relief of roofs and chimney pots and varying architectural façades—a triumph of cubism, a nightmare of magnesium that reflected a pale green light from opalescent tubing recessed everywhere into the city's roof. And through these vast avenues the masses of the Degraded swarmed in aimless and quite effortless contentment.

"Literally," said O'Hara, "tens of thousands. The avenues were choked. It was worse than Trafalgar Square on a holiday, worse than the crush of devotees at the Grand National. Continuously they pressed through swinging doors into the food and slumber chambers of Emporia—vast rooms without the variance of so much as a welded seam, where, in great cauldron-like contrivances, the substance that was manufactured by the sun's rays in the photosynthetrons was constantly available, different foods, colored differently, tasting differently, all piped in from the reservoirs into which the photosynthetrons were drained—all automatic, not a hand raised to achieve the feeding of the populace except that which would guide the ladle to the mouth. The populace was fed—not quite like pigs, but with as little ceremony or appreciation.

"The slumber rooms were uniform. Around the walls were tiers of bunks, each six feet wide and eight feet long, each cushioned with a yielding dry material much like foam rubber but incredibly enduring. It was impossible to tear it, impossible to wear it out from the small friction it received. As a matter of record, it had been in those bunks, unchanged, for nearly two centuries.

"Sanitation? That was one of the major purposes of the Deluge, as they called it—a purging of the city, ridding it of both surplus population and uncleanliness, an alkaline solution that— but wait, I've got ahead of how I learned these things.

"The city of Emporia was impressive. Believe me, engineering reached its peak in those first years behind the Atomic Curtain, when fear and want had been abolished and all the genius of man was channeled into the creation of the perfect civilization—perfect, it seemed! And Emporia was sealed completely, locked in magnesium in its cavern blasted into the rock, its air a manufactured substance like its food, its drink pumped in along the Tube that terminated at Los Angeles, where the enormous purifying plant distilled sea water for half of the continent. But great as were these utterly non-manual works, the most astonishing phase of life was life itself—the horde, the shambling tens of thousands eating there and sleeping there and breeding—

You've always been libidinous. And I suppose you'd think there'd be a furor if a hundred thousand women, nude, came through the streets. But there was none—no furor, not so much as a wolf call, not a whistle in those choked streets of Emporia. One hundred thousand naked women, mind you, their bodies delicately green in that reflected light, frailer than the men, their breasts like pockets turned inside out, their hair as short as the men's and as bristling and their long arms clasping more often than not their strange little babies with the fierce protectiveness of all biological things—the rat fights for its young, and the hare, and the wren— but without real affection. One hundred thousand nude and speechless women, apathetically shambling among one hundred thousand naked men—"

A scene, said O'Hara, from Dante's hell. Men and women without emotion and without souls. Or if souls cannot be bred out of the race, then without the intelligence to express them.

The particular band of the Degraded with which he and Nedra had descended into Emporia now had dispersed among these swarming thousands, but the Son who was guarding them remained, and O'Hara, as they proceeded along a glittering, nameless avenue, passing through several of the slumber and feeding chambers where the masses were eating or lying in their bunks, both together and separately, without shame, no longer could believe that there was any purpose or direction in their movement.

"Where are you taking us?" he asked the Son.

"Toward the Guild," replied the Son. "The Tube from Washington comes there. Also, all the Sons allotted to Emporia are bound there now, to escape the Deluge."

"The Sons escape the Deluge."

"The Sons and all those babies who have the prerequisites of Sons. We collect them from the women after we have tested their intelligence. That is done at birth, their brain waves proving those who will be eligible."

"Tested by a machine?"

"How else?"

"Their mothers don't object?"

"Why should the mothers object? When they have borne them, their task is done. It is we, the Sons, who have the tasks of collecting them and sending them to Washington for training there. It is we, the Sons, who have the task of fertilizing—"

"Only the Sons?"

"The males of the masses are sterile. That task is ours. "There must be many Sons," said O'Hara.

"No, unfortunately. The ratio of Sons to masses constantly grows smaller and nowadays it is only by artificial insemination that the task can be accomplished. You will go this way," the Son said, indicating a door. "This is the Guild."

The chamber which they were now entering differed from the other immense halls of Emporia only in two particulars—the entrance through which they were passing consisted of double doors, like waterlocks, and in the center of the hall the metallic floor was cut away, with steps descending toward a series of still lower and smaller tunnels, the top halves of which had been removed. In one of these semi-exposed tunnels was resting at the moment a huge metal cylinder some sixty feet long. With a hatch at its top into which various of the Sons were now descending, each bearing in his arms an infant, returning moments later empty-handed. After ten minutes of this, the last of the Sons emerged, the hatch was snapped shut and bolted, and the cylinder began moving, disappearing within a second past a valve into its tunnel.

A booming voice now filled the hall. The Sons turned from all sides toward a giant metal mirror, upon which, without apparent source, a brilliant light seemed reflected.

"The infants have departed?" asked the voice, and a chorus of the Sons answered in the stylized manner of a chant. "They have departed, Father;"

"The man who flies has departed?'

"He has just arrived, Father."

"Send him to me. The hour of the Deluge is at hand."

The Son with O'Hara and Nedra motioned them toward a second cylinder now sliding in from its tunnel. "You must go at once," he commanded. "But you alone, not the red-haired woman of the mountains."

And Nedra turned. "You promised me, O'Hara."

"I promised you," he said, watching the Son's atomic gun. He remembered then the sudden, vile extrusion of the belching fire upon the mountain's side. It would happen easily. And now that it was here at last, his reluctance was gone—there was no fear, only an exaltation that was blinding to him, the first quick phase of death. "Are you ready, Nedra?"

"Yes," she said, and turning, drew her arms around him. "Now—"

The voice came booming through the hall. "O'Hara! Wait!"

And in that instant those among the Sons close to them crouched.

"Send both of them to me," the voice commanded, and the light upon the mirror gained intensity, becoming pure incandescence. "Send both of them," the voice repeated. "Will you put away your weapon now, O'Hara?"

He faced the light. "Only when we go together."

"You must go together into the Tube at once. The Sons will not hinder you."

"You are watching, Father? You understand about the gun?"

"Yes, I understand—I watch, as I watch everything. As I know everything. That uniform of yours—the International Patrol. You were based on Wrangell Island north of the Siberian Coast. Before that, you were based in the Falklands, flying southward to Antarctica. Born an Englishman of emigre descent—of American descent. Your ancestors were from this continent, before the establishment of the Curtain. You see, O'Hara? I know!" The reflected light now glowed as would the sun itself, and O'Hara was remembering the clansman's myth—the Sun Beneath the Earth. "You are afraid of me now, O'Hara?" asked the voice. "Afraid of knowledge?"

"I am not afraid of knowledge."

"Then you will come, you and your woman—now, I need you here.

The power of that voice, matched by the sun-like intensity upon the surface of the giant mirror, lent a sublimity to these words that kept the Sons in postures of obeisance, yet to O'Hara the tone seemed instead beseeching, as if the Father were himself afraid—as if dreading lest O'Hara might destroy himself. What else could possibly be the purpose of that display of knowledge of events beyond the Curtain? And that last phrase—"I need you here."

The Father needed him. He knew, as he considered it, that he was going. And Nedra knew it.

"O'Hara—no!"

Thrusting the .38 inside his jacket, he whirled, and seizing Nedra's hands, he lifted her, then going quickly down the steps and through the hatch into the cylinder. The Sons were leaping toward it all at once, and then the hatch snapped shut.

With a tremendous thrust, the cylinder shot forward, hurling O'Hara backward through the space inside. Both he and Nedra fell, landing upon the soft resilience of the foam-like rubber material that had lined the wide bunks of the slumber chambers of Emporia. The interior of the cylinder was barren of all else—a long, completely cushioned projectile that now glided smoothly with the sensation of motion eliminated by the lack of any way of reckoning it, no openings, no vibration, until within seconds as O'Hara managed to regain his balance and got up, seeing Nedra lying motionless six feet away, the cylinder began to lose acceleration rapidly. O'Hara again was jerked off his feet.

And as immediately, the hatch above them opened. The face of a Son appeared.

"You are in Washington," he said. "The Father awaits you."

"Seconds," said O'Hara. Not more than twenty seconds since the hatch had shut, yet in those twenty seconds they had traveled in the Tube from western Kansas to Washington, a speed unthinkable if Washington were where it once had been.

Nedra was getting up.

He had been prepared for Nedra to fly into her tigrish rage and come dangerously toward him, compelling him once again to meet her in the endless struggle of a mountain clansman with his mate— a struggle that had begun to be exhilarating—she did not now so much as look at him. She stood with her eyes averted, her shoulders drooped, her bosom motionless, completely apathetic.

"Nedra?" he called. And she did not answer. She did not move. Her arms were hanging slackly, the palms of her hands limp against her thighs. O'Hara spun her around, looking into her eyes. If she saw him at all, she perfectly concealed it. Her eyes were glazed, her lips seeming loose. "Nedra," he cried, and shaking her, "Nedra, what is it? Do you hear me, Nedra?"

"Yes," she said. "I hear you."

Above them again, at the hatch of the cylinder, the Son was saying, "The Father waits for you. You must come now."

And for an instant, O'Hara heard in the Son's toneless voice an echo of Nedra's—the same flatness, a mindless monotone. Now, in confused panic, he was remembering the relative degrees of contamination he had discovered earlier, low when above the mountains, extremely high both toward the east and west of them and presumably even higher in these atomic-powered cities—remembering too that the people of the mountains had already taken that first stride back toward the dawn of man. And had this sudden intensification of atomic pollution struck Nedra, changing her, since daybreak, into another of these ape-like people?

The thought of it revolted him. His reaction was violent. Unforgivable, he called it—forever unforgivable, for in the next moment he was guilty of that crime of crimes, unthinking passion, the closest that man ever comes to bestiality—these words were his own, the opinion that he voiced in Bloomsbury. He slashed his open hand across her face.

The blow did not stagger her. When he could see again, she had not moved—she was standing there before him, staring at him blankly, a thin smear of blood coming from her mouth.

"Nothing I can say, nothing I've done since, can possibly atone for that," said O'Hara. "For that was the ugly revulsion of a man who strikes his misshapen son, loathing the tortured image of himself. All men are capable of it, as I was capable of it. And even as it was done, while the palm of my hand was aching from the blow I'd struck, the abysmal shame of doing it was squeezing chilling fingers on my heart. And something was changed, something was dead—passion perhaps was dead. She was more to me than passion could possibly encompass after that. A man must get down from the high horse of his masculinity to know what I knew then, at last—I loved her. She was my bride at last. My wife."

He stooped, placing one arm gently beneath her knees and then lifting her unresisting body, and with his head bowed above her, he climbed the steps that led out of the cylinder.

The Son who had been waiting now turned his back upon them, saying, "You must follow me." He began at once, moving with the clumsy gait of the Degraded along the vast magnesium-walled corridor. And O'Hara with Nedra in his arms went after him.

The corridor was deserted. The Son, going in front, was without the tube-like atomic weapon that the Sons had carried in Emporia, the only quick way of distinguishing them from the masses. Yet here, in Washington, the city of the Father, there seemed to be no masses, nor in this long corridor were there any of the bunks or feeding cauldrons of Emporia. The endless procession with the bare feet of the Son soundless upon the metal flooring while O'Hara's heels echoed and re-echoed made it seem as if he were walking alone in the most horrible of nightmares—empty space. It continued undeviating, past the point of bearing, with O'Hara's arms losing any sense of feeling from the dead weight of Nedra's body, until abruptly, without explanation, the Son wheeled toward the wall and waited until O'Hara reached his shoulder. The wall was suddenly slid up before them, revealing a narrow flight of countless small metal steps, disappearing in distance infinitely far above the level of O'Hara's vision.

These steps they now continued to ascend, going very slowly, for O'Hara's iron strength was ebbing, until at last they reached a second level of the city, an immense hall, circular in design and with its walls fashioned of the same glaring magnesium that reflected the green lights recessed into the ceiling—a light that magnified the sensation of astronomical space and emptiness, as if this were an edifice beyond the Earth, and not beneath it. Exhausted as he was, O'Hara still was able to conclude that this vastness was calculated, its purpose to awe, for it could not have had another use. Even the masses of Emporia, the teeming naked hundred thousands swirling in that satellite city's halls, would have been lost in this tremendous glittering void.

At the center of this enormous hall was a cylindrical shaft, and upon reaching this the Son again halted. A second panel shot open and the Son silently indicated that O'Hara was to enter.

"With you," O'Hara insisted.

"I cannot go further," said the Son. "It is forbidden."

"The Father forbids you to go further?"

"Yes."

"What would happen if you did?"

"I do not know."

"You are afraid?"

"I am not afraid. The Father watches me."

"He is watching you now?"

"The Father always watches. You must go now."

"You'll wait for my return?"

"But you are not returning. None who enters does."

O'Hara hesitated. But he knew already that there was no way of returning through the Tube to Emporia and through subterranean city to the plains and beyond the photosynthetron to the mountains. There were no odds at all. It was impossible. His only path was forward to the Father. He turned, and passed through the panel which closed instantly behind him, shutting off, the sight of the kneeling Son.

The floor of the shaft now began rising swiftly. When at last it stopped, another panel opened, and O'Hara with Nedra in his arms walked out into the radiance of the sun itself.

He was uncertain how long he stood there, his sightless eyes aching. And if this brilliance also had the purpose of humbling him, it failed, for anger became defiance, the crazy courage of all trapped animals.

"If I could see," he cried aloud. "If only I could see—"

"You shall see O'Hara," said the voice. "And I rejoice that you have chosen me above death."

As the sentence was done, the volume of the voice was dropping so swiftly that the final words seemed no more than a whisper, close. The brilliancy too was diminishing, and light was taking form and shape.

"When you have seen, the voice was whispering, you will no longer be angry, O'Hara. You too will rejoice. Consider this, all your adult life you have constantly wondered what would lie beyond the Atomic Curtain, what had transpired in these two hundred and seventy years within the two Lost Continents, and here particularly, within the United States—within its Capitol of Washington. Now you are going to know. I am going to show you. To teach you, O'Hara. I have wished so often in these years that it could be told to someone who could understand it. I have thought at times that the man had come, a real Son, O'Hara, for you are not the first to cross the Curtain. But the others were inadequate. They failed me, and I—perhaps I too was not quite adequate. Now you are here. Can you see, O'Hara?"

The glare was gone, but utter darkness had succeeded it.

"I can see nothing. These tricks of light and dark are stupid, Father. If you intend by them to frighten me—"

"It is only the contraction of the pupils of your eyes," the Father said. "They will adjust. Surely I have not brought you here to frighten you. Do you see yet?"

"I cannot—wait!—a wall—"

"You are now at the bottom of a pit. I cannot always trust those who come to me."

"—above me, twenty feet, and on the parapets of it—a bearded man, as fragile as the Twelve Old Men—"

"Yes, I am old. You see me now?"

"I see you now," O'Hara answered. "Very dimly, I see you. They call you the Father?"

"It was wise to have them call me that. But you need not. My name is Bryce—Stephen Bryce—Stephen Bryce, how very odd that sounds! I have not heard my name for better than a century. Let me hear it now—"

"Stephen Bryce."

"You humor me, O'Hara. I thank you for it. But you must come up to me. No, please don't move—you must learn that of all the great machines, only man's body cannot be replaced. Conserve it always. You see, you are rising now. This is that glorious age when the pressing of a button can achieve all things, except the things that matter."

The bottom of the pit was indeed rising, lifting O'Hara and Nedra toward the level upon which stood the reed-thin figure of an aged man, a wisp of a man in robes of shimmering and overlaid transparent cloth, a man with scattered hair no longer white but yellowish as parchment is, the beaked and collapsed face of a prophet, toothless, the pallid mouth moving slowly in the sparse, blanched beard, but the eyes young and large and blazingly bright, their blue made darker by the darkness of their sockets, amazing eyes in a body that was skin-sheathed bone.

"I welcome you, O'Hara," said the Father. "You and the woman from the mountains, welcome. But you are weary."

"Yes, Father," said O'Hara, and then instantly amended it: "Yes, Stephen Bryce, and if it is permitted, if we may rest—"

"This," said the Father, with an indicative gesture, "is called the Dome, a hall useful in that time when many came to me as you have come to me today. The great height of this arched ceiling was designed as you have suspected to be impressive, as if a visitor were standing at the core of the earth—a thousand feet to that ceiling, yet only fifty from wall to wall. A masterpiece of illusion. But through that arch upon your left—that way, O'Hara—you will discover that our architects were not altogether inhuman. Go through into the room beyond. You see? Beds, food and drink, the neccessities. You must rest now. You must sleep. In this room you must shed the apprehensions you have felt. Remember, if I had not needed you, you would not have come here to Washington. Yet I trust," he said, "you will forgive a last precaution. Move back—the door!"

A panel clanged down from above. O'Hara and Nedra were alone.

It was an exquisite room. Hexagonal in shape, its floors were deeply cushioned with a carpeting of woven plastic threads. Its walls were carved intricately in stone so that the semblance of an open window centered each facet and yet there were actually no windows, no exits visible now that the panel had clanged shut. The ceiling was vaulted, fashioned of a glass-like material that shaded from the palest blue toward blue black at its apex. Against the far wall were two immense beds, or divans, side by side, and a refectory table wrought from polished and dark metal, with various bowls and beakers containing the multihued liquid foods of the photosynthetrons.

O'Hara strode with Nedra to the beds. And as he slid her burden from his numbing arms, a strange low music filled the room, the sweetness and ethereal thinness of flutes but with a sustained tone, yet without the throatiness of an organ—close, he thought, to the human voice, in octaves incredibly high and with a quality incredibly lyric. The music of sirens, the music of desire, a music that a man might hear in dreams. But Nedra was at last awakening.

She was lying there motionless, her long rich hair disheveled on the bed, her eyes now wide, her full lips whispering, and as he knelt beside her quickly she was saying, "—not even they could have done this to me. I could have made them destroy me, O'Hara. But you refused, you were too weak, you will be the father of my child—"

He threw himself upon the bed beside her. "No, Nedra, you are wrong, it is not weakness but violence that I hold against myself. We have lost nothing that we had. We retain the privilege of death."

"You believe that, O'Hara?"

"I am certain of it. I have the means here," he said tapping his jacket.

"But you haven't the will. That is the trouble now, O'Hara. This thirst of yours to know what happens next is like a disease. Your hand becomes more reluctant each time you stay it, and now that you have seen the Father what else is there? There are no more wonders. Why do you wait? Let me tell you, O'Hara—"

"Nedra, you are obsessed with dying. Is there no strength in learning to endure?"

"Endure for what purpose? Yes, if there is a purpose, but we cannot escape, we can only sink deeper and deeper into these slick abominations."

"You're learning to think, Nedra, and I'm not sure that it's desirable. Yet less than half an hour ago the fear that you might never think again was terrifying me. What does a man really want?"

"I know what you want. To talk."

"Why, yes," he said. "To talk—"

The opalescent light was dying out. The music now faint.

"To talk," O'Hara said, "and sleep, and wake again. Yes, Nedra, if we can be sure to wake again. Eternal life! Remind me to explain to you—though later on—"

But it was the Father who reminded him, and much later. For when O'Hara awoke the room was filled once more with that opalescent light that symbolized day, for actually, in this city of the Father, this capital of the Lost Continents behind the Atomic Curtain, there was neither day nor night. It was true that there were fourteen hours of synthetic light, radiating from the ever-present tubing recessed into the ceilings of the great halls and subterranean avenues, and these fourteen hours were succeeded by ten hours of darkness in the chambers used for sleep. But there was no real night.

O'Hara, then, awakening into this synthetic day, and finding Nedra still asleep beside him, was in no hurry to arise, but lay there staring toward the vaulted ceiling, remembering Nedra's bitter accusation, "We can only sink deeper and deeper into these slick abominations."

But even if they were forever to remain here, prisoners, would it be unendurable? If their cavern in the mountains had been pleasant, why was it less so here? Suppose that door were never to be unlocked?

Never?

The thought of it was smothering. It was in that instant as if he were strapped down upon the bed, and a cold sweat burst out on his body and he clenched his fists, crying aloud, "Father, Father—"

And the room was filled with a quiet voice: "You are unhappy here, O'Hara?"

The door was locked. The voice of the Father came again:

"I shan't insult you, O'Hara—these are not miracles. It is a simple contrivance. Doubtless you have it beyond the Curtain—electronic disks in the ceiling above you, I can hear you and see you, although I am some distance away in my own quarters. I was preparing to come to you when I heard you calling me. Are you unhappy?"

O'Hara said, "I am not unhappy, Father. I am—shall I call it restless? Caged!"

"I understand—you miss the illusion of choice. You are vastly more comfortable in that room than you were in your aircraft in the Arctic, and within those walls at least you have your liberty. An illusion, I insist—a matter of degree. Yet it is irritating to you, isn't it? I have a remedy for that—the stimulation of your mind. And in time you will achieve patience. There is work for you. While you were sleeping with your woman, I have considered a new concept for the Americas—interesting! The first development in a hundred years, O'Hara, and so delightfully simple that I cannot understand why I did not discover it before. You've seen what has happened to my people?"

"The Degraded?" O'Hara answered. "And the Sons?"

The Father's voice was silken. "Are there none beyond the Curtain who would change places with those you describe as the Degraded? Are there none in your world, O'Hara, as deserving of that ungracious term?"

"I am sorry, Father. I used a clansmen's word."

"And there is truth in it. The physiological facts are obvious. That is why I am vain about my Sons—the same stock; yet so perfectly trained that even you, I suppose, believe they have an intelligence superior to that of the masses."

"I have heard how they were selected as babies."

"And trained! That is the fact of it. Are there still dogs in your world beyond the Curtain?"

"Yes, Father. Our world has not changed."

"Once we had dogs. And it was possible to train them so that they made amazing use of their inherent faculties. They could never be taught to speak, for dogs never had that ability, but they made expert use of their paws and their noses in the way that was inherent to them. Now, the Sons, who are the children of women of the masses, are descended, as are the Degraded themselves, from speaking and thinking men. Like yourself, O'Hara. And I have trained them to recover their lost faculties. Without training you could not distinguish them from the masses. But no amount of patience will instill in them—recover from their lineal past—the power to think beyond instinctive things. We need a new pattern, a thinking pattern. I have wasted too much of my allotted time in trying to salvage. I must create now. That is, you must create, O'Hara—a new caste, a new race."

"That will soon go the way of the Degraded, Father?"

"Yes, in time. The law of retrogression is exact, and for two generations—"

The Father's voice broke off abruptly. Then, in a moment, it came back with amazing sharpness. And O'Hara knew that the Father was speaking now to someone else, and in anger. "Why are you here? You will return at once to your work with the Sons!"

The voice that answered was hysterical. "No, Father—oh, no! I won't return to the Sons. I've seen him on the screen, I know he's here, and I'm going to warn him, Father. He won't surrender to your bloody, murderous—"

"I am calling the Sons," the Father cried.

"Call them and be damned. These arms of yours are so much cheese Father. I can snap them in my fingers. You see? You feel? Pain—pain—you had forgotten what it was, hadn't you? Make the Sons return!"

"The Sons are coming now," the Father said. "You have your choice. Return at once to your work, and the promise that I've made to you—"

"A promise I no longer trust."

"You have your choice," the Father said again. "If I do not keep my promise, you know what lies ahead for you. You do prefer to trust me, don't you, Anstruther?"

The shrill voice rose, "I want to believe! I've got to believe you, Father—"

"Then return at once."

O'Hara heard a sob.

When the Father spoke again, his words came very slowly, "I have been injured, O'Hara. I cannot talk to you today. That imbecile who crossed the Curtain—Anstruther, who knew you when he flew for the Patrol—I'm sorry. You must be patient. Contemplate. Time need mean nothing to you, as it means nothing to me. Nothing, O'Hara! Think. And wait—"

Time need mean nothing. Think—and wait!

These, said O'Hara, were slogans that the Twelve Old Men of Geneva might well have used. "The old," he said, "have this at least in common on both sides of the Atomic Curtain—delay, for change is dangerous. And if they base their thinking on the greatest political fact of both our worlds, the Curtain, the slogan is sound. For we of Europe and Asia and Africa have become completely static, our minds paralyzed by the aftermath of that Third World War, while they—the people of the Western Hemisphere—have reaped the whirlwind of spectacular advance, and both because of that one change—the Curtain. And both of us have lost the future we once had."

In Bloomsbury, with the decadent smell of London in our noses and that strange insight that sometimes precedes intoxication stealing over him, O'Hara's voice now seemed to reach a pitch close to evangelical.

"Which is better?" he was saying. "To starve in Bengal or to shamble naked and unreasoning through the subterranean avenues of Emporia? A hard choice, isn't it? No choice at all, I'd say, if that were all we had to choose between. If that were all, there'd be no hope for men. I wish I could tell you that even then the Father, Stephen Bryce, was less fear-ridden than our Twelve Old Men. But it was not true at that moment. It was to come later, with adversity. The greatest of our teachers.

"Philosophy, old man, but cheap stuff. I am no Socrates, no Kant. At best I am—or was—a pilot for the International Patrol, an observer and no more. It is absurd that I should speculate upon the fate of man when I, in that exquisite room in Washington, could not with accuracy foresee what that strange conversation would portend for me within the next few months. But the fact that Anstruther was alive—and the absolute hysteria of his voice— the realization that he was not far from me within this *terra incognita* shook me, left my throat constricted and parched, I can feel it yet, that parched constriction. And you must yourself, don't you, Arthur? May I fill your glass?"

He was pacing the floor, his pounding tread a counterpoint for ideas that he felt instinctively were much too vast for discussion in that ordinary little flat. And while I helped myself once more from his liquor cabinet he continued speaking, or rather resumed speaking, after suddenly halting nervously and picking up that hand-worn ceremonial club.

"Anstruther, too! And in such mental anguish that the city which I had thought deserted now became at once a sinister catacomb where voices came from nowhere and a man who was everywhere, yet nowhere, was constantly watching me—Nedra and I! The goldfish bowl! Spied on by that old skeleton with the living mind, Stephen Bryce, the Father.

"And yet I thought it bearable.

"But bearable for months? Think! And wait! I did not then know that with those words the Father was sealing us in that room for eight months. Or perhaps sealed is the wrong word, it only seemed sealed—for the door was opened or some undiscoverable panel in the walls rolled up, but only when that synthetic day had passed, only when we were asleep, anesthetized!

"The architects of Washington had indeed thought of everything. This can only be my guess—for neither Nedra nor I actually saw the seal upon that exquisite room broken for the next eight months—but somehow, as sound and air could be piped in, so could an anesthetic that made robots of us each night, dead robots, out of service. And with the coming of each synthetic day there was always fresh food, the gruelly stuff from the photosynthetrons, palatable enough, and the necessary sanitation had been effected by means less final than the Deluge, but other than that we might as well have been within our tomb.

"Dead robots—that was the key to it. The Father was conditioning us. We were locked in a paradise of effortless well-being, the most subtle way of stamping out man's soul, but as with a fever that wastes away the body, so our minds were approaching frenzy through those damned eight months—the frenzy that would break, as a fever breaks, and leave us acceptably pliable.

"Eight months of endless days, each identical with the day before, except that Nedra now was growing big with our child. And I think it was the fact of the small life in her womb that saved us. Our fears were concentrated upon it. Our child, prenatally exposed to ceaseless radiation—was it to be another of those soulless ape men? I believed and still believe that Nedra throughout those months was toughening her resolve, she who forever found the answer to all evil things in death, to destroy the infant if—

"Do you understand now? It saved us. The contemplation of a greater tragedy was restorative, the established principle of medicine, the counterirritant. It also works with minds. It kept me sane—Nedra and the child!

"Then one morning Nedra was gone."

That was the morning of hell. That was the bottom of the pit, the breaking of the frenzy, said O'Hara. For hours, alone, within that hideously exquisite room, he beat his fists against the unyielding stone, or screamed the name of the Father toward the disks concealed in the vaulted ceiling.

"Send her back to me! Send her back, Stephen Bryce! Whatever you wish, ask it of me, but send her back!"

Or, when entreaties failed:

"I have the gun! Had you forgotten, Father? Do you suppose that when at last the door is opened, I shall stand here broken? Or that I shall permit myself to sleep beneath your anesthesia? I have the gun!"

Never an answer. Never the slightest whisper coming from the disks concealed in that room. For the Father understood too well that while there still remained the faintest hope that Nedra was alive, and might return, O'Hara was not going to end his life.

Yet possibly this was not altogether intended as torture, said O'Hara. There was torture in it, and surely the Father was indifferent to that, but that was not the sole purpose of this ninth and most terrible month of solitude. The Father himself had been injured. And a god could not permit that to be known. The Father, too, O'Hara was to learn, had also sealed himself away, using the fraudulent blazing mirrors of his electronic network to direct the hemisphere. He knew—he heard it hour by hour—O'Hara's raging, but his own acute problem and his grasp of O'Hara's mind made any other action seem to him unwise. And the wisdom of rulers is not always gentle.

Think! And wait!

Ten months of that, and the last two months of it at a plane of tension that made thinking seem like the flash of electricity through a vacuum. Thought and contemplation can achieve humility or they can achieve an equally supernormal arrogance of frozen wrath. Yet within a moment it was ended.

For O'Hara awoke one morning with a small cry singing in his ears. He turned upon his bed—and there was Nedra beside him and at her breast was the child.

In every man's life there is a moment that he cannot perfectly remember afterward, for the moment is too emotional to be lived through twice. He has at last approached the reason for his being, and for O'Hara it had come with Nedra. And the child.

He wept.

When he could bring himself to touch them, the child was beautiful, the magic of slumber still doe-like in its wide blue eyes, vigor in the clasp of its small fingers.

"He knows you, O'Hara."

Yes. Why shouldn't he? My child, my son, my own son—yes, he knows me.

"Nedra—"

"Not now." Her fingers touched his lips. "A little while—"

Then the voice from nowhere, absent all these months came back.

"Good evening, O'Hara. You forgive me now don't you?"

Softly, very softly: "It has been difficult for you, but there was no other way. Without my guidance, you would have destroyed yourself, your woman and the child—and not with your gun. You must come to me at once."

"With Nedra and my son."

"They will be safer there."

"It is your word against my thinking, Father. Either they come—"

"Bring them, O'Hara. But keep your weapon ready." The panel through which they had entered months before now was sliding up, revealing the empty corridor beyond.

"You will come into the corridor and turn toward your left," the Father was saying. "Only my voice will guide you. That is correct—now proceed until you hear me. And keep your weapon ready!"

Nedra walked slowly at O'Hara's side, the child asleep within her arms. The panel closed behind them. They were within a seemingly endless metal-lined tunnel that receded in each direction toward infinity, the glaringly reflected light obscuring the convergence of its geometric lines and for a long while they walked as if each second might bring sudden death, completely tense, O'Hara with the .38 in his hand.

"Now you must turn again, this time toward your right," the Father commanded, and simultaneously a second panel opened in the wall. "You must come inside—and put away your weapon now, O'Hara. Only in the corridor was there any danger."

"What was the danger, Father?"

The second panel closed. They were within a vast rectangular hall, its ceiling far above them, azure pale, its walls a fretwork of marvelously carved stone, polished like glass. And deep back into it, against the farthest wall, upon a four-tiered dais of translucent stone was an enormous bed.

"This is where I exist, O'Hara—where I sleep and work, and where you and your woman and the child will live. There is privacy in space and space enough for us. Danger, you ask? A disturbance among some of the younger Sons, Anstruther's group, but I can settle it in time. Approach me closely—here, upon this dais."

The voice was everywhere around them, from every corner of the enormously spacious room, as the voice of a divinity would be, yet O'Hara understood that it was coming from the bed upon the dais, and toward that, with Nedra beside him—Nedra with the sleeping infant held against her breast—he was now moving, as the first man with the first woman must have moved from the Garden, scourged by the voice of wrath. It was like that. It was no less than that awe and humility and perhaps terror, although he knew it was the voice of Stephen Bryce, a wasted man with eyes that burned more brightly than the sun itself.

Sublime, O'Hara insisted.

"Come near to me, O'Hara. For I—cannot get up."

And the spell was shattered. It was the pathos of the words that did it. The Father was helpless, the Father whose mind was the germ of life for these two continents, the only real intelligence within the hemisphere, was lying now upon a vast bed in a vaster hall, a cripple, a brain no longer able to effect for itself the simplest functions of the grossest of the masses.

Yes, the spell was shattered. But a man of O'Hara's stature would finally have rebelled against mere sublime authority, had it attempted to drive him to do the things he normally abhorred. But the authority of a cripple was infinitely more terrible—a cripple's power lay in the innate will of all men to be kind. And had Stephen Bryce so planned it, he could not have planned better. From the moment that O'Hara discovered how completely helpless Stephen Bryce had now become, and how dependent upon him, his own will was faltering.

"You see, O'Hara?" the voice was saying from all corners of the immense hall, although O'Hara now was standing close beside the bed. "At this moment it is you who have the privilege to do what could not be accomplished by the Muscovite—you can destroy these continents. For if I die, these people die."

The lids were closed above the blazing youthful eyes and Stephen Bryce had thus become a wasted, ancient skull, alive but only that. His blue-veined hand lay fragilely upon the coverlet, close to a metal panel that was studded countlessly with unmarked keys.

"You pass the privilege?" the Father said ironically, his voice a whisper within inches of his lips, yet booming from the corners of the hall, an acoustical arrangement that O'Hara did not notice for the first few seconds, so intent was he upon the substance of his words.

"I have delayed for your arrival," the Father was saying, "the Deluge at Emporia. But these ten additional months of life have not surprised them, or are they grateful. My people," he said, and his eyes seemed to burst open, "are incapable of either surprise or gratitude, which limits the satisfaction that I get from playing God. As you observe, I'm not a god—not quite, I suppose, any longer a creature of flesh and blood, but certainly not a god. Few here, behind the Atomic Curtain, are aware of that. Yourself, and Anstruther—and it was also Anstruther who restored to me the realization that neither am I quite immortal. I'd almost forgotten that. You heard, perhaps—a matter of two broken arms and the debilitation that resulted from the shock of it. That is why I am here, upon this grandiose bed, the old lion bearded, O'Hara—the old stag at bay at last. Done for, O'Hara."

The hand rose slowly, fluttering. "And now, the decencies of life. I have things to show you that a woman might not wish to see. And things to tell you that no child should hear, whether it comprehends or not. Send them away—send them toward the wall upon your left, it is prepared for them. At any time you can recall them if you wish, for the slightest whisper on this dais is magnified to thunder—oh, you've noticed that? Send them—at once—the decencies; I have not forgotten."

The eyes were closing. The hand had dropped upon the coverlet. It was as if the Father were already dead. For a moment O'Hara remained beside the bed, then he turned and descended the steps of the dais to Nedra, and after explaining what the Father had requested—Nedra left at once, without a glance at him—he returned again to the bedside of Stephen Bryce.

"Thank you, O'Hara. You are more gracious than the circumstances," said the Father, now opening his eyes again, while weariness dragged at the corners of his pallid mouth. "A new race O'Hara," he whispered. "We need it here. You will remember that I mentioned it to you? Come, now, don't glare at me so sanctimoniously—I am mathematician enough to know that a new race cannot be bred from a single woman, your woman, nor the handful of women I might have the Sons take from the mountains. Are you a student of husbandry? There are books here—behind this dais a doorway leads into the library where I once used to study. Among these books are many from the days before the Curtain, and in that section, if you wish, you may learn all we've ever learned of genetics. We have no cattle now. Our only animals" —the pale lips twisted—"but you know them—men! Your brothers, O'Hara, the masses of Washington and Emporia, New York and Chicago, all our cities. In husbandry, O'Hara, the soundest concept was that rundown stock was easiest improved by crossing the prevailing females with a superior male. The get of any single male is almost limitless, provided—"

"This was explained to me," O'Hara interrupted, "by one of the Sons at Emporia. Artificial insemination."

"I heard his explanation, O'Hara. Yes, the males of the masses are sterile, although not impotent. And actually the tests which we make at birth do not determine intelligence as such, but fertility. The relation of those two factors is no coincidence. The stupid—fertile, once a predominate strain, have bred themselves out with the vanishing of the reason for their existence, which was hunger—the substitution of one physical satisfaction for another. The intelligent—sterile, toward which the ruling classes tended in the days before the Curtain, likewise have passed, and for the same cause—with the necessities of life available to all without effort, intelligence, in itself, lost its survival virtues.

"What now remain are the two breeds that our way of life brought to the front—the stupid-sterile and the intelligent-fertile, a geneticist's dream come true, the fruit of our atomic civilization. We should be reaching the millennium, O'Hara.

"But while we have got the two best strains predominating now, the unforeseeable reversal of the laws of evolution has shoved both strains ever backward, although comparably for each. The keel is on the bottom still, the mast upon the deck, but the ship is sinking. And nature has confounded man once more.

"And so, O'Hara—so through these endless years alone I have been forced to tinker—selective breeding, elimination of the weak, artificial insemination—tricks, all tricks, all little stratagems to stall off the immutable. Each generation slides back further than its sires. Your son—forgive me—will be not quite you, and his son will be neither you nor his mother. And your son's son will see his newborn son with horror. It is exact. But if a new race suddenly were spawned into the hemisphere, recapturing the ground lost in these generations since the Curtain—"

"Father, you'd still be tinkering."

"But the possibilities of this tinkering are extensive. Beyond the Curtain, fortunately, exists an inexhaustible source of uncontaminated sires."

"How would you get them here?"

"That is your task."

"My task? I could not count upon a providential thunder storm to get me through the Curtain again."

"Providence we cannot reckon in planning the future of a hemisphere, and never have. It is true that chance—pure chance—enabled you, and Anstruther before you, and others now dead before both of you, to pass through the Curtain. But it was not Providence. Any man flying in the correct direction at the exact second that you were flying—and at any point in the Curtain—would have got through."

"I'm not sure I understand you. At any point in the Curtain at that exact second?"

"Within those exact ten seconds, O'Hara, hundreds of pilots in your International Patrol must ram into the Curtain every decade, yet if all of them were to hit it at the correct speed, flying the correct course, at the correct time, they would all get through. Chance enters into it only in that you happened to be doing all of these. Once each year, and for an interval of ten seconds, our Carolina reactor shuts off automatically and the Hanford or West Coast reactor takes over supplying the power for the Curtain. That has been happening now for the two hundred and seventy years since the establishment of the Curtain—the reactors were so arranged in the beginning. Completely automatic, you understand, as are the Tubes, the photosynthetrons, the East and West Coast distillation plants, the Deluges—as everything must be within this hemisphere. And there is this interval of ten seconds between the shutting off of the Carolina reactor and the generation of the Hanford reactor—ten seconds in which the Curtain does not exist!"

O'Hara closed his eyes. The taste of blood, saline and hot, was in his mouth—his heart now pounding with trip-hammer force. For here, within a sentence, was the determining great secret of the two halves of the earth—"There is an interval of ten seconds in which the Curtain does not exist!"

"It cannot vary by even a fractional concept of time," the Father was continuing. "And there, O'Hara, is how your task can be accomplished. You have your known factor of time, and in the lower Rockies, you have your plane. When it is brought to Washington, it can be duplicated on a more adequate scale, for the Sons, under guidance, are not bad workmen. Time and method are problems we can master, and there is only the issue of your willingness to obtain from beyond the Curtain—"

"My willingness? Do you believe, Father, that men—men as I've always known them, not your masses and Sons—would voluntarily enter into this proposition?"

"Do you believe that they would not? For a full belly, for a life without exertion, without the strain of thought—really, O'Hara, I have not forgotten what your world was like."

"Remove the strains they know, and they will discover other strains. In time, for instance, they will rebel against becoming your automatons."

"I am aware of that—I am now dealing with Anstruther. But that at least is a problem I can solve. Let me show you how I deal with human problems, O'Hara—let me show you the city of Emporia, where you first saw my people. Observe upon the wall behind this dais a metal screen, such as you saw in every hall and every corridor of Emporia, and as exist in every city of this hemisphere, even our dead cities—remember Spokane? The giant tower with its solarium? Remember you were curious and flew down close to it? Remember Denver? Those cities we abandoned soon after the establishment of the Curtain, as soon as our subterranean metropolises were built—for in those days we were not certain just how quickly the nations beyond the Curtain might construct atomic plants. True, we had our scintillometers, we were constantly on our guard, we had our rockets ready, but the physical plant could be built, prepared for instant operation, and we had by then no accurate reports of what your scientists might be thinking—we had learned that thinking was more vital than the last incidents of construction. We had no surety except our rocket barrages that you would not get these suppositional plants into production before we could destroy you, which meant of course that we too might be destroyed. We had with us the frightful memory of that Third World War, and how very close the outcome seemed at first. So we took no risks; We went beneath the earth, leaving dead cities where once we had lived. We built new cities up into the Arctic, outpost cities, as far as the northern coast of Canada, leaving only that chain of mountains, where the engineering problems were prohibitive, beyond the network of our automatic civilization. Now, this metal panel—" The Father's fragile fingers poised above the unmarked keys. "I touch, as you observe, and instantly you are seeing what is happening across the continent in Emporia."

The screen above the dais now glowed. And when the brilliant light adjusted into patterns, O'Hara saw the glittering corridor outside the Guild, the hall of the Sons at Emporia. The shambling naked tens of thousands of the masses passed before his eyes, as aimless as he'd seen them when he had been there, the women with their babies in their arms, the nude and hairless ape-like men, feeding by thousands at the photosynthetron troughs, sleeping by thousands in the wide-bunked slumber halls—a mass of life as purposeless as maggots, living and devouring.

"The Sons again have gone within the Guild," the Father said. "And now I touch this key—"

Above the corridors of Emporia, slots opened in the ceilings and from them poured a tide-like wave of palely amber liquid, cascading down upon the swarming masses, engulfing them, yet as O'Hara watched, those caught up in the tide were vanishing—not sinking down, but actually vanishing, while those who fled in screaming panic, milling as a scalded colony of ants might do, leaping above the fallen bodies of those trampled in the crush, when once touched by the amber tide jerked back from it, but where an arm had been, a leg, a head, was nothing.

"Dissolved," the Father said. "The Deluge is a caustic solution that will cleanse Emporia of all filth, all population except those in the Guild—all that should not endure. Observe—this key the solution now is pouring down through slots beneath the corridor, draining into that pipe within the Tube which carries it—and them, for they are only liquid now—into the Pits of Yellowstone, the continental sewerage plant, where the caustic is decanted and restored to tanks for future use. You see approximately three hundred thousand of these—call them men!—disappearing now, all except the Sons. Observe the screen—it flashes now inside the Guild, and this is even more adroit."

The pattern changed, and when it reshaped, O'Hara recognized the vast hall of the Sons, and saw them staring as they knelt, obeisant as they watched the metal screen within their own hall. That screen, inside the Guild, was glowing now, the brilliance of the sun upon its surface and a booming voice exhorting them—the Father's voice as O'Hara had first heard it in Emporia.

"That voice," the Father said, "my own, also is automatic, the electronic impulse which released the Deluge also started the voice. All these details were co-ordinated in the beginning and are now effected through batteries of integrocalculators here in Washington. The single touch of a key sets in motion the chain of events, another key modifies it or ends it—although at all times I can shift these operations to manual and direct them step by step. Suppose now we go to one of the slumber chambers, distant from the heart of Emporia, where the Deluge has only now begun. You will see them asleep or in their more intimate existence, and you will realize how really painless all this is."

"No, Father," said O'Hara. "No, Stephen Bryce. No—more."

"Compassion, O'Hara?"

"Disgust. Loathing."

"For me. I can understand that. When I was younger there were times when I felt it too. But how else can the problem of overpopulation be solved, O'Hara?"

"You have the means. There are no births except at your direction."

"You would have me deprive the women of the masses of their sole amusement, which is the bearing of children? And further, you forget the declining ratio of potential Sons among the newborn—to keep constant the total of Sons, the birth rate of the women of the masses constantly must be stepped up—we must have more babies, more population to select from, but our supply of food material is constant, adequate for a constant population, which through these periodic Deluges I achieve. An instant's agony—no worse than that experienced in that painless institution of your hemisphere, the electric chair—avoids the months and years of slow starvation which your own estimable system, O'Hara—the system of your hemisphere—enforces. Which do you actually believe to be less cruel?"

"But in our hemisphere there is no volition—"

"The truth is, isn't it, that no one will accept the responsibility for managing society?"

"We have had such men. We called them monsters."

"You are not yet quite adults. But I have lived now for almost three hundred years. I was born before the establishment of the

Curtain, while a people of your hemisphere were loosing upon our cities a murderous rain of warheads, destroying among others the city of my birth, killing my father and my mother and my small brother—I have lived, O'Hara, long enough to remember the monsters of your hemisphere, and remember them acutely, not as vague names in history. And also I have lived long enough to recognize the immutable facts of a mechanical world, and to lose, I suppose, my childish scruples. And yet, had I any choice at all in these matters, had I less responsibility, had I someone to lean upon, someone with the physical abilities that I no longer have—yourself, O'Hara."

"I reject you, Stephen Bryce. For after all of your excuses you remain a monster who has lived too long to value life."

"And will live long enough to fit you into my purposes."

"If I don't destroy you now."

"Destroy a cripple? You haven't the capacities for it. And destroy all of my people in this hemisphere? You call me a monster, O'Hara? Come now, tell me—is that the ethics of the world beyond the Curtain nowadays? To shrink from necessary cruelties to perform those that would be incalculably more terrible?"

"It is a matter—a matter of intentions—"

"Bosh! Kill millions to spare thousands—that isn't even good economy. Spare the inhabitants of Emporia, but not spare me—and not the tens of millions of these continents who depend upon my knowledge? And not yourself? And not your woman, O'Hara? And not your child? Let's try to avoid these absurdities—you are going to do as I wish you to do, at least until I have taught you how this panel operates the integrocalculators. Is that not true?"

O'Hara met those blazing eyes a moment. Then his own eyes closed. "Yes, Father. It's true."

The Father smiled wanly. "I welcome you again. You may join your woman and your child now, for I must sleep. I am exhausted by the rare experience of argument. Later on, we must work together on the problem of Anstruther and the younger Sons. I shall need, I think, more than my brain for that. For at this moment, just beyond the door through which you entered this hall, they are coming now, the danger that I warned you of. And he, whom once I welcomed as I welcome you—he who is screaming that he means to save his comrade of the International Patrol, yourself—is motivated chiefly by another vision that he saw upon this screen, a vision that has cracked his fragile brain—it was the woman, Nedra. Another complex from your world that I'd forgotten."

PART FOUR

O'HARA put down his empty glass.

"I have had enough of this," he said, and got up, as an angered lion might get up—that kind of throttled wrath, restrained only by the dignity of his huge and thickly muscled body, for the pent-up loathing that he had felt for Stephen Bryce—the Father, the only brain guiding the destinies of the hundreds of millions swarming through the subterranean cities of the Western Hemisphere—was burning through him, even here in London, in this flat of his in Bloomsbury, much as if he had gotten into his veins a dose of that caustic solution that he had seen dissolving the masses of over-populated Emporia.

"You see?" he asked, and whirled abruptly toward me, his darkly tanned face twisting sardonically beneath his tousled dark hair, his blue flight jacket of the International Patrol now completely unbuttoned, for the drinks we had had and his rapid pacing of the floor of that little flat and the pace of his report, and above all his tension, had dappled him with sweat. "You see, do you—I'm utilized! I've lost whatever grip I had. Or perhaps I never had it. When there's no stress, we can all of us think ourselves cucumbers. But when I was walking at last away from that immense bed upon the dais in Stephen Bryce's unthinkably vast hall in Washington, my pity for the Father was drowned in disgust for any man who could do what I had just seen him do, and I dreaded him more than I feared the dangers now loosed in the endless corridor outside the hall.

"For I could deal with Anstruther. Insane or not, Anstruther could not seem too dangerous, the way that I remembered him. His rather womanish blue eyes and fair hair and his romantic boyishness—weakness, I told myself—could never be formidable.

Yes, I could deal with Anstruther. And as I left the Father and went toward the distant wall where Nedra was waiting with my infant son, I meant to do it.

"Let me make the situation clear, I had been without hope. It had seemed incredible that I could escape with Nedra and my son from the labyrinth of Washington, retracing my way along the glittering and utterly deserted corridors through panels that slid open without detectable human motivation, back to the Tube and through it back into Emporia, now a dead metropolis, and up again by its only shaft to the surface of the earth and through the patrols of the Degraded in western Kansas once again into those mountains where Nedra's kinsmen were. No one—I had had the clansmen's word for this—had ever escaped once he had sunk into the cities of the lowlands. It was that absolute hopelessness that had driven me unresisting forward to the Father, and yet now—

"Now I believed there was a way to do it. I had only to learn from the Father the mechanism of the integrocalculators, the key-studded board he kept beneath his blue-veined hands, and to make my peace with Anstruther who surely understood this maze of a city and who, as the Father himself had said, controlled a dissident faction of the Sons, and the way would be clear for Nedra and my child and me.

"That's hope for you. The impossible at once becomes a very simple thing. I had only to do this, and only to arrange that. I wonder now how I supposed the Father, so readily to be outwitted, had been able to endure for two hundred and seventy years behind the Atomic Curtain. The truth is of course that I was not thinking—I was engaging in the opposite of thought, which is hope. And hope blinded me. Or rather, purpose blinded me. I had been so long without either."

He had been, he said, quite certain of his direction when he started walking away from the dais. He had seen Nedra going toward the apartment built into the distant wall, and he had thought that he had only to go that way himself to join her. Yet in the absorption of his speculations he walked for some fifteen minutes without the distance once occurring clearly to him, and it was only the sensation of walls closing in upon him that finally halted him.

He was in a corridor. Somehow he had passed from the vast hall of the Father.

"I was to learn that in the city of Washington there were no walls as we know them. They had the thickness and the height of walls, but the Father, constantly watching in the screen above his bed, could with the touch of his little finger disarrange and reassemble those immense, sections of stone and metal in a thousand patterns, all preconceived it is true, to cope with all conceivable situations. I was to see the giant gears that could elevate within an instant the lowest depths of the city to the topmost level and transfer the Dome itself, that amazing architectural illusion, into the very bowels of the earth, miles below the muddy bottom of the Potomac. In all of the city only the Tube was fixed, and that solely because the shifting of its continental span was too monstrous an engineering feat even for those masters of the early days immediately after the establishment of the Atomic Curtain. It would have involved the balancing of the crust of the earth itself, and as in the case of Archimedes with his global lever, where was there such a fulcrum?

"But the city, Washington, was a myriad of interchangeable parts, and at no moment since its construction could there possibly have been a master plan for it—nothing that any enemy could definitely say was thus and so, the plexus here, the exact place to strike at. Within the broad limit of its thousand patterns and countless thousands of lesser integral dispersions it existed only as the Father wanted it, and through his keyboard could instantly set it up.

"I say that the lone exception was the Tube. That is true, the Tube was fixed, but its terminus could be sent whirling away from it, sealing it off. Conceive of the city, if you wish, as a series of spheres, one within the other, like a child's gyroscope, revolving when the impulse came from the integrocalculators, or expanding through the integration of chords from a larger outer sphere which then contracted into the lesser orbit. Too tough? It was for me.

"It was much too tough a problem for me, and when I found myself enclosed within the comparatively narrow confines of that corridor, beyond the Father's—and Nedra's hall—I felt for the first time since Nedra's return with her newborn child that complete and imbecilic frustration that must come over those poor deviled rodents that psychologists force to pop through little doors to establish their reflex patterns. I stood stock still, my brain suddenly as empty as the corridor about me, numbed beyond comprehension for how long I do not know, until at last I became conscious of the spasms of my fingers."

And within the passing of the next five minutes, said O'Hara, his mind went through the progressive stages of the full cycle of evolution—inert at first, then active only as a salt solution might react electrically, then numbly timorous as a hypersensitive vegetable, and finally aware. The worm recoils from surfaces too hot or cold. He was aware like that, until somewhere along toward the rapid reassertion of the human mind he met and conquered, if not fear, at least the impossibility of fearing.

To fear, he said, and to know the reason for it, constitutes the greatest single stride up from the primal ooze.

"Nedra!" his first cry was. And then, "Oh, Father, Father, help me! Help me—"

And the voice came to him gently:

"You see, O'Hara? Are you so measurably superior to that dawn child who worshiped the fire that burnt him? You call upon me now as if indeed I were a god, and solely because I seem to injure you."

"Father, you mock me."

"Yes, O'Hara, I mock you—but only to help you regain your reason. There is something you should know, O'Hara—you must understand that a man who has lived in authority as long as I have has seen all the pitifully few reactions of men under duress. As you were walking away from me, I knew that you were considering how you would plot against me. I cannot read your mind, but given the man you are, trained as you are, it was inevitable that you would react in that manner. I could, I believe, reduce all this to an understandable equation, just as I can shuffle about the components of this city into the pattern I desire without thinking in detail of the various phases of it. The integrocalculators do that detail thinking for me. That should be comprehensible to you, for all these little mechanical marvels were rooted in the world as it existed here before the Curtain, and exist now beyond it. Equations of the brain—we had the fundamentals of them in the years before the Third World War; and the origins of spatial architecture lay in those experimental buildings in which the walls were movable, of course only horizontally, but not remote in mathematical technique from the vertical and spherical construction of this city. A matter of imagination only, isn't it?

"And memory, O'Hara. My memory for the keys upon this board, and the integrocalculators' automatic memory of the meaning of successive stabs of power.

"And so I think I can write the equation of your being, O'Hara—an equation in terms of the years you have existed and the times you have faced death and love—I must include love, however ephemerally your poets think of it. Yes, love, O'Hara, for there as you undoubtedly have suspected is a complex thing, mystical beyond the caress of a woman's arms or a baby's breath, intellectual beyond the tables of multiplication that you studied as a youth—the soul of man in fact. Surely you've recognized it as that. Your woman of the mountains, Nedra, lacks your capacity for love, which after all is tenderness, and so you do not understand her always, do you, O'Hara? The soul—you would dispute this with me? Then take the next gradation below Nedra that we have within this hemisphere, the people of the masses. What essentially have they lost? Yes, you do know that! Their souls, the capacity for love, decreasing in direct proportion to their retrogression. If they possessed it there might be some hope for them—but they do not. Oh, yes, O'Hara, I can write that equation—physical and mental strength, and the capacity for love—or soul—these are the algebraic terms of man. I bore you?"

"My wife and my baby, Father?"

"Safe with me. You see, I even ape the attributes of a god—the things you love forever are attainable by keeping faith with me. Hostages, shall I say? As the pledge of immortality keeps your kind in hostage. Yes, they will be here with me awaiting you, when you have finished the task I set for you."

"The task?"

"Ultimately your task will be as I have outlined it for you, the return to the Eastern Hemisphere to obtain those sires of future generations of Americans. But now before that can be possible, you must salvage Anstruther for me."

"But you yourself, Father, told me Anstruther was mad."

"Demented, yes, by the vision of the woman Nedra. But he can be salvaged. He must be salvaged. For if I lose you, O'Hara—should something go wrong during your flight back into the Eastern Hemisphere—I will have at least Anstruther. And I have no time now to depend on the chance again that some adventurous or befuddled pilot of the International Patrol will crash through the Curtain."

"You'd risk a madman with the task you set for me?"

"Only if I must. I don't belittle that risk. But for that matter, how sure am I of you? Once beyond the Curtain what pledges your return except the woman you love? And that reed is too thin to be my sole reliance. You must reclaim Anstruther for me, you must bring him to me, where I can get at him."

"I am to be his Judas, is that it?"

The Father's voice, a silken whisper in that glittering corridor, lashed out. Your posturings annoy me. We are not discussing morals, we are discussing what you will do. Have you so soon forgotten the months you spent alone in that magnificent little room? And Nedra and your baby?"

"Whom you dare not harm! They are your only hold on me."

"Don't underestimate what I dare, O'Hara. Nor overestimate your value to me. I could decide, if I must, to work with lesser tools if necessary. But as for your scruples if I had wished to destroy Anstruther, he would be dissolved by now. I can do it at this moment, simply by touching the key beneath my finger. No, you would not be destroying him by bringing him to me. You would in fact relieve me of the possible necessity of eliminating him."

"You are too clever a logician for me, Father. But I refuse."

"Do you indeed?" the Father said. "Then I must show you something. As you observe, the walls of the corridor are now rushing suddenly away from you, O'Hara—"

And instantly he was swallowed in space, a void, the ceiling and the walls vanishing toward infinity, miles, within a second, so that he felt impacted into himself, shrinking, yet knowing that the macrocosmic city still contained him. And even as he clung to that shred of reason, the floor beneath him began to sink, so that once again walls were surrounding him as he descended. And presently far above him a metal surface closed darkly while the wall upon his left began receding and the segment of floor that bore him followed it at a speed so terrific that his senses could not bear up under it, and he blacked out.

He was lying face down when he recovered, and for a long while he remained there, unable to move, then at last he heard a faint, strangling cry, and lifting himself by driving his knuckles hard against the floor, he saw not ten feet from him, behind a translucent wall, Nedra and the child—Nedra holding the baby far above her head and swimming frantically in water that was rising rapidly around her throat.

Almost at once the water was above the level of her head churning in from invisible sluices that must be somewhere across the translucent room, and Nedra turned a despairing face toward him and then sank beneath the surface, although continuing by her desperate struggle to keep the baby's head above the water. He could see her mouth open as if to scream to him. He could see the violent threshing of her legs and he knew instantly how long that could last, and he plunged his shoulder against the translucent wall, as if to smash it.

But the wall yielded back from his weight as if it were a jelly, pliable but impervious, for he could not get through it. With his giant's strength he could smash his fists within inches of her body, he could drive his fingers toward her and grasp for her threashing arms and legs, but he could not quite feel them—he could not quite touch them. He could not save her.

She was kicking desperately again, the fur kirtle working loose from her body in the fury of her struggle, and once more she managed to drive her chin above the surface of the water, and continuing that frantic treading she was keeping the baby from drowning while O'Hara, ramming himself continuously into the pliable wall, slashed with both fists in futile efforts to reach her. Now suddenly he heard Nedra's choked voice, above the splashing of her body, as if the sound track of a movie had resumed after some minutes' silence:

"I can't, O'Hara—can't keep—going—"

And she sank once more. This time her sagging legs were not able to support the child above the surface, and her arms sank helplessly, the child revolving slowly in the water toward her, wide-eyed, grasping with its tiny fingers, and O'Hara saw them both drifting downward in that aimless, dying way that half-buoyant matter has.

"Father!" he screamed. "Stephen Bryce—"

"Yes, O'Hara," the gentle voice came from the space about him. "Yes, I understand. You see, I have already reversed the flow of the water. The room is draining."

O'Hara could not speak. He sank upon his knees; watching the level of the water drop toward the bodies drifting on the floor of the translucent room. And almost instantly that room was drained. And Nedra was lying with the baby beside her, her arms limply—unconsciously, O'Hara knew—enfolding him, and the water now dripping in small rivers from her loose, rich hair that had swirled like a shawl across her body.

"They need my full attention now, O'Hara," the Father was saying very softly. "You must go now upon your mission—I will be with you constantly, I will be watching, and when it seems wise I shall talk with you. But remember, whenever I wish it, I can again return you to a translucent wall like this one that will yield to your touch without ever admitting you, and beyond it, so very near to you, Nedra and the child will drown."

"She needs you quickly, Father—"

"And she needs your voice to sustain her. Speak to her;"

"Nedra," he whispered, unable to believe that she would hear. But her eyelids opened. "Nedra," he whispered, "if I am able to return—"

Her lips were moving now. "You will, O'Hara."

"I will! And no matter what you're told, never believe—"

"I shan't, O'Hara."

Then the sound track was dead again and he knew it. The Father, lying upon that immense bed within that incredibly vast hall, wherever that now was in Washington, and watching in the screen above the dais, had shut off the key that had made Nedra's and O'Hara's voices audible to each other, and was himself speaking again.

"I have regretted doing this, O'Hara. But if all the regrets of my life were to come back upon me suddenly, I should as surely drown in them as Nedra and your baby were drowning a moment ago. Now I promise their lives to you, if you are faithful. The walls again are receding, as you see—"

The walls were receding and the floor upon which O'Hara stood was rising and Nedra and the baby in her arms had vanished once more into that chaos of shifting walls and floors and ceilings, and again O'Hara was conscious of the rapidly increasing velocity with which he was moving through the space of Washington— conscious of it only momentarily, and then the black pall of vertigo smothered him.

But the voice that pervaded the spatial geometry of the underground metropolis never stopped speaking to him, counseling him even as he lay in a coma, as if it were a dream voice, the voice of a god that was dimly remembered from a childhood revelation, and very slowly, as his senses returned to him and once more he could see the tangibles of metal and stone and his own flesh, he began to feel as if the voice spoke only to himself, O'Hara—as if those about him, later, could not hear it. This became an obsession that he never clearly recognized for what it was, the Messiah complex in its early stages, the conviction, never really questioned by himself, that the omnipotent being of the Western Hemisphere spoke only to him and listened only to him, an absurdity that ten months before—when he was beyond the Curtain—he would have derided. In the end when he was done with delusions, he was to understand how well the Father realized the magic of the Voice from Space, a psychological device that was implemented by physical control over those whom O'Hara loved.

"You must get up now, O'Hara," the voice was telling him. "For even at this moment Anstruther is approaching you— Anstruther does not yet know where you are, nor is he actually searching for you. He is in fact going about the futile business of trying to find his way into this hall where I exist—he and his dissident Sons, relying upon the juvenile techniques of your mythical Monte Cristo, digging or boring or cutting, completely unaware that within an instant's time I can transfer him twenty miles away. Anstruther does not know the secret of the integrocalculator and will never know it, even should I be forced to use him if you fail me. But do not fail—and you shall know that secret, O'Hara. Some vessels will contain water and some will contain hydrogen, some will contain molten magnesium and some will contain only eiderdown, but few will contain them all. You will, O'Hara—you will contain what you must, I think—so long as I keep my fingers on the fibers of your heart. Arise."

O'Hara got up. He was standing in a small circular room at the end of one of those glaring corridors, as if in running he had come at last upon that point in infinity which the corridors always seemed to promise, a room with a diameter of forty feet, its sheer walls rising to a dome that opened on a tiny patch of brilliant blue, much like the blue of O'Hara's now shapeless uniform. Was it the sky he saw, the heavens that he'd known before descending into the subsurface warrens of this lost atomic world? He did not know—illusion had become so routine that the fact seemed always suspect now. Yet it could be the sky, a pledge of things to be, as Nedra and the baby had become in memory.

"Are you listening, Stephen Bryce?"

"What is it now, O'Hara?"

"The ceiling—?"

"A symbol. And only you in this hemisphere can understand it."

"I don't."

"It is inevitable, O'Hara, that the mechanics of this hemisphere as we have been forced to organize it would tend to create in your mind the impression that I am divine. Is that not true?"

"It is stronger than an impression, Father. If you have lived, as you say, nearly three centuries, if you control this spatial city and the Curtain and the Tube—and I know you do—it becomes extremely difficult to think of you as mortal.

"You see? In spite of your reason, in spite of the scoffing tone you force into your voice, you are beginning to believe. The genesis of faith is most often the misinterpretation of truths. And so I have made that tiny patch of celestial heaven visible to you. For you—and you alone—must understand that I am not God, that I am not immortal, that I am subject to the laws of nature and eternity regardless of how long I manage to evade them.

"That patch of sky is there to bolster your sanity, O'Hara. For you must be sane. No matter how deeply involved you may become in the game of playing the Chosen Son, you must retain your sanity, or the purpose of the game will be defeated by the zest of it. Remember this, you have few realities to cling to—that patch of sky is one of them, and the senile tremor of my fingertips, and the receptive loins of your wife, and your baby's cry, and the inerasable memory of the world beyond the Curtain. Cling to these, O'Hara, for you will need them. Anstruther is approaching."

Anstruther was indeed approaching, but O'Hara was not prepared for the manner of his entrance. As the voice died away, the metal sheathing of the corridor immediately beyond the circular room bulged suddenly and then became molten, flowing down from the living rock it shielded in a silver stream, and a great yellow mass of fire erupted out into the corridor, becoming instantly a mottled red and magenta that in turn, and as instantly, was a fuming cloud, gray and black and flecked with ocherous matter and roiling constantly within itself, until in a fraction of time it was sucked up through recessed ventilators in the flame-seared ceiling, the fumes and the fire and their resultant heat gone simultaneously, so that O'Hara who was crouching only twenty feet away felt only that first scorching blast, as if the fire door of a furnace had swung open, and the next moment smelled the sweat of it drying on his skin and the sharp odor of burnt hair—his beard and eyebrows crumbling at his touch. The flash left him blinded. Then he heard a cry:

"O'Hara! O'Hara! Thank God I am in time."

It was Anstruther's voice. And the joy of that cry, the jubilating ring of overwhelming relief in it, brought tears involuntarily into O'Hara's sightless eyes. He stood there weeping as if suddenly he had come blundering against his only friend.

Nor did he question that Anstruther was his friend. All the warnings of the Father moments earlier were lost in this excruciating feeling of reunion and deliverance. He was saved, he was freed at last of the exhausting nerve-drag of these long months in the Western Hemisphere, behind the Curtain, never daring once in all that time to trust even the woman he loved, never completely, and menaced, even while he slept, by an omniscient and omnipresent living fable—the Father.

Now, at last, he felt, here was a man from his own time and world, and with his own sense of what a man should be—Anstruther. He stretched out his hands.

"Anstruther, I—can't see—"

"The blast," Anstruther explained briskly, and immediately strong arms were lifting O'Hara's helpless body. "We have a remedy for that. Don't be afraid, O'Hara. You're safe now, you're free. We who have had to live with Stephen Bryce know what that means. All slaves are blind."

O'Hara asked, "But wasn't my blindness your doing?"

"Yes. But there are blindnesses that don't involve the eyes."

"Mine does."

Anstruther laughed softly. "The physical man. You were always that, O'Hara—always concerned most with the health of your body and doubtful of the health of other men's minds. Forget your eyes, that is nothing," he said, and as he continued speaking, the sound of his voice moved away, and O'Hara realized that it was not Anstruther who was lifting him. He was being lowered now, coming to rest upon a cushioned bunk. Anstruther was saying, "We were not expecting to find you beyond that last wall, O'Hara—it was the Father we expected there. Stephen Bryce," he continued harshly. "And if we had found him—if we had found him we would have no time for you. I am going to bathe your eyes. This will burn some, but if you clench your hands—"

O'Hara felt live coals inside his skull. His spine arched tautly upward from the bunk and whorls of flame shot through that portion of his brain that stored the memories of color—purple, yellow, green and the red of blood. Sweat drenched him. Then the tautness broke and his eyes felt cool again and wet, and he collapsed.

"Can you see now?"

O'Hara opened his eyes. Beside him, hulking nakedly, his ape-like body crouched as if to lift O'Hara once again, one of the Sons now held the vial that Anstruther had just passed to him, and behind him were other Sons each bearing the shining tube-like weapon that O'Hara had first seen beyond Emporia—armed Sons, in this, the empty subterranean metropolis of Washington, the danger that the Father had first warned him against, and led by a man equally naked, though frail, rigidly erect, his bright blond beard fringing downward upon his narrow chest, his pale blue eyes made more myopic-seeming by the tiny capillaries that had burst in their irises, a face with an intensity of purpose that made normal strength seem weak, a face to which emotion supplied a look of superior courage, a zealot's face.

"Give me your hand," Anstruther said, and clasped it.

O'Hara sensed the torrent of emotion in that touch.

"You are one of us now," Anstruther said. Then he turned to the Sons. "This man is my comrade, my brother. This man will be your brother. He too has come into your world by some power infinitely beyond our understanding, and he too will join strength with yours in overthrowing Stephen Bryce who calls himself the Father."

Involuntarily, the Son beside O'Hara bent his knee and said, "The Father," whispering it, reflexively devotional. Anstruther took no notice of it.

"The Deluge," he was saying, "has just been loosed upon Emporia. The tens of thousands who dwelt there have gone now to the Pits of Yellowstone. Some among you were born there, in Emporia, and your mothers are no more. Stephen Bryce has destroyed them. Do you understand what I am telling you— Stephen Bryce has destroyed your mothers as he will destroy you when the need for you has passed. As he would have destroyed me long ago had he dared. Do you understand?"

"We understand," the Son beside O'Hara said. "Stephen Bryce, the Father—"

"Who calls himself the Father!"

"—who calls himself the Father, has loosed the Deluge on Emporia. And will loose it on us."

"Unless we destroy him first."

"Unless we destroy him first," echoed the Son. And the others said, as if it were a litany, "Unless we destroy him first."

"We are not free until Stephen Bryce is dead," said Anstruther.

The chorus answered gravely, "We are not free until Stephen Bryce is dead."

"We are prepared to die—"

"We are prepared to die—"

"To free those who come after us."

"To free those who come after us," the Sons repeated.

Anstruther clapped his hands. Instantly, in unison, the Sons sank down where they had stood and lay upon the floor resting their faces torpidly upon their heavy arms, and instantly they were asleep, some forty of them, lying in a grotesque ragged row with Anstruther still standing in their midst, though silent now, his blue eyes peering down at O'Hara upon the bunk.

"They are like newborn infants," he said finally, a strange tenderness in his voice. "They drop to sleep at once, O'Hara, forgetting the danger of their future, oblivious of the horror of their past, slipping down into the sweet senselessness that their exhaustion craves. Do you know how long we worked to reach this corridor?"

O'Hara said, "They don't know what danger is. But you do, Anstruther."

"Six days and six nights without stopping to rest. If time down here were measurable," Anstruther continued raptly. "Working all that time, searching endlessly, sure that at last they were nearing Stephen Bryce, yet when again they realized that once more I had failed them, they sank down to sleep as you saw them do, trusting me, O'Hara, to lead them past this failure finally to triumph."

"Anstruther, you're mad."

The pale eyes closed. "Is it mad to work against the worst tyranny the earth has ever known? Then I am mad."

"But you can't win, Anstruther. You can't beat the Father. If he wished it, he could loose upon you at this instant the Deluge that he turned into Emporia. And these poor, stupid and deluded Sons would never awaken from their torpor."

"It is not the loss of his Sons that stays him, O'Hara."

"Nor would it be you or I, were we to endanger him. He is watching you now, he hears what you are saying, and if he believed—"

"I know all this, O'Hara," said Anstruther wearily, and sat down upon the cushioned bunk, now cupping his zealot's face within his soft, small hands. "I know Stephen Bryce and his power. Yes, he'd destroy me instantly if he believed that I endangered him. But he does not think that I do. His faith in himself is quite as absolute as my abhorrence of what he has done to these people. Look at them, O'Hara—they're men! Or they were men, their fathers were men, before Stephen Bryce stamped out their souls. And they can be men again."

"If you continue to lead them?"

"Yes, if I—if anyone continues who believes in them."

"Is this the reason for your revolt against the Father?"

"Could there be another reason?"

O'Hara nodded soberly. "You, too, might aspire to be the Father."

"And if I were—"

"You see, the thought is in your mind!"

"If I were," continued Anstruther, "I could not possibly do worse by them than Stephen Bryce has done. But I will never be the Father, O'Hara. Didn't Stephen Bryce tell you that?"

"He is listening to you now." O'Hara warned.

"I'm sure he is. He knows every word I've said, perhaps he knows every thought that I have had, since I came through the Curtain. That is why he does not dare to use me unless he must. But there's another reason why I cannot waste my days in dreaming that I might become the Father in his stead—a reason that dispels the curse of vanity that all men are prey to. I can live for two years only with the amazing medications that Stephen Bryce and his fellow scientists of the early days developed, and then my illness, a cancer of the brain, will destroy me as surely as the tyranny of Stephen Bryce has destroyed these men. Do you think that a man with a destiny of death could think only of ambition?

"All men have a destiny of death."

"That is true enough. All men have it, but with most men the time is not fixed. How long have you been in Washington, O'Hara?"

"Eleven months."

"And has it seemed so long?"

"Incredibly long—and incredibly short, too, like a nightmare of the instant before awakening."

"A nightmare of the instant before awakening—that is how you sum up these eleven months. And I have only twice that long to live, and to me too a year seems like a nightmarish instant—two instants of life before me, O'Hara! That makes ambition an impossible mockery. Would you dispute it?"

O'Hara looked steadily into Anstruther's pale, straining eyes. What was he searching for in them, he asked himself. For arrogance? For the bright marsh fires of insanity? For weakness? None of these were there. For Anstruther, once the charming and imaginative boy, had gained stature, and the boyishness was gone. And even as with Stephen Bryce, himself facing the same approaching certainty of death, the purpose of his being now was solely the future of the hemisphere.

It was impossible to doubt Anstruther's motives. To question his methods, yes—but not the motive behind them. Which was true also of the Father. O'Hara could loathe the individual acts of each, yet at the same time he respected their sincerity. It was a cosmic irony that these two men, instinctive enemies, opposites, should be working toward a goal that was identical, yet by their natures working toward it through irreconcilable methods. For Stephen Bryce meant to breed out the race of the Degraded, both masses and Sons, while Anstruther believed the elimination of the Father, as a move toward a new environment, would solve the problems of the continents.

As for O'Hara himself, he could not choose between the cold science of the Father and the emotional approach of Anstruther, but stronger at the moment in his heart remained the horror of Emporia. He held out his hand.

"I believe you, Anstruther."

"You mean, don't you, that you want to believe me?"

"That's it," O'Hara answered simply. "I do mean that. I want to believe you."

"Good! For it is more important to me that you should want to believe me, despite any uncertainty in your mind, than that you should believe without question. Faith itself can be shattered, but the yearning after faith is indestructible." He took O'Hara's hand, and at last got up from the bunk. "Tomorrow," he said, "or when we next awaken, we resume. Now tell me, for you must have come recently from Stephen Bryce, which was the direction and what the distance? Back along this corridor how far?"

"I cannot tell you, Anstruther."

"But you came into this room—"

"Unconscious," said O'Hara, which was the truth as far as it went. He did not dare to mention the integrocalculators. Yet as warily he drove from his mind the memory of Nedra and his son sinking down toward the bottom of that water-filled room. His path in this struggle seemed obscure—his feeling was to follow Anstruther, to help him and these sleeping Sons, and yet he could not bring himself to follow absolutely, he could not reveal the Father's purpose, nor could he permit himself to think of Nedra and the baby, for agitation would defeat him. He must grope through this, betraying neither Anstruther nor the Father. Nor himself.

The middle ground, he told himself—the middle ground, always seeming to both extremes contemptible, weak and confused. And perhaps confusion really was the virtue of it, veering this way for a while, then that, but persevering devious and without dogma toward the goal, toward saving Nedra and his child. Was that contemptible? He could not think that it was. In the first phase of mankind, before codes and ideologies, there had been only the preservation of the family and a dim concept of God—and so, O'Hara felt, would be the final phase.

"I was unconscious," he repeated.

"Then we are lost again," said Anstruther gloomily. But instantly his eyes were light again. "It does not matter. However long it takes, we will find our way to him. We have come in a straight line this far, and we will continue it until we reach the outer shell of Washington, which must be close to this room. Then we shall cut back again through the heart of the city, never leaving between the lines we cut the space that Stephen Bryce's vast throne room occupies. Somewhere, someday, we'll find the heart of this."

O'Hara asked, "You too, Anstruther, were unconscious when you left the Father's hall?"

"I have never been there. After I crashed in Patagonia, the Sons brought me to Washington through the North-South Tube, which plunges underneath the Gulf of Mexico from Yucatan—the second of the two great Tubes that are the arteries of these continents. As you know, there are smaller, lateral Tubes—"

"I know very little, Anstruther. And I ought to know."

"The two great Tubes," said Anstruther, "converge at Washington, the Transcontinental and the North-South Tube. The lesser Tubes branch off to all key points, to the Pits of Yellowstone and to the vast plutonium plant in southern Colorado-"

"I flew into its radiation zone," O'Hara said, remembering.

"—to the Arctic outposts in Alaska and Labrador, to the plants in South Carolina and at Hanford that generate the Atomic Curtain, to the major population centers. You, whose family was once American, would know the names of most of them, but they are no longer cities as you and I remember cities—they had no purpose now, except as warrens for the masses. No trade, no growth, no manufactures. A few repair shops at strategic points, with almost nothing to repair, though they have the skill for it. Everything has been done here, everything is finished, and only man—or what is left of man—is subject now to change. That has been true almost from the day they established the Atomic Curtain. At once, behind its absolute security, the moral fiber of the masses started to decay. Only the elite, the scientists, were able to preserve a kind of integrity, for all too soon they were confronted with the challenge of the retrogression of the masses of the continents, the reversal of evolution, resulting from the gradual pollution of the continents by their atomic-powered plants in every phase of life. But after those first scientists, there were no more—no minds that came out of the masses had the capacity for exploratory thought. And gradually these scientists died off through these three centuries, until there was only the last of them, the Father, Stephen Bryce. No, I have never seen the Father's vast hall—he did not raise me from the pit when I arrived."

"I recall the pit," O'Hara said.

"He raised you out of it, up to the level where he stood, because he had to take that chance at last, to trust his life with you, O'Hara. Or possibly he knows you better than you know yourself. That was true with me, for I was not antagonistic when I stood beneath him in that pit. But he sensed the path I would choose, siding with the Sons. He has not let me come into the hall. Instead he comes into the Guild of the Sons, or in the corridors, appearing in some manner that I do not understand, emerging despite locked doors and seamless walls. It was in the Guild, upon the screen, that I first saw you and the woman, Nedra—"

"Yes?"

"—and knew that with your help I might at last destroy this tyranny. Soon after that, I tried to come to you. The Father intercepted me in the corridor. Do you know the rest?"

"You broke his arms?"

"And he broke more than that. He drove me away, though promising again to let me go on with my work among the Sons. That was the task he gave me when I came to Washington, teaching the Sons, trying to make them seem like men, as you and I and Stephen Bryce remember men. Now I am trying to fulfill that task, but now I find that Stephen Bryce opposes it." Anstruther crossed the room and dropped upon a bunk. "Yet I shall fulfill it. With your help, O'Hara," he said quietly, "before I leave the Western Hemisphere, I shall fulfill that task."

He did not move again. The sound of his breathing became the quiet sound of sleep.

O'Hara's brain was staggering with fresh doubts. Surely the Father, whom he knew had heard all this, understood now that he could not reclaim Anstruther. Nor could O'Hara say with certainty that if the thing were possible he would attempt it now. This too the Father, who boasted of the equations of the mind that he could write, must know. Somewhere in this morass of unattainables and doubts must lie a deeper aim.

"O'Hara?"

"Yes, Father?"

"O'Hara, you must not question me. You must not think that you can challenge me. You are wavering, O'Hara—despite the evidence of the translucent room, despite Emporia, despite the shifting of your body through the space of Washington, you are not yet convinced that what I wish to do within these continents will be done. You have permitted your reason to be shaken by emotion, and yet I know that in the end of this you will not fail me. You must leave that room now. You must walk into the corridor—"

O'Hara leaped up. "You are taking me away from Anstruther?"

"Yes," said the Father patiently. "I must take you away for a while, for there is much that you must learn. Go into the corridor at once, for I am sending an anesthetic into that little room, as I once sent it mercifully to you when Nedra bore her child. Keep walking, O'Hara—further—and further—and you must close your eyes, for this will be very swift—"

O'Hara clenched his fists against a sudden rush of pressure. His knees were buckling and his mouth stretched wide and in the blackness that swirled over him his senses reeled. "You may approach my bed," the Father whispered.

And it had been done. O'Hara was again inside the great hall of the Father, just below the dais. The Father's feeble hand was beckoning.

"Just so far, O'Hara, and watch my hand upon this board— don't think that if I relax my touch upon this key you could save Nedra and the child. I do not like to threaten you, but you have permitted Anstruther to convert you, O'Hara. The absurdity of defying death for a mistaken altruism does impress a man your age. But do you really believe, O'Hara, that I am as wicked as he thinks?"

"I saw the masses dying in Emporia. I saw my wife and baby sinking in that translucent room."

"Cruelty is comparative, O'Hara. And not all of it, anywhere, is personal. Do you suppose that I alone shaped this hemisphere and am alone responsible for the evils in it? You must go now into the library behind this dais, O'Hara—you must read how these things really happened. I did not alone erect the Curtain, I did not build the atomic reactors that made the Curtain possible. I did not make the initial choice. All these things were done, after the Third World War, by men who were mature when I was still a child. I inherited the conduct of these continents as you have found them. I have built nothing, achieved nothing, save to stay alive for two hundred and seventy years while all my peers were perishing.

"Two hundred and seventy years," he whispered. "Surely that would amaze the doctors of your world—surely one at least of them would wish to return with you through the Curtain solely to learn how I have lived this long. And it is so simple—I prolong my life the way your doctors empty bowels. I take little pills, O'Hara, that any chemist of your world can easily compound. Yet were your doctor to come through the Curtain for this secret, I would not talk with him of how to prolong life, but of euthanasia. I am tired, O'Hara.

"And now you too think I am a tyrant. Let me tell you this, O'Hara—were I to cast aside this keyboard and forget the masses that you think I tyrannize, what has happened at Emporia would be multiplied in deadliness a thousand times. No, not by the Deluge but by the scourges it prevents, pestilence and hunger.

"Who do you condemn for pestilence and hunger in your hemisphere? The truth is, isn't it, that you consider them unavoidable—yet by the Deluge I avoid them here. And by preserving life within my brain, long after I have lost the joy of life, I do maintain these continents as they carne to me.

"Anstruther calls this tyranny, I happen to call it my duty. But perhaps you think Anstruther is right about it. Perhaps I should summon him here and explain to him the working of the integrocalculators through this keyboard. He could destroy me then, and assume my functions. And he could continue, for the two years that remain to him, to try to awaken in the dead brains of the Sons the spark of their bred-out intelligence.

"Do you know his possibilities of success? If all atomic pollution of this Hemisphere were suddenly to end and decontamination were in time achieved, then in this pollution-free hemisphere Anstruther could breed a race of thinking men, starting with the Sons and the women of the masses—in time he could do it. If he could live five hundred thousand years he might accomplish it. But he has just two years.

"But let us suppose he had his five hundred thousand years. What do you think would happen to his youthful altruism in that time, when I, within a modest three centuries, have become such a callous tyrant?

"Now you must go into the library, O'Hara, and later I shall show you how the integrocalculators think for you, and still later you must see the City of New York, the restored city, duplicating to the last dirty tenement that city of the twentieth century that was ravaged in the Third World War. And I think then that you will begin to understand the broader aspects of a tyranny like mine. You will perhaps discover that from evil sometimes comes a little good.

"For I am granting now that the Atomic Curtain is an evil thing. It has brought this hemisphere the security we sought, both against aggression and want, but what has happened here is infinitely more tragic than war. Grant it—the Curtain is evil. But what do you think it is that keeps the peace for Europe and Asia and Africa? What unifies them, O'Hara? It is only the terror of what exists behind this Curtain. And if they of your hemisphere thought tomorrow that the Curtain could be pierced, what do you think would happen to that peace and unity? And if indeed this hemisphere were helpless, what do you think your continents would do to us?

"So in that respect, at least, the Curtain is not altogether evil. For all those that it has destroyed within this hemisphere, it has saved equally as many on your side of it.

"But as you observe the integrocalculators, notice that we are not really helpless. I can still enforce this peace. If I touch this little key, I release toward the major population areas of your hemisphere a barrage of rockets that would make the holocausts of the Third World War seem trivial. When you return home, O'Hara, if you must tell them that the Curtain can be pierced, also remind them that the piercing works both ways, and that what seems to be the possibility of conquering this hemisphere—breaching these centuries of peace—is in fact a terrible delusion.

"And observe, O'Hara, as you study the integrocalculators, that the charted position of the Atomic Curtain depends solely upon the adjustment of regulators for latitude and longitude. And were I now to touch this key—this one!—the Curtain would everywhere advance, crossing the seas, pushing through your helpless continents, but leaving in its wake as it progressed only the wastelands of radioactive pollution. Remember this, O'Hara, when you speak to your comrades of the International Patrol. With the quiver of my finger I can wipe their aircraft from the skies.

"And also observe, O'Hara, that the scintillometers of Washington are working perfectly. And were the scientists of your Eastern Hemisphere to set in action any new atomic ovens, I would know it instantly. I could release my rockets. I could advance the Curtain. They would have to move very swiftly to forestall me, O'Hara. And I do not believe they could do it soon enough.

"Yet even if you had such excellently trained scientists, and could set up your reactors and place your warheads in your rockets and launch them before my rockets or my Curtain were to reach you, your rockets would thunder down only upon the wastelands that compose the surface of these western continents. You would destroy our photosynthetrons, the source of our food, but that is all. You would not reach our subterranean cities, or the vast reservoirs of food and water beneath the surface or the intricate tunnels of the Tube. You would hurt us, yes—but you would not destroy us, O'Hara. And within minutes, then, we would as surely wipe your continents clean of life as with this shaking hand I wipe the perspiration from my forehead.

"Such is the actual power this keyboard—or what it stands for—gives me. Anstruther thinks I am the tyrant of a degraded race, and the degrader of it. I could as easily become the master of the entire earth, were I to wish it. But I don't, O'Hara. My burdens here are sufficient. Is this the thinking of an evil tyrant?"

O'Hara said, "Tyranny is only a word, Father. But Emporia was a fact."

The frail hand collapsed upon the Father's breast. His eyelids flickered jerkily above his blazing eyes and for a moment the rise and sinking of his bosom ceased. The pale lips parted, the fingers seemed about to slid from the keyboard beneath them.

It was the fingers that O'Hara leaped to seize, for he remembered what the Father had warned him, that if the pressure ceased, Nedra would drown inside that translucent room. But the Father's sinews stiffened. His lips again were moving:

"Not yet! Not yet! I am not dead."

O'Hara recoiled. And as he stood there the horror of Emporia seemed vague beside this new horror, that all life of this hidden hemisphere depended in these instants upon a brain that was hovering so very near the line between the living and the dead. The Father's life was life for millions now.

"I did not die!"

It was a cry of triumph. The voice was hoarsely jubilant. "I did not die!" the Father cried again. "But do you know how close it was? So near that I could see beyond. And I am ready!" his eyes opened very wide. "This problem must be resolved, and now. While I consider it, go behind the dais into the library. You will find more than books to amuse you there.

O'Hara moved backward slowly. In his mind was the apprehension that those fingers might in death relax their pressure on the key. But the Father whispered:

"Go quickly, O'Hara!"

"But Father, if you die while I am absent?"

"Then instantly you will be with your wife and son, free to make your way back to the mountains, if you can. I am giving the integrocalculators the impulse to accomplish that. Do as I tell you and you have this pledge. But—I shall not die! Now, go."

O'Hara turned and descended the steps and passed through the door behind the dais. It slid down behind him. He was standing in a tremendous tiered hall, stacked from floor to ceiling upon each wall with books, while occupying the center of the hall were countless exhibits of machinery and clothing, weapons and utensils, all the implements of the civilizations that had been piled one upon the other here in this subterranean capital of the Western Hemisphere. Against the farthest wall was an immense bright screen, like those that he had seen in the corridors and public buildings everywhere upon the continent, and on this screen, at the moment that he entered, Nedra was visible.

Nedra was nursing the child. At the sound of O'Hara's cry, she looked up slowly, as if she was expecting to find him in the room with her, wherever that might be, until finally her eyes were raised, and O'Hara knew that she was peering into the screen in that lost, small room of hers.

"Nedra," he called to her, "does my voice come through to you?"

"Oh, yes," she said calmly, "and I see you on the screen above me. It is as though you were standing here beside me."

"Do you know where you are?"

"But surely you recognize this little room, O'Hara."

It was the exquisite room in which they had spent so many months together, the perfect little room, hexagonal and thickly carpeted, its ceiling vaulted and displaying shades of blue that darkened toward the apex. "Yes, I know that room," O'Hara whispered bitterly.

"And do you know your son?" she asked, and pushed the child gently from her breast. She was as he had last seen her in that translucent water-filled room, lying upon the floor—completely nude, her majestic body serenely recumbent, her deep breasts forward as she rested on her elbow, watching the child, which now rolled from his back upon the floor, and smiling up into the screen began to crawl toward it, O'Hara pressed his face into his palms. "How long have I been gone?"

"I do not know, O'Hara—perhaps two days, perhaps two months. There is no way of telling time in the cities of the Degraded. There is no sun and no moon, and no need for time, for time is a measure of accomplishment and nothing is accomplished here. We exist, and that is all."

The child sat up. He yawned.

"He must sleep now," said Nedra, and moved quickly to pick him up. "We must not talk, we would disturb him—"

"Nedra, this is not possible. We're speaking as if we were together in that exquisite little room, yet only hours ago—or days ago—I saw you drowning, and I unable to break through the yielding wall to save you from it. And only hours after that—or was it days or months?—you suddenly were back with me in that exquisite room, bringing the child, after those endless days and nights of solitude in which I did not know—"

"What troubles you?"

"Time troubles me. Time and the vagueness of what has happened in it. And you trouble me, Nedra! This is not the way you were, content to have a semblance of me showing on a screen."

"Ah, you see, O'Hara?" She smiled. "This is that dying process that I warned you of, this is what happens in the cities of the Degraded. You mind is steeped in clouds. You are frantic now, but soon enough you will not care. You will not know it. And that will be much worse than that death which could have come easily for us upon the mountain. Remember now? Remember that you told me we could always die?"

"Yes, Nedra, I remember."

"We cannot do it now."

"I can die now, I can climb these tiers of books and leap—"

"But I cannot. And you would never leave me."

O'Hara bowed his head. At last he asked, "Where were you all that time I was alone in that exquisite room? Where was the baby born?"

"I was with the Father. A woman of the masses was with me."

"I have seen no masses here in Washington."

"Nonetheless they are here. Millions, millions—like those we saw jammed together in the corridors of Emporia, jamming the corridors below the upper levels of the capital. They exist, down there, as we exist up here—as worms exist within concentric rings in a decaying log. The baby is sleepy, O'Hara. And I am sleepy too."

She stretched herself upon a couch that he remembered, holding the baby closely in her arms, and she was smiling drowsily up toward the screen when the light upon it ebbed.

"Nedra! Don't leave."

"But I am not leaving. As long as the Father wishes it, I shall be here, as close to you as if we were upon two couches in this same exquisite room, able always to see each other and to speak."

"Which is worse than death!"

The light was gone upon the screen. Her voice, sleepy, came to him once more. "Are you sure of that? Are you so certain that death will not be this way?"

And he was not certain. Nothing now seemed certain. Nothing had reality. But soon, re-echoing Nedra's words, he would not care. He would not care!

Days passed. At least the glow would come again upon the screen and Nedra would be there, talking to him as though they were together in that exquisite room, smiling or laughing at the child upon the floor, angry when O'Hara's frustrate calls awakened it, scolding. Or whispering through the darkness on the screen.

"Nedra, Nedra—"

"What is it, O'Hara?"

"Where are you in that darkness? Let me hear your voice. Speak to me, Nedra!"

"But I am here."

"Yes, you are there, wherever that may be, and I am here, in this enormous room of books, entombed in centuries of written facts while you—you cannot see, but now I touch this screen, my hands are feeling for you in that dark, toward the whisper of your voice. And touch cold metal! Nedra—"

"Yes, O'Hara."

"It does not matter to you that we are apart like this?"

"But you sent me away from you, O'Hara."

"And you will never forgive me."

"Oh, yes. I do forgive you, O'Hara. But I shan't pity you, as you seem to wish. I have not forgotten that when you wished to talk of solemn, stuffy things, philosophizing with the Father, you sent me to bed. And you'd do that again, for all men do it. It is only in the night, like this, when you want me, O'Hara, that our separation is a torture to you. Why don't you read those books?"

He pounded both his fists against the metal screen.

But there were nights when O'Hara did read. Dust had collected on these volumes now for better than a century, the last archivist's entry being dated 2124. And the name signed to it was the Father's—Stephen Bryce. It was a daily journal that O'Hara discovered on the last shelf at the far end of the hall.

"It has been a tragic mistake," was written in beautiful, rolling script. "We have gambled and lost. Maria died last week—and today, when I tried to awaken him, Wilson's hands were clutched around the crucifix he always wore, as if with his last breath he prayed forgiveness for our sin. I am now the last of us, unless in the mountains beyond the Mississippi, where the pollution is not so intense," some of those who fled our perfect civilization still exist in their imperfect way.

"Yet in this last week of his life," was written on the yellowed page, "Wilson developed his ultimate formula. He could have taken it and been with me today. He preferred instead to die.

"And I prefer to die. But what of these creatures whom our blunders have brought forth upon these continents? Is it not my obligation to keep striving to redeem our race? Am I free to choose life or death? I think not. I must live. I must preserve what we have left while I continue seeking to regenerate. For to any problem there must be an answer. There will be one for this!!"

Some mathematical calculations followed, and then came the notation:

"We wanted too much. And we have got too much for us. Along the way somewhere we let our aspirations push us past the point of prudence, yet it was not wrong for us to aspire. Perhaps even now, if I were to lift the Atomic Curtain—but I don't dare! I cannot trust Eurasia even now. I must work this out alone."

And at the bottom of the page, as if it were an afterthought:

"One way out is the volume on the first shelf of the left front wall."

O'Hara found it. The covers of it were stamped cleanly from magnesium, and as he picked it up, seeing only that it must contain a single metal page, the hushed voice of the Father filled the Library.

"You have it now, O'Hara. Place it inside your jacket, for you do not yet need it. Remember my pledge, that if I die, you will be instantly with Nedra and your son. I am sending you down now to the integrocalculators. As before, hold your breath, open your mouth—this will be very swift and terrible for you."

There was a great rush of chilling air and the library went black, and in that blackness O'Hara felt himself exploding, dying, passing through death into magnetic space, becoming part of space, losing identity. Then out of this serenity he felt himself congeal again.

He was standing before a vast oblong machine, inside the glass casing that enclosed it. There was no entrance to the casing. And beyond the glass, upon all sides, a pale gray depthless liquid kept the casing perpetually suspended.

"Observe it quickly, O'Hara," came the Father's whispered voice. "For soon your nuclear heat will disturb it. Already its counteractors have begun to hum a warning to me. You are the first to have passed into it since it was suspended there, insusceptible to shock, beyond all foreseeable change. And you must be the last. You have streamed into it in the mesons and neutrons that compose you, and what you think is flesh and blood, your body, clings together only through the wave lengths of your brain. You have no real finite shape or substance now, you are only what you think. And you must think! Absorb it all, and quickly—this is the key, O'Hara! The board I hold is only to assist your focusing your brain. It is recorded, isn't it? Now, you must return—"

The chill air and the overwhelming blackness smothered him.

When he revived he was upon the library floor, kneeling as if in prayer. He raised his eyes. "It could not be," he whispered. "It did not happen—"

"What did not happen?" Nedra asked him, and was visible upon the screen. "And where have you been these weeks, O'Hara? Where were you all these nights I tried to call you to the screen?" Her voice was petulant. "I am beginning to wonder now, O'Hara—you told me that you came from beyond the Curtain but you seem to be marvelously at home here among the Degraded. And except for your ages, you and the Father are becoming much alike. Did you really come from Washington when you approached my mountains in your flying thing?"

O'Hara shrugged. Was this so different from the tirades of the housewives of London, Cairo or of Stockholm? Were women anywhere, once they were mated to their satisfaction, different? Except for the ceremonial warclub that she'd left behind in her cave in the Rocky Mountains, Nedra was as women were everywhere.

"Did you really miss me, Nedra?"

"Yes. Of course I did."

"Of course," he sighed, and started walking toward the tiers of books.

But much as he learned in the library during the ensuing weeks, it was his journey through the Tube to New York that taught him most of what America had been before the Third World War. The subterranean city, built since the establishment of the Curtain and glutted with its multimillions of naked and hairless masses shambling along from feeding hall to feeding hall, sleeping together indiscriminately in those wide cushioned bunks everywhere along the city's corridors and herded always by the Sons with their atomic guns, was another and larger Emporia, and from the density of its population must itself be approaching a similar Deluge. It would be coming any day, the Son attached to O'Hara anticipated.

"Only the Father knows the hour," the Son explained. "He counts the masses as they multiply, and when there are too many for the Tube to feed, the Deluge mercifully will come."

"You call it mercy?" asked O'Hara.

"Yes, that is the word that we were taught."

"It does not hurt you to know what happens to the masses?"

"Hurt me? I do not understand. I am in the Guild when it occurs."

"But one of these women who will be dissolved may have been your mother. That one—she who carries her baby against her breast—she may indeed be your mother. And these—your sisters, and if they had received the training at the Father's schools in Washington that you received, they would have been as you are, articulate, able to comprehend—"

"Are you referring to these females?" the Son asked, puzzled.

"Don't you know the word *mother?*"

"It was not taught to us. It must be nonessential."

"But you do know about the birth of babies."

"Oh, yes, an entirely artificial process."

"The female who bears the baby in her womb nonetheless is its mother. It is her flesh and her blood that sustains it before its birth, and there is nothing artificial in that phase of it. Her blood has fed you. She has felt the pain and I think she must have felt some joy at your birth. Yes, despite your customs, despite the soulless processes the Father has enforced, or been driven to enforce, the word should mean something, it is not nonessential, and you can never aspire—"

"One moment, please!"

"—you can never aspire to emulate the men your fathers were, decades ago, unless—"

"One moment, please," the Son repeated courteously. "For I remember something that happened once, which has sometimes disturbed me. I had been sent to collect the babies for the measurement of their brain waves, to determine those who should be sent to Washington to become Sons. There was a female who resisted—"

The Son fell silent. He was staring at O'Hara, but his eyes were vacant, unseeing, or seeing very dimly back into the past. Then his voice resumed in a whispered hush:

"And I though that was—beautiful."

O'Hara paused a moment. Then he asked, "What did you do?"

The Son glanced hastily toward the great screen in the hall. He straightened his back. "I destroyed her at once. She was consigned to the Pits of Yellowstone."

"And did the Father know that?"

"The Father," replied the Son, "knows everything."

"Yes," said the Father's voice, while a blazing light came suddenly upon the screen. "Even what you are thinking now, O'Hara. But I did not know that he remembered—I did not think it possible. I suppose I must consider it as dangerous. If you will come this way, O'Hara, toward the screen, I shall give you another little lesson in morality—"

And O'Hara did as he was told, leaving the Son who now was kneeling with his eyes downcast. Another Son came forward, aimed his tube-like weapon at the kneeling, hairless ape-like hulk, and fired. The Son who had remembered vanished in the flame.

"You have seen enough of the subterranean city," said the Father presently. "You must go now to the island where the ancient city stood, O'Hara. And then to the Monument."

The Tube beneath the river took O'Hara and his new escort to the island where a shaft ascended. O'Hara emerged again for the first time since he had descended into the earth at Emporia. His eyes involuntarily swept in every direction, seeing the swift, free-flowing waters of the mighty river, the strangely wonderful irregular contours of the earth, and above all the sky—the limitless pale sky that seemed, as it had never seemed before, celestial—the heavens, freedom, not of man. His lungs were gulping deeply of an air he had forgotten.

"This sight amazes you?" the Son beside him said.

"It awakens me."

"You have been sleeping?"

"Dreaming."

"I understand dreams," the Son said sympathetically. "In Washington they taught us what they meant. They are a memory of things we should forget—and do forget when we awake."

"You dream?" O'Hara asked.

"Oh, yes—all of us dream sometimes. Even the masses. We dream of cities such as this before us, great heaps of ruble, and fire is raining down upon us and we die in heaps untidily, or live untidily, and our bellies are empty, and we must fight with One another. These things were actuality before the early days, before the destruction of this city that you see ruined before us. Here," said the Son, "a tower once stood. Now, as you see, it is only some bits of metal and crumbled stone. Our ancestors lived in whole corridors of such towers."

"I know," O'Hara said. "I have seen photographs of it within the library at Washington."

"But there was no resemblance to the photographs," the Son explained, "only miles and miles of heaped up earth and flame-seared rubble with rusting beams and steel protruding from the surface. Small stunted shrubs had sprouted in the ruins, and a strange yellow leafless vine that matted itself thickly close against the ground. A jagged fragment of stone blocks was thrust far up.

"The greatest tower of all. Hundreds of feet it soared above the earth, yet when the rockets came, it crashed as quickly as the least of them. They say that some of those who dwelt here managed to escape, being shielded from atomic fire by those whose bodies lay above them, and so they fled across the river, living for a while upon the surface above where we have built our subterranean city. But most of them died of diseases that some of the rockets brought. A few at last went north, toward what was then called Canada—"

"I know," O'Hara said. "I've read of it."

"And more died there. Only the strongest then were able to escape toward the west, perhaps into the mountains where they say a strange new race now dwells, huge red-haired creatures, as large as yourself, with short arms and stiff spines, unprepossessing creatures and enemies of the Father."

"Unprepossessing?"

"Yes. But do not take offense. Since you have come from Washington we do not mind you. I have heard it said," he whispered, "that even the Father himself—is not like us. Nor should he be, of course," the Son said hastily, and resumed his speech: "There were in this ancient city some ten or more millions of inhabitants before the Third World War, but they were situated very stupidly, grouped together densely, and we have avoided that mistake in rebuilding our new subterranean New York. Also as an object lesson of how foolishly our race once planned, the Monument was built—a replica of the ancient city as it was before its destruction. We go there now."

For four days O'Hara wandered through the empty Monument.

The fifth day, he stood before the great screen in the Guild of the subterranean city across the river and listened to the Father's voice.

"Have you seen it, O'Hara?"

"I have been there, Father."

"Is there more you wish to see?"

"Nothing."

"What did you think of it?"

O'Hara said, "I thought this, Father: that kind of city could not possibly have grown up behind your Curtain. There is too much of the greatness and the cheapness of the human soul in it. There is too much of free and human aspiration, unsafe for you perhaps, maudlin I feel certain, yet almost by the fact of these defects fare more glorious in its total achievement than all the glittering corridors and vast chambers of your geometrical metropolises."

The Father's voice seemed melancholy, "That is true, O'Hara. What you say is true. Yet only my Curtain could have saved that city. Such is the paradox that I have faced alone through all these years, until this hour. You must return to me now. I have solved my dilemma. And possibly I can solve yours."

PART FIVE

O'HARA went alone into the cylinder that rested at the terminus of the Tube within the Guild of the Sons in subterranean New York. The Son who had attended him, standing by to bolt down the hatch, glanced covertly toward the great screen in the center of the hall.

"You will see the Father?" he whispered.

"Yes, I will see the Father," said O'Hara. "If he wishes it."

"I have always heard his voice come from the screen."

"I have never seen him. A Brilliantly unbearable radiation comes upon the screen and that is all."

"You wish to know what he is like?"

The Son drew his brutish body up to its great height, his long arms swinging loose, his weak eyes focusing intently upon O'Hara's face. He was in that moment at least something more than subhuman, for a beseeching huskiness came quickly into his voice, not the piteous whine of an animal but the humility of a man.

"I wish to know what he is like," he whispered.

"He is like yourself."

The Sons jaw muscles flexed. His nostrils flared.

"He is not as large as you, or as strong as you, or as content as you," O'Hara said, "but he is more cunning, and more consciously merciless—"

"Stop that! He listens."

"—and he would destroy the one man who would lead you back into the glory of your kind, the lost glory of the fact of being man and not a soulless animal. One man alone would help you, Anstruther—"

"Stop it! Don't speak again!"

"Then you have heard of him? The word is traveling. And once the word again is on the lips of those who would be men, no power as yet conceived—"

"Liar and renegade! Beast of the upper earth—"

The Father's voice came wearily, "Enough, O'Hara—do not preach to him. Our problem has been solved. Descend."

The hatch clanged shut, O'Hara felt the shock of the cylinder's sudden acceleration and sprawled helplessly upon its foam-like cushioning, and as before, when he regained his feet, the quick deceleration flung him down again. And the hatch was opening.

"The Father awaits," a Son above him said.

But this time there was to be no long ascent by corridors and stairs and shafts to reach the awe-inspiring architecture of the Dome. When he left the cylinder, a panel opened in the wall beyond the terminus of the Tube, and after O'Hara had passed through, the Son stepped quickly back, the panel slid down instantly, and in the rushing dark O'Hara heard the Father's silken voice, now faint, now roaring through his brain, now very faint and weak again:

"I am returning you at once to Anstruther. When you have regained your senses, awaken him. You have only to tell him that you have at last remembered the way to reach me. He and his Sons will follow willingly enough.

"But this time I shall not guide you by my voice. A panel will open in the corridor beyond the point at which Anstruther blasted through. Lead them through that panel. Ascend the stairs you will then find. At the top of them, push up the metal covering. And you will find yourselves before this dais."

O'Hara gasped, "Anstruther was that close to you?"

"Anstruther always has been that close to me, but men who live by their emotions never quite achieve their goals. He feels. I think. That is our difference."

"Ah, Father, there is more than that."

"So you believe, O'Hara. Emotion is contagious, and you have caught the fever of it—but few men ever catch the fire of thought. You will, you will! But until I have rid you of this delusion you are useless to me. When you are here with Anstruther we shall then see how altruistic tyranny can be, when it is based on thought. And how completely senseless and destructive pure emotion is."

"I will not betray Anstruther to you."

"Do you forget your wife and child?"

"I will not betray him."

"You saw her agony when she was struggling to keep the child afloat?"

"I see that agony now, Father. It is my agony. But I will not betray Anstruther. Do as you will, but quickly, Father—in this final cruelty be merciful."

"My hand is on the key, O'Hara. Must I?"

"Quick!"

"I commend your resolution," said the Father quietly. "Now I promise you that I will not destroy Anstruther, nor will I detain him from the fate he wishes for himself. Is this enough?"

"You promise this?"

"You can enforce it. I cannot work through you unless you wish." The Father's voice sank to a whisper now. "Open your eyes. For you are in that small point in infinity—the room that seemed forever unattainable, the end of these long corridors of Washington. Anstruther and the Sons are sleeping there with you. Awaken them and do as I have said."

O'Hara was now conscious of opening his eyes. The illusion that the Father's voice was audible only to himself was overpowering at this time, for had he not been violently in argument with the Father in this room, where Anstruther and the Sons still were sleeping? Anstruther had not moved from the bunk across the room, or had the Sons stirred from the grotesque line upon the floor where they had fallen. Or, it seemed, had O'Hara himself moved since he first had sat there on the bunk, discussing with Anstruther the Father's tyranny. And all that seemed to have intervened since then—his return to the Father, his weeks of study in the library behind the dais, his strangely visual life with Nedra by means of the screen, his descent down to the unattainable integrocalculators, his journey through the Tube to the three cities of New York, and his surprising colloquy with the Son who first had guarded him there, the Son who had remembered that a female once had fought to keep her child and who had thought that it was somehow beautiful, and who had died for thinking that none of these events that had transpired since he first left this little point that was infinity now seemed a portion of his conscious life. They were only dreams, he told himself.

"Yes, they were dreams, only the product of disordered sleep," he told himself.

Then his hand touched something sharp within his jacket. It was the metal book—the way out that as yet he did not need.

And so it was no dream. O'Hara returned the book to his jacket. He crossed the room and bent over Anstruther. Would it be a betrayal now to awaken him and lead him as the remembered voice of the Father had commanded? Yet it was true, his reason told him, that he himself could enforce the Father's promise neither to destroy Anstruther nor to detain him from the fate he wished for himself.

"Anstruther," he whispered.

The Sons stirred sluggishly upon the floor. One of them hunched himself up to his feet. Another fumbled for the shining tube of his authority.

"Anstruther," said O'Hara, shaking him.

The Sons were focusing upon him now with their weak eyes, and moving toward him silently, their faces blank, seeming malignant in their utter lack of expression.

"Anstruther!" cried O'Hara, whirling toward the Sons. "Wake up, Anstruther!"

And Anstruther leaped up. The pale blue of his eyes was swallowing the pupils. "Yes—yes, now!" he cried. "The hour!"

The Sons fells back, as silently as they had advanced, their hands loose on the shining tubes they swept in little arcs.

O'Hara said, "I can lead you to the Father."

"Yes—I know—"

"But you risk your life. The Father may destroy you."

"Yes."

"The choice is yours."

"I have no choice. I seek him."

"Then follow me," O'Hara said, and turned into the corridor. Anstruther and the Sons came after him.

Beyond the blasted wall a panel opened in the seamless bright magnesium, and when all had passed through it and began to climb the steps, the panel shut them into darkness, O'Hara halted now and turned again.

"You have your atom guns. You can blast your way back into the corridor. I must tell you that the Father knows that you are approaching. He asked me to lead you."

"Yes. Lead on."

"I will not do it, Anstruther. Despite his pledge and despite the logic of his argument to support it, I will not lead you further into what is certainly a trap for you."

"What is the way to go?" Anstruther asked impatiently.

"But what do you hope to accomplish?"

"All that any man can accomplish—to meet with evil and combat it."

"Regardless of whether the Father is evil, you cannot combat him. Your only chance of ultimate success is to avoid him until the Sons and the masses everywhere will rise against him."

"But unless I meet him, they will never rise."

"You mean unless you die?"

In the darkness their voices had sunk to whispers. The turgid, thick-nosed breathing of the Sons made hearing difficult, yet neither of them noticed it. For each of them knew both the questions and the answers that must come.

"Yes. Unless I die."

O'Hara knew now that Anstruther could not be stopped. He had set for himself this course toward inevitable death; he had been constantly seeking it; he meant to give the Sons whom he had taught and the masses that he had not yet been able to teach, and might never have been able to teach, a martyr.

Still, O'Hara refused to lead Anstruther to the Father. It was Anstruther himself who pushed O'Hara aside and strode upward at last through the darkness until his groping hand touched metal above him and he thrust against it and it yielded to him. He climbed slowly out of the dark into the brilliance of the sun above him and disappeared into it. And when the Sons too had passed and vanished, O'Hara followed.

Anstruther was standing rigid and defiant halfway up the dais toward the enormous bed from which, as O'Hara emerged among the cowed and kneeling Sons, the fragile hand of Stephen Bryce was beckoning to them all. And beyond the pitifully small mound that Stephen Bryce's wasted body made beneath its coverlet, Nedra was standing with her baby in her arms—Nedra magnificently tall, robed in the thick, rich tresses of her auburn hair.

And of those gathered there, herself, Stephen Bryce, Anstruther and the Sons, and O'Hara, only Nedra seemed tranquil. Only Nedra seemed waiting for what must now happen with serene indifference—the total serenity of woman everywhere who knows that after blood is shed, she conquers.

It was Nedra's indifference that inflamed O'Hara. At the foot of the dais in that incalculably vast hall, with the hairless nude bodies of the Sons now hulking between him and the bed upon which Stephen Bryce was very slowly dying, and below Anstruther who had frozen halfway to the bed, O'Hara reckoned his chances.

He might just reach Nedra before the atom guns of Anstruther's Sons obliterated him. He might get there, but it would only be to die with her in his arms. He had had that chance before, to die with her, and he repeatedly had rejected it—he rejected it now, for it was to live with her that he wanted. Yet with the fever of death about that enormous bed O'Hara could feel surging within himself—the mad and heroic drive toward immolation, to die with Nedra, as she had wished before.

The Father spoke sharply. "Stay where you are, O'Hara!"

A Son's hand touched him. He whirled and drove his fist into the hairless face, exulting in the splattered flesh and bone.

"O'Hara, stop! Nedra will not die and does not wish to die, and you yourself will not die unless you wish it. You have a mind—you must use it."

And Nedra said, "Wait now, O'Hara."

"Yes," said Anstruther, "wait. This is my hour."

One of the Sons was now pressing his shining weapon against O'Hara's back, but his eyes were moving irresolutely, watching both Anstruther's upraised hand and O'Hara's half-crouched body and aware—constantly and fearfully aware of the silent small form prostrate on the enormous bed above them. And the miracle of the vast hall, that the Father's voice was a senile whisper when heard upon the dais but an overwhelming and god-like roar a few feet from it, gave those Sons further from the bed the strange obsession of listening to a deity's words come thundering from dying lips.

"It is indeed Anstruther's hour," said Stephen Bryce, and the Sons pressed forward to the steps of the dais.

Anstruther lowered his hand. "You have brought me here at last, Stephen Bryce," he said, "into this hall which is the symbol and the origin of your power. It was for this meeting that my craft was guided by a power more sublime than yours through the Atomic Curtain into Patagonia, and that the Sons then sent me northward through the Tube, that I might meet you here and take from you those keys and their control of the integrocalculators I might once again restore these people to the dignity of men—"

"You hear, O'Hara?" said the Father. "None of this springs from Anstruther's will. This is the classic attitude of the Messiah. Avoid this attitude, never believe that what you do is not the fruit of your own thinking and your volition."

Anstruther's own voice now again was audible, but he was looking past the Father and the keyboard now, toward Nedra.

"—and to restore the dignity of woman's motherhood, the peopling of the earth, the sacred adoration of their sons—"

"Worship comes from within," the Father said. "It does not need Messiahs to restore it. This is emotion speaking, blind emotion."

"—deliver to me now the keyboard of the integrocalculators. The weapons of the Sons whom you debased are turned upon you now—"

"You see, O'Hara, this violence will not be his. He has aroused the Sons, he led them in revolt, yet when the climax of it comes he shrinks from recognizing that the act is his. He blames the Sons, or pins it on a power beyond us all, and in this way he sheds responsibility for what he surely knows must end in death for all of us if I so will. This is the way of emotion, this is the weakling's way, O'Hara, this is the maddened posturing of a fool insensible to all except how he must seem just now in Nedra's eyes—the Chosen Male, the Dedicated Man. And she is seeing him that way! Don't you foresee how all of this must end, O'Hara? One moment more—"

"Answer, Stephen Bryce," Anstruther cried. "Answer, or die. Give me the key!"

The Father's voice broke coldly now into the sudden hush. "No, my son, I am sorry—the key is not for you, and I cannot now save you from yourself, as I had wished to do. For the worst of all human diseases is upon you, the one disease for which we never yet have found a palliative—your own vanity."

"Give me the key!" Anstruther screamed out in hysteria. "Or by my own hand, I—"

"Anstruther, stop!" O'Hara cried.

The kneeling Sons rose up in sudden frenzy, leaping for the steps. And in that moment of confusion Anstruther struck wildly downward at the Father's skull. The sound of it was like the bursting of an egg, Anstruther rocked, as if it were himself that had received the blow, and then, his arms extending cataleptically, he gripped the keyboard and drew back with it.

The Sons, now milling on the dais, seemed lost and leaderless, a shambling herd again, until from their slack ape-like mouths issued a low, despairing wail, as animals in panic raise their senseless cry, then all at once, as panicked animals will swerve, they turned toward Anstruther, their long arms lashing out toward him.

"No," cried Anstruther, reeling back. "No, don't—this was for you!"

But a wild horror was upon them, a bloodlust born of their shocked sense of guilt, and their immense hands tore at him, gouging at his eyes, ripping his face to sheds. He rushed beyond the enormous bed upon which the Father lay inert, and reaching Nedra, flung himself prostrate at her feet, then raising eyes that welled with sudden tears he sobbed, "We might—have led them! You and I—"

The Sons went swarming after him. Nedra was standing motionless, serene-dazed or serene, O'Hara could not tell. Anstruther's hand slid down along her thigh, and then, defiantly, he smashed his fist into the myriad of keys upon the board. Then the tide of leaping hairless bodies swept down on him, and as O'Hara snatched Nedra away from them, Anstruther screamed again, a scream of agony that rose half muffled from the writhing mass. They tore him apart, dismembered him, lay wallowing in bestial fury in his flesh and blood.

"O'Hara! O'Hara!"

It was the Father's voice. The hall's vast walls were now receding toward infinity, and from above, sped by the impulse that Anstruther's blow upon the keys had loosed, the intricately embellished ceiling now was plunging toward them and a great roaring from a greater distance drowned the babbling of the Sons. The Father's hand rose up. And fell. O'Hara bent down to the bed.

"This was the solution of the problem. Death for both extremes, O'Hara—death just a little earlier than it should have come. Now both of us, Anstruther and myself, commit into your hands the redemption of these continents. You understand, you hear?"

"Yes, Father—yes, I hear."

"You must go back through the Atomic Curtain. You must convince them that our skill can save their continents from their real enemies, hunger and disease. You must convince them, O'Hara, for this is their last chance, I think, as it is ours. Convince them that we want their colonists to build again, as they once built, a new and stronger race within this hemisphere—new blood to strengthen ours. And then return quickly, for it will be your task to carry on my work, to avoid my mistakes, to practice the restraint I should have shown, ridding this hemisphere at last of its pollution—"

"But the Atomic Curtain, Father?"

"You—will—pass through. The keyboard—quick! It is a means of concentration, of translating thought into fact. Think and the integrocalculators will respond. Think quickly—take your woman and your baby in your arms and concentrate—the Tube—"

"You, Father?"

"—to the Pits of Yellowstone. You see—?"

The roaring from the space around them now drowned out the Father's voice, and his eyelids shriveled shut. And while the Sons at last turned from Anstruther's mangled body and knelt down in worship at the bed, slots opened in the rapidly descending ceiling and the amber torrents of the Deluge came cascading down.

O'Hara cried, "The Tube! The Tube! The Tube!"

Darkness engulfed him. A great wind shrieked through his last consciousness. Long after that, it seemed, he was wrapped in a silence that was endless and sublime, as death might be, yet he felt certain that it was not death. And after that, long after that, he sensed that he was in the cylinder within the Tube. He struggled up, Nedra was lying at his feet, her baby locked tight in her shielding arms.

And so the Father had disclosed in death this final truth to him, and they had escaped through it—the actual power of thought. It was destructive thought, intensified with Anstruther's mind and focused through the keyboard, that had freed the impulse that caused the integrocalculators to disarrange the spatial structure of the subterranean capital, then loosing in the great hall of the Father and indeed all Washington the devouring torrents of the Deluge. And it was his own thought, O'Hara's thought, attuned to these integrocalculators which once more had moved his body through these walls of stone and seamless magnesium—his body and Nedra's and the child's—streaming as Stephen Bryce had sent him from the library downward, unchained energy, and now into the cylinder of the Tube that at this moment hurtled them toward the west.

Deceleration flung him forward in the cylinder. When its momentum died he crawled to Nedra, lying motionless.

"Nedra," he called to her.

Her lips moved silently, as if the trick of speech were lost to her. Her sluggish breathing seemed a part of that subhuman torpor he had seen before, when they were in the Tube arriving at its terminus in Washington. And as before, her apathy enraged him. It was the fury of a man who cannot dodge his guilt. He recognized it now. He stayed his hand.

"Nedra," he said, "however wrong I may have been before, this time—this time at least, I have been right. We are returning, Nedra, rising from these depths, and you must help me rise this time. Do you hear me, Nedra?"

Her lips moved painfully, "I do hear you, O'Hara."

"We have escaped," he cried. "We've gotten out of Washington despite your fears. And you yourself, this time at least, refused the chance to die."

"No one escapes, O'Hara."

"But that is the worst of all delusions, for we have done it. We've gotten out of Washington at last, and if we can do that, we can go on."

"Where would we go."

"To your people in the mountains. And after that—"

"It has never happened."

Grimly he answered, "They have always told you this, that it could not happen. Perhaps that is why it has never happened before. Perhaps it is part of your people's philosophy of death, your hankering after death—perhaps they were afraid to have it happen, Nedra! For nothing is impossible when men are willing to endure, and to dare, and most of all to think."

"It cannot happen, O'Hara."

"It's going to happen now," he warned. "And since I must, I shall make it happen in the one way that you really understand. Give me your hand."

"I can't—"

Deliberately, he swung his open palm sharply against her face. Nor this time did he loathe himself for striking her. He struck again, and as her chin came slowly up, he said, "Yes, Nedra, yes, it's happening," knowing that if he could dislodge her one obsessive thought—and he was doing it—she would become again the Nedra he had met and conquered in that mountain amphitheater months before.

He was being very calm, a paradox of gentle brutality and masculinity, when her own hand shot out and seized his throat.

As he staggered back, her long nails slashed his cheeks and she came after him, not sluggish now but lithe and murderously quick, and leaped upon him, locking her strong legs around him, and thus driving him down hard upon the cushioned surface of the cylinder while her tensed fingers stabbed toward his eyes.

O'Hara rolled from beneath her. The apathy had vanished from her eyes. What he saw in them was that wild, tigrish mating lust of the Nedra he had loved, and loved now, and must conquer or as surely die. Again she pinioned him, again tearing at his face, and with a final desperate thrust he broke away from her and staggered up. She leaped for him at once. Through the blood in his eyes, he saw her chin and swung for it. And this time it was she who dropped.

She lay at his feet. Her fingers moved unguided and found his ankles. She dragged herself toward him, painfully, and when he saw the fierce and untamed admiration in her eyes, he flung himself down blind with desire.

Yes, there were limits to the possibilities of thought. There were some things that called for more than the will to endure and to dare, as he had meant it, and it was arguable, he now confessed, that these might be the most important things of all.

In that little flat in Bloomsbury, the floor of which he had been pacing all this time so constantly, O'Hara now paused, shrugged his great shoulders and reached toward the glass that had remained untouched for better than an hour while he had told me this. He was back with me once more, back in mind as well as body, from those lost continents beyond the Atomic Curtain. He was back to the dirt and the poverty and the insecurity of the world as he had known it as a boy, and as if he felt the change was too abrupt he lifted his glass to the level of his eyes, and staring moodily into it, whispered:

"To Stephen Bryce, the Father."

"To Stephen Bryce," I echoed.

O'Hara smashed the glass against the wall. Then he turned again to me and the smile came once more to his wide, strong mouth. "Well, he's gone, has Stephen Bryce, for nothing human could have cheated the Deluge pouring into that vast hall in Washington—Stephen Bryce and his adoring Sons who turned at last against their self—appointed Messiah, Anstruther. But don't think that I would discredit Anstruther. He was more than a man. He was a force, a spirit—the little, stupid things Messiahs do die with them, but their message, the cause for their being, lives on and grows. And so it will with Anstruther. He gave them a word they had forgotten—men. And some will remember and spread it. Yes, Anstruther in death can triumph over all those masterworks that trammeled him in life. And I—"

A low cry came to us from the room beyond. O'Hara whirled, his dark eyes seeming to flash fire. His great fists tightened quickly, then he forced them open, very carefully, as if it hurt him. He stared a moment longer, and then he said:

"There's a little more and I must finish it. I left you with us in that cylinder of the Tube, its momentum gone, and Nedra and myself completely one again, but not free yet, still trapped. I must get us out of that. It is too much like the ending of a chapter in those serials you used to write—you're hanging from a cliff, and the pond below you swarms with hungry crocodiles. You're slipping, you're certain to fall—but we mustn't worry too much. With a quick flourish of your pen—I suppose you actually use a typewriter—you'll whisk away the crocodiles and place a haymow in the pond to receive you gently when at last you fall.

"With myself and Nedra and our baby it was not quite that easy. We were sealed inside the cylinder. And no Son now appeared above us at the hatch. We were sealed in there as completely as we had been sealed, months before, in that exquisite hexagonal room in Washington. But now there was no omnipresent voice to lull us, and we meant to try.

"The hatch was kept rigidly in place by a thick metal spring, protecting us from the vacuum of the Tube during our passage. I glanced around that empty cylinder for some sort of lever to pry against the spring, and then absurdly—for the first time in months—I remembered the pistol strapped inside my jacket. Now I drew it out and fired twice against the coiled metal before it snapped. The hatch sprang open.

"We climbed out warily. Once more we stood in a deserted corridor of glittering magnesium, its endless distances reaching toward infinity. But this time no one opened panels in the walls for us. We marched, a long, long march to nowhere, prisoners still, yet knowing this time in our hearts that space alone could never vanquish us. Nor were we wrong, for finally we made an oblique turn and there before us lay the Guild. And as we entered it, the Sons rose from their knees before a blindingly bright screen. And a god's voice was droning:

"'Now they will come to you—this darkly bearded man and this red-haired woman with a boy child in her arms. Take them to the surface of Emporia, and there deliver them unto the Son who guards the valleys toward the mountains. He must see that they reach the mountainside and leave them there. This is your task. This is your task—'

"The voice droned on repetitively in that same pitch of godliness that I had first heard in the subterranean city of Emporia, beating the order endlessly into their brains until it was—as so much of their guidance was—hypnotic. A voice from the grave—rather, a voice out of the depthless Pits of Yellowstone. Yes, Stephen Bryce's voice, recorded sometime in the hours before his death while he lay waiting for Anstruther and myself to come to him. Knowing that he was to die, and planning to achieve in death the goal he sought for me. And I had thought he would not open panels in the walls!

"Now the Sons were rising from their knees, and they came at once to us—they never doubted that we would be waiting there—and motioned that we were to follow."

The ensuing march, led by the Son whose duty was to take them to the surface, had nothing of the horror of their first descent into Emporia, for it had been the swarming masses of the Degraded that had made it horrible, the shambling tens of thousands, naked and vilely apathetic, aimless. Now there were no masses. And the Son now marching with them knew what he was doing.

"Are you not lonely here without the masses?" asked O'Hara.

"Lonely?"

"Do you not miss those who were swallowed by the Deluge here?"

"Oh, no."

"You realize what caused the Deluge?"

"Yes. The Father caused it."

"And if I told you that the Father too was swallowed by the Deluge?"

"That could not happen."

"But if I say I saw it happen?"

"No," said the Son. "For even now the Father speaks to us. And even now the Tube brings new food from the photo-synthetrons. And soon the Tube will bring more females to repopulate Emporia."

"Do you not know what has occurred in Washington?"

"None of us ever knows what has occurred in Washington. It is not necessary that we know, for the Father speaks, and the food continues coming, and the water from the oceans of the west, and we the Sons need nothing more than that. No," said the Son, neither obstinately nor shaken, "we need nothing more, and we need to know nothing more, not while the Voice still comes to give us tasks."

O'Hara himself, certain of what he knew; certain of what he understood must yet be done, could not feel in this moment of such faith that all of this, the whole vast system of existence and regeneration stemming from the fixed impulses of the integrocalculators, must in time run down. For one brief instant he forgot the Father's constant warning that he must not put his trust in miracles, and it seemed possible that these lost continents could go on as they were, unguided, automatically, until their retrogressive doom in time left these glistening corridors only the moist warm droplets of the primal ooze.

And was that actually so terrible? Might as well feel pity for bacteria as for these mindless creatures. But then, in New York, there had been that Son who had recalled a female of the masses who had fought to keep her child. And that Son had remembered it as beautiful.

However dim, perhaps not sharper than the anguish of a wobbly tooth, the anguish of the soul was not yet gone from them. And on that anguish he could build.

"This is the shaft," the Son beside him said.

So O'Hara and Nedra and their child ascended once more to the surface above Emporia and went across the multihued coiling of the photosynthetrons and again upon that long march into the upland valleys. And there the Son turned back.

"Good-bye," O'Hara called to him.

The Son stood silently. His weak eyes focused for a moment, then he shook his head. "But you will be returning," he said. "The Father frees you for a purpose that is known to him. When you have achieved it, he will send us again to take you back to him."

"You do believe that, don't you?" said O'Hara. "You do believe—"

But the Son was gone.

For the next five days O'Hara and Nedra and the child wandered higher into the mountains. And the beauty of growing things, the trees that soared toward the intense blue skies, and the soft thick mosses and grass beneath their feet, and the birds that fluttered suddenly off when they approached, and the frogs and insects that hopped away or crawled from under rocks, the bite of the wind that came whining down the far white slopes ahead, the gaggle of water searching its path through pebbles, the heat of a true sun in the heavens, all these—and freedom from oppressive walls and more oppressive destiny—awakened them slowly from the long timeless stupor of the lowlands. Nor did they know how deeply, if how troubled they had slept.

"I am hungry," said Nedra.

"I shall hunt for food."

"You have forgotten how to do it."

"An empty belly is a rapid teacher."

"But what will teach you to become a man again?"

"That too I shall learn," O'Hara laughed. He had not laughed for months.

The third night of their wandering it snowed, and they took refuge underneath a ledge of granite, and Nedra toiled for hours with dry bark and some twigs until she had a fire. But a very small fire.

"I am cold now," she said accusingly.

"I shouldn't wonder," said O'Hara. "The fact is, Nedra, you've got to put on some clothes. Which means, I'm sure, that I shall have to get to providing them. I had forgotten what a chore it is to be a husband in this world."

The snow did not stop. On the fourth day of it O'Hara shot a giant timber wolf. Its flesh was coarse and its hide, when they had baked it out, had an amazing stench, but Nedra fashioned it into a sort of kirtle, not so expertly made as that which had concealed her sex the first time that O'Hara saw her, but serviceable.

"Beyond the Curtain," he said, "men buy perfumes for their women but I doubt, Nedra, that any ever bought a perfume such as this."

"You do not think that I am beautiful in this?"

But it had been a long day's climb and O'Hara was weary. He did not feel that he was in the best of shape for battle. "Yes, Nedra, beautiful," he sighed, and for this night at least she let him lie a coward.

On the sixth day, as they were trudging slowly upward along a snow-drifted trail, the brush ahead of them parted suddenly and from it stepped the gaunt, commanding figure of the clansmen's Elder, his Colt aimed menacingly at O'Hara's breast.

But Nedra said, "Is this the way you welcome us? Where are the others of the clan?"

And they came out of hiding along the trail behind the Elder.

It was not a time for conversation. The Elder now turned his back upon them and began to lead the way, and the clansmen closed in quickly around them, and together at a trot they proceeded along the trail toward the sandy chasm.

In the days that followed, with Nedra reigning placidly once more within the deep gloom of the cavern, O'Hara prepared himself for what he knew must follow. Now that he was free, now that he felt himself again a factor in his destiny, he was reluctant. It was the Elder who at last convinced him, after hearing one night the strange abominations of the lowlands.

"It is a time of strange things," said the Elder cautiously. "I too have heard and seen strange things since you were with us. Do you recall the day you vanished in the valley? Those of us who escaped the Degraded continued on until we reached the lake that had the black water. In time we returned here with it, and made the long copper pots that you designed upon the walls of the cavern—"

"Oh, yes, the still for refracting petroleum."

"—and then we prepared the water that you wished, the colorless water, to give to the flying thing. We wished despite your absence to send it into the air. We took the colorless water in jars and we placed the jars before the flying thing and waited. And presently we heard a voice that spoke the way you spoke when you first came to us. Again and again, as a wolf calls for its missing whelp, it called for you: "O'Hara—O'Hara—come in, O'Hara! This is Tournant calling, this is Wrangell calling—can you come in, O'Hara?'"

"Tournant!"

"The voice kept saying that. Yet there was no one in the flying thing, no man to speak these words to you."

"Of course! Of course! A voice—the wireless—speaking through three thousand miles of space. And through the Curtain."

"Is this not strange, O'Hara?"

But O'Hara seized his arm. "The voice! The craft! And you took the fuel there? Then I—I can fly again!"

It was that overwhelming yearning to be taking off again that sent him rushing to the cavern.

"Nedra!" And when she turned. "I'm going to fly again."

She wiped the baby's mouth. She rubbed her hands together slowly, with sand between them, to rid them of the fat of a wild fowl she was roasting. She placed a log upon the smoldering fire.

"Where will you fly?" she asked.

"Does it matter, Nedra?"

"Yes."

"All right, I shall go straight up as long as the motors will push me, and then I shall circle around as a condor might do it, and I'll feel like a condor, too, a king of the skies—"

"I am going with you."

That sobered him up. And he took her hands: "There is a chance, always a chance, that the flying thing will fall. And the baby, Nedra, your child—our child?"

"The baby is the clan's. But I, O'Hara, am yours."

"But Nedra, if I—well, if I don't come back to these mountains—?"

"Ah." She smiled. "I knew!" And clenched the ceremonial warclub and advanced.

It was the Elder who managed things. At dawn they departed, the men and the younger women of the clan going swiftly upward through the heavy snowdrifts and O'Hara with Nedra trotting grimly among them until at last they reached that upland meadow where he had first set his craft down on the continent. The craft—and the jars of fuel—waited there.

Nedra got into the cockpit. Then O'Hara directed the task of clearing a runway through the snow. When they had finished, O'Hara climbed in, touched his instruments very carefully, then touched them in earnest and felt the living throb of motors. They coughed and then died.

"Once more," he whispered to himself. This time they roared.

The Elder flung himself face down into the snow. The younger clansmen scattered. O'Hara shook his fist at them. The craft shot forward. Before it reached the wall of trees it knifed into the sky.

For some minutes O'Hara was too busy with the glory of his wings, driving higher, soaring, to observe that Nedra had now shut her eyes. The ticking of his scintillometer broke in upon his absorption finally, its millroentgen count a steady .285. Then he heard a more staccato clicking, and it was Nedra.

"Here, your teeth are chipping. Take this jacket, Nedra."

He pulled it off. And the metal book that he had taken from the library in Washington dropped onto his knees. He closed his eyes, and when he opened them, he flicked wide the covers. Upon the single sheet of bright magnesium was this: "December 20, 12:35:01 P.M. Save for these ten seconds, only you can do it."

Nedra called his name but he did not hear her. His mind was working like an exquisitely refined machine. He was counting, squeezing the fractional lost months and weeks and days and hours, the minutes and seconds of the past twelve months into a pattern, calculating time, estimating his position by the daytime pinpoints of the stars.

"O'Hara, O'Hara! Our mountains have vanished—"

December 20—and precisely at 12:35:01 P.M—and for the ensuing ten seconds.

Sweat poured from his body. Infinitesimal memories arranged themselves. He could not be certain. But then he could never be certain again on this side of the Curtain. To the day, yes! And to the hour and possibly quite close to the minute—but never to the second! He would have to feel his way into it, watching his milliroentgen count, and if the Curtain was there, he would have to turn back. Yet this fuel would not last him back from the Curtain to Nedra's mountains. It would be a chance—a frightful chance.

"O'Hara, tell me—"

"We're going through the Curtain, Nedra."

And she nodded somberly.

At fifty thousand feet O'Hara leveled off. As he accelerated past two thousand miles an hour he checked and rechecked his calculations of the day and hour. His problem, as he analyzed it, was to reach the Curtain before 12:35:01 P.M., and to continue swinging into it and away from it until—at the miraculous proper moment—his scintillometer reading dropped below the danger point, and then, upon the inward arc of his ellipse of flying, to smash through.

It would be best to approach first in a dive from his maximum altitude, at his maximum speed. It was true that he might thus smash into the Curtain before the ten-second interval in which it did not exist, during the changing of the reactors, but at least this time he would know what he was about to do—he would not be senseless from a bolt of lightning.

This was his plan. And it worked.

It shot him back across the Arctic, deep into Asia, deep into the hemisphere of Delhi, Rome and Paris and the Twelve Old Men of Geneva.

"You've got to have luck for anything like that," O'Hara admitted. "The luck of a Columbus. Would you have bet on us?"

He laughed, then he corked the bottle. There would be no more tippling in that little flat in Bloomsbury.

"I would not bet against your luck, O'Hara."

"But there was more than luck to it," he answered. "For I was beginning to learn the most difficult of the arts—to think. The Father had taught me how to start learning. Ninety-nine hundredths of the best motor you and I have got is never used—ninety-nine hundredths of each of our brains lies idle. Perhaps in Washington I learned to use another hundredth. At least I had begun to learn how to learn, and once that has begun no problem can remain insoluble."

"Almost the words of the Father," I pointed out.

"Yes, almost the words of the Father. And if you link them with the words I found in that magnesium book—the words I forgot in my extreme concentration upon the matter of the ten seconds in which the Curtain would not be before me—if you recall those words—"

"Only you can do it," I quoted.

"—then you know why I am here tonight," he said. "Do you think I'd desert them?"

"Desert whom, O'Hara? Your son?"

"Yes," he said, "my son—and the Son who remembered a woman of the masses who had fought to keep her child, that Son who had died for thinking it was beautiful and the tens of thousands of others now shambling dully through those subterranean corridors, their bellies full, without anxiety as we know it, yet haunted—dimly haunted by the memory of love. For Stephen Bryce told me that tyranny is in essence not the existence of a tyrant, but the debased minds of the people, and it is their lost faculty of love that most debases them. Of course I'm going back to them. Do you know a comparable challenge?"

"We have a challenge here," I insisted. "The deserts of China and Africa, the hunger of our billions. What you have learned— and what you know of guiding us—can end all that."

"Are you trying to convince me?" he smiled, and took my hand. "Listen carefully, Arthur Blair—tonight I am returning through the Curtain. Don't ask me how, for I have told you, the words in that magnesium book, the moment when the Father died in Washington—I am going back! I know I am going back despite all that the Twelve Old Men and their Security Bureau may attempt. I shall be there in Washington tomorrow. I will have much to do, and for the next three months you will not hear from me. But when those three months end my voice will come to you, not on a screen that blinds you with its incandescence—by wireless, Arthur Blair. I shall be speaking for the Western Hemisphere to you and all these billions. For you need us. And we so greatly need you. My voice will come through the Curtain, and when I am finished speaking there will be no Curtain. I will have lifted it forever.

"We can save our two worlds, Arthur, but it won't be easy. The Twelve Old Men, those timid guardians of the past, are going to fight you. You must fight back, and fast—inform the peoples. Give them the facts, the dangers most of all. Don't raise false dreams, for nothing is accomplished without sweating. Yes, you have got your work cut out for you, Arthur—and only you can do it!"

He freed my hand. He stooped, and when he rose again, he held the ceremonial club tight in his hand.

"I'm going to open that door," he said, "and for just one instant you'll see the most magnificent woman on this earth. Then out you go, old boy! Stand back—stand back!"

THE END

If you've enjoyed this book, you will not want to miss these terrific titles...

ARMCHAIR SCI-FI & HORROR DOUBLE NOVELS, $12.95 each

D-141   **ALL HEROES ARE HATED** by Milton Lesser
AND THE STARS REMAIN by Bryan Berry

D-142   **LAST CALL FOR DOOMSDAY** by Edmond Hamilton
HUNTRESS OF AKKAN by Robert Moore Williams

D-143   **THE MOON PIRATES** by Neil R. Jones
CALLISTO AT WAR by Harl Vincent

D-144   **THUNDER IN THE DAWN** by Henry Kuttner
THE UNCANNY EXPERIMENTS OF DR. VARSAG by David V. Reed

D-145   **A PATTERN FOR MONSTERS** by Randall Garrett
STAR SURGEON by Alan E Nourse

D-146   **THE ATOM CURTAIN** by Nick Boddie Williams
WARLOCK OF SHARRADOR by Gardner F. Fox

D-147   **SECRET OF THE LOST PLANET** by David Wright O'Brien
TELEVISION HILL by George McLociard

D-148   **INTO THE GREEN PRISM** by A Hyatt Verrill
WANDERERS OF THE WOLF-MOON by Nelson S. Bond

D-149   **MINIONS OF THE TIGER** by Chester S. Geier
FOUNDING FATHER by J. F. Bone

D-150   **THE INVISIBLE MAN** by H. G. Wells
THE ISLAND OF DR. MOREAU by H. G. Wells

ARMCHAIR SCIENCE FICTION CLASSICS, $12.95 each

C-61   **THE SHAVER MYSTERY, Book Six**
by Richard. S. Shaver

C-62   **CADUCEUS WILD**
by Ward Moore & Robert Bradford

ARMCHAIR MYSTERY-CRIME DOUBLE NOVELS, $12.95 each

B-1   **THE DEADLY PICK-UP** by Milton Ozaki
KILLER TAKE ALL by James O. Causey

B-2   **THE VIOLENT ONES** by E. Howard Hunt
HIGH HEEL HOMICIDE by Frederick C. Davis

B-3   **FURY ON SUNDAY** by Richard Matheson
THE AGONY COLUMN by Earl Derr Biggers

MUSIC SOOTHES THE SAVAGE ROBOT

For unremembered eons the god had slept. For a million years it had quested through the star worlds of its dreams, until it lived only as a faint legend in the race memories of mankind. But now the time had come for man to recall its name, and to worship it once again. Noorlythin arose and went out into the world of men—with his robot minions.

The High Mor wanted all Earthers dead…including Kael McCanahan's father and the rest of their crew. With the flame-tressed Flaith, McCanahan fled through filthy sewers and the dusty desert—only to be confronted by Noorlythin!

But McCanahan's father left him a valuable legacy…the means to destroy Noorlythin, and his minions once and for all. If only McCanahan could keep it away from his enemies, and rescue the lovely Flaith…

CAST OF CHARACTERS

KAEL MCCANAHAN
This spacefaring Irishman didn't have time to properly mourn his father's passing, and was confused by his legacy—a harp string!

FLAITH
Her temperament was as fiery as her hair, and her beauty had gotten her far on this world. But now she had to rely on her wits.

THE HIGH MOR
This ruthless ruler of Senorech killed McCanahan's father while he slept, and wasn't afraid to kill others he deemed undesirable.

NOORLYTHIN
An immortal and powerful being, a God long forgotten. Obscurity no longer suited him—he longed to be worshipped again.

THE DOYEN
These primordial gods of space simply couldn't tolerate one of their own going rogue…

SFARRAN TROOPS
They were unstoppable warriors! Their numbers seemed unending; and they were only too willing to die before capture.

.

THE WARLOCK
OF SHARRADOR

By
GARDNER F. FOX

ARMCHAIR FICTION
PO Box 4369, Medford, Oregon 97504

*For more information about Armchair Books and products, visit our
website at…*

www.armchairfiction.com

Or email us at…

armchairfiction@yahoo.com

CHAPTER ONE

THE McCANAHAN came awake in the pearl mists of a Senn dawn, staring upward into the round blue muzzle of a Thorn blaster. The handgun hung in the air without visible support, its trigger moving slowly back. In an instant, it would lash out at him with a thousand tares of destruction.

He whipped the bedclothes into a geyser of silk and moonylon, and dove naked over the edge of the bed to roll on the floor and turn over and over. He brought up against the chair where his uniform belt hung, and fumbled blindly for his service holster.

The blaster spoke in a soft whoosh of yellow flame, and the bedclothes puffed once, billowing into a thick, reddish smoke. *That would have been me, instead of the blankets, if the Little People had not come in my dreams to whisper in my ears of Flaith's loveliness,* the McCanahan thought, and tore loose his addy gun.

His wrist steadied, and he touched the stud. The blaster, hung on a tensor beam, went red, then white, and began to melt in droplets all over the thick Morrvan carpet of his officer's quarters. The tensor beam, held by a minute mechanism inbuilt within the handgun's butt, let loose, and the blistered, melting thing thudded to the floor.

"It was a close thing," Kael McCanahan told himself, sitting there naked on the floor.

It had been the Sfarri who had sent the gun. The Sfarri, who hated the men of Terra with a hate like a fierce, blazing flame; who would not scruple at assassination to gain their aims.

"WARLOCK OF SHARRADOR"
ARTIST UNKNOWN

They were a cold, efficient breed of men, these Sfarri. The far-flung Galactic fleet ships of Mother Terra, stretched in a thin line between the stars, had crossed addy beams and searirays with their slim vessels a thousand times. Almost always, Terra lost her ships. Almost always, those far-ranging Sfarran ships smashed the eagle-blazoned Terran cruisers, and fled like laughing ghosts into the black infinity of space.

No Terran ship had ever captured a living Sfarran. Somehow, with the barbaric philosophy of Hara-Kari, they committed suicide. It never failed.

And slowly, but remorselessly, the ships of Terra and the Solar Combine were pushed back and back, away from the Rim planets and the close vastness of the Sack worlds that were so rich in every mineral, jewel and foodstuff known to man, and even in some that Terran man had never known.

The Solar Command had ordered Kael's father, Sire Patric McCanahan, Fleet Admiral, with Captain Raoul Edmunds and Commodore Kael McCanahan, to Senorech, there to make at last parlay with the High Mor who ruled the Senn. They were to offer alliances and trade agreements.

Too many times, at the foot of the great ruboid throne of the Senn ruler, had young Kael McCanahan seen the thin, hard lips of the High Mor twist cruelly as he lashed out at the gray-haired Admiral. Too many times had the red flush of fury crept up past his tight white uniform collar with its crimson Commodore braid encrusted thick on its rich surface, as he listened to the High Mor explaining to his father the fact that the men of the Solar Command were no match for the relentless fury of the Sfarri.

The High Mor, it was plain, was eager to ally himself with the Sfarri.

In return, the Sfarri would rid him of these annoying Terrans.

THE Thorn blaster that lay melting on the thick pile of his officers' quarters was the opening shot in the extermination program.

The McCanahan let the breath from his lungs in a sudden relief. He sat with his back propped against the leg of the chair, and the hand that held his own Thorn shook so that he put his wrist on his naked knee. He was a tall man, a man grown hard and fit with the mechanical fitness that was the hallmark of all officers of the Solar Intergalactic Command. Blond hair was cropped close to the conformations of his head, giving his face a hard, carven look.

The mark of deep space was in Kael McCanahan's eyes, and in the catlike walk and movements of his big body. He had been processed as only Spacefleet officers were processed, in these days of the Empire, with a cold precision to his mind and a careful hardness to his body.

He came off the floor and began to dress, sliding into the white uniform with its crimson facings, pushing feet into highly polished jet boots. His mind went to his father, the Sire Patric McCanahan, who was Earth representative at the court of the High Mor, overlord of Senorech.

"If they've made their try for me, they've already made it for him," he told the room.

He buttoned his white jacket that had the golden eagles at collar and cuffs. He whipped the leather service belt around his middle. He fastened the black blaster holster to its pivot.

The door opened to a fingerpress, and he was out in the long, metalloid hall, moving with long strides. A woman came out of the shadows to meet him, running.

"Kael! Kael—wait!"

It was Cassy Garson, in her white nursing uniform that was always a little too tight for her curved body. Like many other Earth officers on the distant planets of the empire, the McCanahan had fond memories of the Nursing Auxiliary of the Fleet. Cassy Garson had been a lot of fun, on a dance floor, or under the curved canopy of a canal boat, or on the silken cushions of a reflexifloor.

Her soft hands caught his, and he could feel her body's tremblings as she came against him. "Kael, you've heard! Oh, Kael, I'm scared! What'll they do to us?"

"Talk sense, Cassy!" he snapped, knowing his nerves frayed and jumpy because of the metal thing he had melted in his room. He softened his voice, and told her of it.

Her dark eyes were frightened things. "They killed your father tonight! The same way, probably. A Thorn blaster was found a foot from his gloved hand. It looks like suicide. The High Mor has sent word that we're to leave. All of us. No more Earthers on Senorech!"

Cassy whispered in the stillness of the corridor, "We've orders to be aboard the *Eclipse* by noon. To chart our course for Antares. To get out of the Rim planets and stay out."

The McCanahan drew a deep breath. His tight collar choked him, and a vein swelled and throbbed in his hard face. "He's afraid of the Sfarri. Sfar is close to the High Mor's home galaxy. May the gods curse a man so driven by fear he'd murder a man who wished him nothing but good!"

Cassy shook against him. "Kael, let's rouse the others! We've got to be on the *Eclipse* by noon!"

THERE was nothing he could do now, nothing except swallow the bitter truth that he was running from a fight; that he was leaving his dead father on an alien planet with not even a shamrock to blow in the breeze above his grave. His father, one of the Bloody McCanahans, who had scratched their names on graves from Mars to Makron, who had been born to the service of the golden eagles, and now lay with no man to whisper a prayer over his dead body.

McCanahan shook himself like a cat stretching after a sleep. The anger boiled within him, locked inside his guts by his tight lips. "I'm going to get his body, Cassy. I'll take it back with us for decent burial."

Her hands tightened until the red nails cut into his flesh. "You're a fool, Kael McCanahan! A stubborn fool that's walking to his death! Don't you understand? That's just what the High Mor wants you to do! He'll have his dragon killers waiting for you, like cats standing at a mouse-hole in the kitchen flooring!"

"Let them wait," he growled, but her hand dragged him along the corridor, to door after door of the fleet barracks. They roused the honor guard, eighty men in all, the most allowed on Senorech by the High Mor. Men tumbled from their bunks with sleep glazing their eyes, but they wakened fast enough, with Cassy and the McCanahan to whip them into action.

They found Captain Edmunds of the *Eclipse* half dressed. A small, chunky man, he showed the years of his service in the crows' feet at the corners of his eyes and the faint silver that threaded his curly black hair.

"I'm sorry, Kael. You're The McCanahan now, but that doesn't mean a thing, not after what's happened. Get aboard the ship. I'll bring the men, and whatever they want to take along."

Cassy said, "I've alerted the nurses. They'll be ready at blast-off time."

Within an hour, it was done. Sober men in white uniforms were filing out of their quarters by twos and threes, with their warbags slung over shoulders or hanging by, leather thongs from their wrists. They moved across the city in a body, nurses in their center, their hands wrapped on the walnut butts of their service blasters.

McCanahan lost himself five minutes before Captain Edmunds took them out of barracks, toward the silver bullet that was the *S. I. C. Eclipse.* He stepped from Cassy Garson's side, into an intersecting corridor, and moved down a flight of steps to the basement. It was easy, down here among the great heating tubes, and dynamos, to stand and wait until the boot falls faded. Cassy came once to a ramp, and called, but her voice echoed hollowly in the cellar unanswered.

Twenty minutes after they were gone across the city, the McCanahan was sliding through the shadows cast by the monolithic buildings, and moving along the broad avenue flanking the Jaddarak canal. Ahead of him were the white bulks of the government buildings. Somewhere in those towering multi-windowed edifices, his father lay dead, with a Thorn blaster close to his hand.

He reached the high stone wall of the gardens and was hoisting himself over the red and stone wall top when a dark-faced Senn caught sight of his Earther uniform and screeched the alarm. The McCanahan cursed in his throat and dropped to the ground inside the garden, his jet boots printing their soles deep in the soft loam of a bed of Thallan sunflowers.

He made for the arched doorway at the near end of the gardens. At a run he came into the darkness of the groined arches. He knew his way through these labyrinthine tunnels. With his father, he liked to walk in the cool corridors where the manacled takkaprots screeched their birdlike songs and the colored waters of the fountains made a rainbow of moving brilliance.

The hoarse, brazen pitch of the bry-horns was startling in the Senorech morning. *They'll be roaming these halls with their blasters cutting at every shadow, he thought. Sooner or later one of the shadows they shoot at will be mine!* He had to reach his father's suite, had to kneel there and do what must be done for Patric McCanahan, as Patric had done to his own father before him.

They might expect him to come as he was, expect him to fight his way to his father's side and kneel to whisper a prayer for him over his dead body. On Earth it would be expected. Expected and guarded against. But Senorech was not Earth, and on Senorech things were rarely done for emotional reasons. The McCanahan yanked his Thorn from its sheath as he slid into a telepetor and twirled a dial. If they were expecting him he was ready.

Curiously, the suite of rooms was empty, save for the crumpled man who lay in a white uniform with gold and platinum aigrettes on the shoulders, and red tykkan braid looped under a crumpled arm. McCanahan went to his knees, and his lips moved. In the custom of spacemen everywhere, from the domed tunnels of the Moon to the hellcraters of humid Brinth, he put his hand to his father's wrist and whispered, "I swear by the blood that bonds us, you will not have died in vain. I will make the report, and investigate the reason for your dying."

It was a simple thing, that oath. Many men had spoken it, until it had become a part of the creed of those who roamed the star worlds. It prevented tragedies, and saved lives, for once the reason for a man's death, was known, preventive precautions were taken, so that many men who otherwise would have died, lived to walk the palm terraces of Mars and sail the tossing seas of Acherner. The histories of space featured and explained it, and glamorized its usefulness.

But as the McCanahan let the words trail from his lips, he cursed and looked down at his palm, where part of his father's wrist had come off, to stick to it.

He grimaced, and then reason came into his head. His father was recently dead, no rotting corpse. "Plastiskin," he breathed, and leaned down, ripping with strong fingers at that wrist, carefully built up to hide something.

Around his father's wrist was wrapped a length of silvery wire, thin and fine. The McCanahan leaned forward and untwisted it.

It came away and danced in his fingers, reflecting the blue glow of the wall mercurilamps.

"A harpstring!"

He sat on his ankles and forgot that a mile away the *Eclipse* was warming its takeoff tubes. "Now why in the name of Brian Boru did father hide such a thing on his wrist? He played no harp, nor anything else that ever made music!"

BUT this was no time to solve puzzles. With a snap of his fingers, he rolled up the silvery wire and bound it tight about an ankle, then thrust his foot back into his service boot. He went to the window and stared down at the splashing fountains and the sunflower gardens half a mile below him. The walls were lined with Senn guards, inside and out, and men with the High Mor's red dragon insignia on their cloaks moved here and there in the shrubbery, slashing at ferns and jungle vines with their swords.

"They'll tire of that soon enough," he decided. "Then they'll come through the palace itself, a floor at a time, working the place over with the point of a dagger and the muzzle of a Thorn."

They would be expecting him to hide. They would be expecting him to keep retreating ahead of them until they trapped him high above, in a cloud-room or on a rooftop. A Senn or a Sfarran would act like that. They would do the smart, the sensible thing.

"Faith, my belly tells me it's the smart thing for myself as well," the McCanahan muttered. "But my head tells me something else again!"

He wandered the rooms of the palace until he found the wallgrille of an atmosphere tube. With the edge of his service knife, he worked at the screws until the plate came loose from the wall. He crawled into the tube and replaced the grate as best he could. Then, sliding and levering himself from curve to curve of the tube, he began moving downwards.

When he came to gentle loops, in the tubes, he let go and slid. It took him three hours to get down, but when he came into the cold metal coils that could duplicate the atmosphere of fifty planets, he was below the search level, and as good as a free man walking the streets.

"Except for the uniform," he told himself, glancing down ruefully at the white and gold resplendence of his fleet garb.

In ten minutes he was crawling up through a street grille, and heading for the space docks.

He was moving up the Avenue of Emblems, with the gleaming bullet that was the *S. I. C. Eclipse* towering above the buildings, nosing its point skyward, still half a mile ahead of him, when he heard the announcers. The words were just sounds, at first, like the pennons flapping above his head from the tall poles, each a gift of the United Worlds.

His mind was torn cleanly with a thin, hard grief, for he was remembering his father, and the way of his smiling and his gentle voice, and the fun they had shared together on the Klisskahaenay Rapids in a boat, or in the crisp darkness of space, with the stars beckoning and his father pointing them out to him. And his handclasp when he left for the Academy, his letters, his visits at holidays when the needs of the Empire were relaxed enough to free the Admiral from his cruiser. It was a good companionship, that of his father and himself, born of their mutual need when his mother died on Aldebaran.

And now it was over. No more would he see that smile or listen to that voice or wonder how it was that his father knew so much more than he about so many things. They would never hook a lyskansa-fish or blast a Martian boar with needleguns. They would never find new foods in restaurants that—

"—under penalty of the red dragon! Repeating! Space Commodore McCanahan—Kael McCanahan, Earther—is to die on sight. All guards are hereby warned. McCanahan must not leave Akkalan. He is to be shot on sight, under penalty of the red dragon! Repeating..."

It sank in after a while. He drew back into the shadows, and the harpstring tied to his ankle pained him, as if it whispered with his father's voice. *They're afraid of me and what I can do to them*, his mind told him. *They don't even dare let me get close to a space communicator panel!* But why? Why? The McCanahan shook his head and looked down at himself, neat and trim in the gold and white space uniform.

"It's a card with my name on it asking that they shoot me," he told the shadows. *"I've got to be rid of it or swallow a dozen blaster-beams."*

They would be searching the space docks just about now, minutes before takeoff time. They would almost dismantle the ship to find him. And there would be others, blasters in their hands, stretched all around the field. They would shoot on sight, to kill, or they would suffer the fate of the red dragon; and no one in his right mind cared even to think about that punishment, that took a man a month of agony to die.

McCanahan stripped naked in the shadows and bundled his uniform into a ball and weighed it with his boots. He made a compact bundle and threw it up, through the lengthening shadows, onto a low, sloping roof. Let them find that when they could! Then he turned and ran on the sun-warmed bricks, away from the field, toward the dirty alleyways that were the Akkalan slums.

"Now where in the name of the family leprechaun could a man who is stripped to his buff hope to find a shelter in this unholy town?" he asked the wind as he ran.

McCanahan thought of Ars Massen, a little dark man with a colossal thirst for the pale yellow fire that was Senn wine. His lips twitched as his memory ran on the nights they had spent together in the lowland taverns, sampling every liquid that the skills and arts of men could brew. Ars Maasen traded in lyss furs, and spent his profits faster than the fierce little desert tycats could breed and run to his traps.

With Ars Maasen he would find Flaith.

CHAPTER TWO

THE cities of the Senorech had been built half a million years ago when their primates first modeled clay from mud and water. As the years piled knowledge on their shoulders, their buildings grew and expanded, but they still showed the heterogeneous planning the first Senn had put into them. A man could lose himself in the slum quarter, where the dragon police rarely came, for the High Mor was content to close his eyes to the manner of a man's profit, providing he paid a good tax at the end of the year. Under the creaking signs and iron grille balconies, in the dark street shadows, even a naked man could run free and unmolested.

He came to a square of light and an open door under a carven tycat. Carefully he crept closer listening to the song a hundred throats were bellowing through the smoke and the wine fumes. He came inside on soundless feet and stood sheltered by a solid oak railing.

Flaith was a breath in a man's throat and a catch at his guts, lovely in bronze moiré, her amber shoulders bared to the curve of her breasts, the moiré slashed teasingly down a naked side to the swell of a white hip. She leaned on the wooden tabletop, and her slant eyes were clear, and her crimson hair a flame caught in the blaze of a wall torch.

The McCanahan let his eyes linger on her loveliness, but it was the little dark man, with the scar across half his face and a full foaming tankard at his mouth, that he had come to see.

He drew back his arm and threw the pebble he held.

Ars Maasen felt the sting of the rock on his forehead. He lowered his mug and swore by a dozen gods at the ill manners of men who would toss rocks in the middle of such a song. And then he felt Flaith's white fingers, and the dig of her long red nails in his forearm.

"It's Kael!" she whispered. "He's naked and alone!"

"For shame! A fine boy like that and—"

"Hssst, you byblow fool!" she warned. "Go to him and see what he needs!"

She pressed the key to her dressing room into his hand, and when he had slipped through the men and women toward the door, she stood so the others could see her. On tiny golden feet she climbed from chair to tabletop, and her bare arms were amber serpents writhing in the crimson half-light.

"The Snakes of Slaamsheel," she called to the players, and a roar of delight went up, for this was an old ballad, and the flame-like Flaith dancing with skirt to mid-thighs across the tabletops, set the blood bubbling in a man's veins.

The McCanahan caught the fire of her throaty singing just as Ars Maasen whipped the cloak off his shoulders and flung it about his chest.

"A full belly, is it?" the dark little man asked. "Wine or Puban ale or maybe both?"

"I'm sober as the snakes Flaith sings of, and as mean!"

Ars Maasen caught the madness in his voice, and grunted, "Come quickly, then. This way, across the sill and through the alley to her doorway!"

When they were moving into the shadows of the alley, Kael told him of his father's death, and of the orders of the High Mor that made him lower than a Tuuran-peddler. And as the words came through his teeth, the raw fury that twisted him showed in his eyes. "They blasted him without a chance for a fight—the way they tried to blast me! Now they're hunting me for a reason only the Shee fairies could know!"

"Easy, boy. Easy! Talk as you want —it helps ease the pain under your navel. But don't let the hate shake you so. It blinds a man."

The little trader turned the key in the lock and the stout wooden door opened inward to a tiny room where an oil lamp cast a dim yellow glare on a dressing table and stool. Costumes hung from a peg-rack on the wall above a tycat-skin couch.

"Flaith's room," he muttered. "Only she comes here."

The McCanahan sat on the couch, and with elbows on knees he looked at the floor and began to swear. He cursed in low Martian, and in fluent English, in high Centauran and sibilant Antaranese. "May the foul fiends of Mars' ten hells gnaw his belly! May the imps of Iseen claw his eyes from now 'til Doomsday! If only Hobgob himself were alive, and here to flyaway over Cureeng with his mean little soul!"

ARS MAASEN chuckled, and Kael McCanahan bit down on his tongue and glared hard at him. The little man moved to the dressing table and lifted a golden carafe. He went to pour the fiery liquid it held, then turned to glance at the McCanahan. He shook his head and went across the room and gave him the carafe.

"There are times when a man can't quench a thirst, no matter how much he drinks. Take it all."

Kael tilted the carafe and let the smoky quistl slide into his mouth. After a long while he tossed the carafe aside, and drew air into his lungs. He came to his feet and walked up and down.

"I'll need clothes. Some sort of disguise, I can talk their language well enough. I'll make out until the heat ebbs away and I can come back for him. The High Mor! A god and a priest to a god to these heathen Senn! But he's a man, and man can die, slowly and in great pain, when he's hated!"

Ars shook his head. "Go away, yes. But forget this vengeance for a long time. Maybe forever. You'll live longer that way."

Kael put out his hand and lifted the dark man off the floor and shook him. "He murdered my father! Burned him while he slept, with a Thorn blaster on a tensor beam! No way to strike back! No chance to fight for the life he loved!"

He put the little man down and patted his arm. Ars rubbed his chest where his jerkin had pinched his flesh. "You're a strong man, Kael McCanahan. But not strong enough to buck the High Mor on Senorech! I tell you—"

The door came open and Flaith slid in, away from the reek of winey air and the sound of roaring voices. She closed and locked the door and set her back to it.

She was a woman to stir the pulse of a man, in her bronze gown with its slits and deep neck, and the tight fit of its cloth to the swell of her haunches. Her slant eyes with the long curving lashes, the red fullness of a moist mouth and the smooth forehead low under the flaming hair had made her the darling of the quarter. She looked at Kael with her anger bright in her green eyes, and her lips thinned to a tense line.

"Before you speak, Flaith," said Ars Maasen suddenly, "let me tell you he isn't drunk, except with hate for the men that killed his father."

When Ars was done with the story she was in front of Kael whispering softly, "Kael, forgive me! A woman can be a fool! I was one just now, with the thoughts I had of you."

"It doesn't matter. Nothing matters any more except the man I'm going to kill some day! They won't let me leave on the *Eclipse*. They're going to keep me here and hunt me down. And I don't know why!"

Flaith whirled and went to her dressing table. She fumbled at a jar, lifting the lid and dipping her fingers into jet cream. She said, "I'll change the look of your face, Kael honey. Wipe away its hardness and its pain. And somewhere here in all these clothes will be something to fit you. Ars, look among them!"

For an hour the McCanahan sat while they worked on him, and when the hour was done, he stared at himself in the mirror and swore by the eye of Balor himself that no man on all Senorech would know him.

"You're as big and as strong." Ars grinned, studying him. "But you look like a traveling singer, with those short curls and the shadows under your eyes. A man who sings to a woman and loves her, and runs with the dawn!"

Kael snorted, but Flaith nodded.

"A singer or a player of music. Can you use those fingers to coax a tune from anything but a pretty girl?"

Kael laughed. "And what would a man whose family came from Galway be playing? I remember a night I sang of love to a woman on a balcony over the canals of Shar Lir before I put the harp aside and coaxed music from her flesh."

Faith flushed and scowled, then bubbled laughter.

"You used a harp, that night, you faithless rheenog! A harp that I bought and put aside with my tears, like a moonstruck school girl!"

She fumbled in a chest and drew it out. The lamplight caught its thirty strings and made them glitter. Her fingers stroked it, and her eyes were tender as she lifted them to his face.

Flaith shrugged her shoulders. "I'm crazy. I'm moonstruck and as mad as the ghouls that haunt the rim of Braloom! But—I'm going with you!"

And when Kael would have argued, she put her fingers across his lips and shoved him toward the door.

"Wait outside! Neither you nor Ars nor any man we meet will know Flaith for the shameless little gypsy she's going to turn into! Do you think I want those fingers coaxing music from that harp for anybody but me?"

CHAPTER THREE

THE old rock road from Akkalan to the cities of the Inland Seas is long and broken. Deserts spin their sandy webs across the shards of its ancient cobblestones. Gaunt black ruins of forgotten cities can be glimpsed dimly in the fading sunset, at the foot of the Samarinthine Hills, or standing atop the stone slabs that mark the caravan routes from Pint to Kanadar. Few used the old stone road, and the few who did travel it were so wrapped in their own cares—for this was a road much frequented by criminals and their like—they had no thought for the man and woman who sat by the edge of a running stream, twenty feet from the crumbled side of the highway.

Kael's long fingers swept the taut strings of the silver harp, and a burst of clear sound came flowing forth in a wild, free call. And then the sound was softening, deepening, and in it was something of the peat bogs of Iar Connacht, and something of the chill wind that sweeps the Finnihy from Kenmare to Killarney. A soul wept bitterly in the strings' twanging, with the tears of Deirdre staining its cheeks, and the terrors of Strongbow's son clutching its middle.

"Ai, to be like Ossian, with the power to move men to laughter or to tears with the playing of his fingers on the strings," he whispered to Flaith, where she lay with her chin pillowed on a white fist, staring at him. "But a man does what he can with what he must, and I'm not one for blaming the tool in my hand. It's a good harp."

"It was made by Brith Tsinan," Flaith told him dryly.

The McCanahan opened his eyes at that, and held the harp so as to admire its fluted curve and ornate column. He touched the strings again and they wept at the deftness of his touch. He moved them again and made them laugh.

Flaith wriggled her naked toes to the lilting rhythms he drew from the strings. Across the star lanes and the paths of distant planets, men and women had carried these tunes, and though they lay as dust in their graves, something of their memories sat in Kael McCanahan's fingers this day.

He made the harp sing of Tara and the great hall of Cormac MacAirt, of the baying hounds that ran in the hunts at Clonmell, and the cursing stones of Monasteraden.

The girl rolled on her back in the grass, and the worn cloth of her blouse grew taut across her breasts. "Teach me words to put to those songs, Kael McCanahan," she whispered, "and we'll eat well from the coppers and silver bits we take in the marts like Clonn Fell and Mishordeen."

"Words? Songs? I don't know anything about those. Make up your own words while I play to your ears and the sunlight, and the joy of being alive!"

And at the thought of life, he thought of death, and remembered his father lying on the floor with a Thorn blaster close at hand, and remembered Captain Edmunds and Cassy Garson and the rest who had lifted from Senn in the *S. I. C. Eclipse,* and what had happened to them after that!

He stood suddenly. The scowl was black across his face as he lifted the harp. He threw it from him roughly. Its strings screamed angrily as it skidded across the ground.

"I sit here and play music, and my father calls to me in whatever grave they gave him! I ought to be thinking of finding the High Mor and choking the life from his throat with these hands!"

Flaith put her long fingers to her red hair and shook it free to the breeze. Her slant eyes brooded at him as she remembered that day—weeks back—when they had stood outside the walls of Akkalan watching the destruction of the *Eclipse* under the cruiser beams of the High Mor's space fleet.

Kael had watched, sick and twisted. "That rotten mother's son ordered her smashed! He couldn't find me, so he played it safe and killed them all!"

He went mad for a little while, and Flaith clung to him with sharp nails digging into his arm and back, screaming in his ear. Only when she buried her teeth in his neck and tasted blood did he come back to sanity.

Now, remembering all that, and knowing how the death of his father and the destruction of the *Eclipse* ate in his middle with a sort of sharp, acid bitterness, Flaith watched the McCanahan lift the harp from where he had flung it. A silvern string was curled up, snapped by the rocks across which it had skidded.

"Now, how can we replace that?" Kael wondered. And then his fingers were slipping off his boot and lifting loose the harpstring he had taken from his dead father's wrist.

"It isn't a d-note," he told Flaith, "but it will have to do. I'll not touch it oftener than I must."

He attached the string, and tested it with sweeping fingers. He growled, "Only Ossian himself would know the difference."

The McCanahan brooded less and less in the days that followed, and as they moved along the road that bent in a wide arc about Drekkora and beyond the snow-topped hills of Sharn, he slipped back into the Kael McCanahan she had known in the taverns. Laughter came back to his lips, and he turned more and more to the harp, coaxing magic from its strings, that seemed to soothe his spirit.

As he played, Flaith hummed with him, and words came to her lips, words that matched the wild, clear music, and she sang these words to the ancient melodies, and at last they came to Clonn Fell.

THE stalls that lined the Square of the Balang were hung with priceless tapestries from the looms of Beinoll and Drithdraga, and were bright with the potteries of Lamanneen. Men and women of city house and desert tent brushed through the stalls, fingering the wares, haggling over prices, dipping into leather purses for stored coins. Many there were whose fingers waved to the sounds that came from the big fountain in the square where a tall man sat and played a silver harp.

No man would have known the McCanahan in this brown stranger with the naked chest gleaming through the rents of his worn, dusty jerkin, with his loose cloth trousers fastened at naked ankles with metallic cording. And no man would have known Flaith in the dark-skinned gypsy wanton, with her midriff bare above her flapping skirt of transparent teal and below the woven halter that bound her breasts. She was a gamin who laughed and swayed her hips as she sang, and her eyes flashed and flirted with the slack-jawed farmers in from fields and furrows.

A sudden jostling took the farmers and the merchants as they listened to the harpstrings. They made way sullenly for the file of Sfarran warriors who came shouldering a path arrogantly through the press. They were tall, handsome men, their lean faces swart and dark. They looked like fighting men; trim in black and gilt field uniforms. Their black eyes moved everywhere, missing nothing.

Now the Sfarran detail was closer to the marble fountain where Kael sat with Flaith huddled close against him. He could feel the shiver run through her bare arm where it pressed his side.

She whispered, "They look for us," and her dark eyes surveyed him, studying his disguise. He could read the approval in them.

The Sfarri glanced at them and passed on.

A man cursed softly from the shadows. There was a wild flurry of capes and sandaled feet. A peddler, with a scraggly gray beard flowing across his chest, ran like a frightened rat from a group of Kash cattlemen and into a thick thong of rug merchants from Stig.

"A rykinthus peddler," whispered Flaith.

Kael felt the fury rise in him. The Sfarri governed the people of this planet as they might a herd of cattle. There was no emotion in the chase. It was hunt a man down, capture him! Take him to the Sfarri tribunal, where an atomic disintor ray would blast him into thick white powder.

The peddler ran past Kael on shaking legs.

In his darkest eyes Kael read the angry terror that lay deep within him. Teeth gritted, Kael moved clumsily, bumping into the foremost of the Sfarri pursuers, throwing him off balance. Two others ran into him and fell heavily to the cobblestones of the square.

The Sfarran officer rose, tight-lipped at this clumsiness. His hand went to the holster of his addy-gun. Kael rammed a fist to his middle and slid sideways, his harp still in his hand. With a backward lash of his arm he drove the harp's heavy crown into his temple.

The blow knocked the harp from his hand. He scrambled after it, where it lay on the cobblestones. His fingers missed as he snatched at it and swept across the strings. At the harsh, discordant sound that rose into the air the Sfarran officer who had been reaching for him fell awkwardly to the stones, sprawling lifelessly.

Other Sfarri were falling too, as if the breath of life had been blown from them. They lay here and there beside the fountain, like dead men.

Kael stared dumbly, hearing the shouts of the people of Clonn Fell falling back from the lifeless Sfarri.

Then he whirled and slipped in among the crowding merchants and farmers, pretending that he was driven by stark terror.

A moment of wild, flurried movement, and he was free, darting behind a wooden wagon toward the heavy drapes of a carpet stall. Flaith was shrinking bad, also losing herself in the milling mob.

Kael saw her, dove toward her.

She cried out! "What was it? How'd you do it? What killed them?"

"I don't know! We have no time to play guessing games!"

He caught her hand, dragged her into an alleyway where the massive stone walls of ancient buildings towered high above them. The dark shadows they cast lay like shielding hands that shrouded them in sudden darkness.

Flaith panted, "You touched your harp! It made a sound! That must have done it!"

"I know all that! But for the sake of your unborn children, stop talking and run!"

THEY went swiftly through the narrow streets, burdened only by the silver harp. Under a stone archway, Kael swung to the right. A small figure stood in the doorway, beckoning to them. It was the bearded peddler Kael had saved from the Sfarri.

"This way," the peddler called. "Lunol forgets no man who saves him from death!"

An oak door opened. From it, a stone stair led down into a pit of Stygian blackness. The peddler put a hand on Kael's belt, dragging him down into the gloom.

They went swiftly, toward a stream of water that rushed and gurgled darkly between two narrow paths of brick that jutted outward from the sheer rock walls.

"The sewer system of Clonn Fell! Quickly, along the ledge! Gods be with us! If the Sfarri follow and clap their hands on us they'll throw us to their torturers!"

The peddler whimpered in his fear as he scurried along the narrow brick ledge. Kael and Flaith ran after him. Soon their sandals were wet with the accumulated filth and slime of centuries. They moved swiftly, with the dim light of tiny bulbs, high in the domed ceiling, guiding their feet.

They went for miles through the sewer, deep down under the streets of Clonn Fell.

When they emerged into bright sunlight, they stood on a wide beach where the gray, cold waters of the Taganian Sea rolled restlessly.

Flaith sank on a rock, one hand pushing back her thick red hair. Kael read her weariness in her haggard face.

"Why were the Sfarri after you?" he asked the peddler. "What did you do?"

Lunol shrugged. "I dwell in the Clith Korakam desert that stretches from the ocean here to the cliffs of Kamm."

Kael frowned his puzzlement.

It was Flaith who explained. "The black tower of Balzel lies in the Clith Korakam desert. It is a place forbidden to all people of Senorech."

The old man whimpered his fright. "I saw a man come out of that tower. It was many months ago. He was a tall man with a bald head and scrawny, withered arms. And yet there was something in the manner of his walking, something in the way he held his head, that sent a cold chill of terror down my spine!

"Since then I have had dreams. Terrible, frightening dreams! Dreams of places where no man has ever been! The Sfarri have been hunting me since then. It took them along time to find me, but now—"

Lunol shrugged. "From here it is not far to Clith Korakam. Once I am on its no sands man will ever be able to find me! I've spent all my life on those sands. I know them as I know the fingers of my hands."

Kael looked at Flaith. "Sure, they'll be after us, too, now! They know what we look like. They'll want us for helping this one get away."

"What can we do?"

The old peddler smiled. His swart face lighted under the loose cowl of his kufiyah.

"Come with me. I will make a home for you on the desert where none shall ever find you."

Flaith said, "Perhaps they won't know about us. We left the Sfarri lying like dead men, remember!"

Lunol looked his interest.

Kael said, "I touched my harp and the Sfarri fell like poisoned insects. Why they fell I do not know. Do you?"

Lunol shrugged his shoulders. "I am an ignorant man. I do not know about these things. But this I do know. If we do not go into the desert, sooner or later the Sfarri will find us!"

They set off across the sands, past the high-humped rocks that were beaten and weathered by the fierce storms that ravaged the planet. They struggled across the burning wasteland, their throats choked with the heat and the sand.

The sun glowed down on them, making sweat run in tiny rivers that plastered their robes to their flesh. The hours went by. Night came, and they slept where they fell, exhausted.

With the sun, they were up and moving. The days came and went, long eternities of heat and thirst, through which they plodded in the shifting sands. They were tiny motes of life against a backdrop of level, desolate loneliness.

They crossed ancient beds of rock, where once, in forgotten eons, a sea had rolled. Here Kael had to lift and carry Flaith, for her thin sandals were gone, and her white feet were red with blood where the stones had cut them.

They went on and on. They stopped at an oasis, here and there, to quench their thirst in the cool waters of a subterranean spring. They ate of the dried figs and bits of hard black bread that Lunol carried in his girdle.

Toward dusk of their sixth day on the desert, Lunol cried out. They focused eyes salt-encrusted with dried sweat where his finger pointed.

"There! See yonder, and know Lunol did not lie!"

THERE was livid fear in the eyes of the old peddler as he gestured at the glistening black pile of the tower lifting upward from the sand. It was almost as if he expected to see something dark and fearsome slip from the basalt blocks and come hunting him.

"It's been there for thousands of years," he whimpered. "Even when the balangs roamed these sands, the tower was there."

Flaith came close to Kael. "I'm frightened! There's something wrong with it."

Kael snorted and walked forward through the sand, ploughing his way where the wind had piled thick granules. Flaith ran a few steps after him, her hand seeking his arm. Behind them, could hear the peddler moaning.

"I tell you," he chattered, "I've seen it come out of the tower on clear nights when there wasn't a wind stirring across the sand. It just moved around, all white and shining, making the sand lift and whirl, like a storm down off the Barakian hills. It was cold. Terribly cold! The sand was frozen solid where it had been."

The McCanahan stared at the tower. It was tall, formed of black basalt, a thick column of rock that was windowless and seemingly doorless. At the base of the column was a long, low building that stretched on either side of the tower for forty feet. Two red pylons, carved and polished, stood like pointing fingers at its ends.

The old peddler was wringing his hands. "It wasn't human, that thing. It could kill as easy as a harlot winks! Once I saw a hare run past it. It stretched out a thin wire of that cold white stuff and touched the rabbit, and the rabbit died. I'm afraid!"

Kael turned and caught the old peddler, yanking him to him.

"You've bleated and brayed ever since we got out of Clonn Fell! Go back if you want!"

The old man's eyes glazed in his brown face. A wind stirred the wisps of whitish hair that straggled from under his kufiyah, and the springs of thin beard that fluttered on his chin. He seemed to shake himself, and at an effort, his eyes cleared.

"No! No! You saved me from the Sfarri. I told you the tower was the only place where the Sfarri never came, on all of Senn. But to go to the tower, to meet that thing—"

The McCanahan let the old man go, gently. He was ashamed of the burst of rage that had shaken him. He drew in a lungful of the hot desert air. He was alone on Senn. His comrades in the *Eclipse* had been destroyed. The High Mor was seeking him across a world, and to have this peddler whimpering his fear in his ears was proving too much.

He said gently, "Sorry, old one! Sooner or later the Sfarri will come here to the tower. After they have searched all Senn. They will find us. Maybe inside that tower—"

Lunol shivered. "No man can live inside the tower. No man can approach it. Death strikes down all who try! I've seen too many animals run close to it and—hofff!—they go up in smoke! There's a band of death all around it. If you go too close, you'll be the one to turn into smoke!"

Kael McCanahan shrugged. "As well go up in smoke as die under a Thorn blaster held in a Sfarran hand!"

He went on alone.

Flaith whimpered, watching him. She crouched, her long-nailed fingers digging into the soft flesh of a white thigh. Her eyes were wide, frightened.

He went twenty feet, then thirty. He grew smaller, walking across the flat stretch of dunes toward the great black tower.

As he walked, the McCanahan threw his blaster, fastened on a length of rope, ahead of him. If some electrical force was probing, it would seek out the metal of his addy-gun and shatter it.

Nothing happened to the gun.

He walked on and on.

No death struck at him. Now he stood under the shadow of the great gateway that was formed of a queer, sleek marble that held green fire frozen beneath its glazed surface. He put a hand on the gate and pushed.

To his surprise, the doorway opened, noiselessly.

Kael moved under the arched gateway, into a region of dim light and sharp black shadow, where a towering pile of glass and metal bulked huge in the center of the hall.

And then his legs crumbled beneath him, and Kael McCanahan went down, onto the tiled yellow flooring of the tower room.

CHAPTER FOUR

HE FLOATED bodiless in space. The stars swirled about him, moving endlessly in their orbits. This was death, he knew. But it was a strange form of death, for here and there he could recognize familiar constellations, saw nebulae and galaxies that he knew.

This is not Noorlythin!

The voice swirled about him, rumbling out of the black stretches of space itself. The McCanahan could feel eyes on him, hidden eyes that probed at him, lancing through him with the remorseless certainty of a surgeon's electroniscalpel.

This is a Terran. A man named McCanahan. He is frightened!

He was within the tower. Only Noorlythin could live in that trap of hell. I do not understand!

Something touched him, as gently as a spring breeze off the sea. And with the touching, the eyes of Kael McCanahan came open to the robed figures that floated between the stars. He tried to see their faces, but only a blinding whiteness, returned his stare, under the low hoods of the robes.

Seek not our faces, Terran. To you, we are as the sun!

His tongue was thick and swollen. He mumbled. He swallowed, as if to clear his throat.

"Where am I? Who are you? I walked into the tower and—"

What had happened to him on that yellow floor? His knees had buckled and he had gone down with an intangible force crushing him. Kael shook his head.

We are the Doyen. An ancient race, a race of once-men who have lived out the span of our lives a million centuries. In that time, we changed. Our bodies evolved upward from their primal shape, striving always to progress to that last, final shape of all.

"Noorlythin? He is one of you?"

Once he was. But Noorlythin could never forget the adoration that was showered on us by the Sfarri. He hungered to be worshipped as a god, as once he was, many eons ago. Noorlythin turned his back to us, the Doyen. He has gone back, resuming the primal shapes of the men whose race is young.

Fear came to the McCanahan there among the stars. It crept in through the unspoken words of the robed things, clutching at his mind with frozen fingers. He shook uncontrollably before he could assert himself.

"This Noorlythin. You seek him?"

He has broken the Doyen law. He has become as an animal. With his powers, he can be a god to any primal race. No primate can stand to him, and well he knows it. When he is ready, when he has used the Sfarri to conquer all the primal races of the galaxy, he will ascend into the living sacristy of the Temple of Sharrador. There, once again, he will be worshipped with living sacrifices, with orgies that only a primal race can conceive and execute.

The McCanahan said, "You aren't telling me all this just to talk."

You are a poor servant. Your flesh is weak. Yet must we use you against Noorlythin!

"How? How can I help?"

And then all space was shaking, flowing in a liquid stream, inward toward a whirlpool of light that swam around and around, sucking the stars and the black deeps of space into its maw. And as the stars and space flowed faster and faster, so flowed the McCanahan stretched and lengthened and tortured...

HE SAT on the yellow tile of the ancient tower. A tumble of red hair shifted and tossed before him as Flaith's white hand shook him. Beyond her, near the open green marble door, stood the peddler. His eyes burned with the fright in his face.

"Kael! You were so still. I thought you dead!"

She helped him to his feet. He swayed, almost retching with the pain that spasmed his muscles. Flaith was a blur of white before him. He put his hands to her soft shoulders, and his fingers dug in. He held to her, as to reality.

Slowly the floor solidified and steadied beneath his buskined feet. The pain slid away, slowly, then with greater speed.

"Out there," he said thickly. "Things. Bright things. Maybe made of energy itself. They spoke to me. Told me about something named Noorlythin. It was as if I was suspended, in space itself. Want me to help them.

Flaith came against him until the hard tips of her breasts burned his naked chest. Her voice was a flow of terrified sound.

"The Doyen! They are the Doyen! We on Senn always thought they were just a myth, like the balangs! They are gods, Kael! The gods of all space!"

The McCanahan grunted. "Well, gods or not, they want to make a servant out of me. They want me to help them round up some character named Noorlythin."

From the doorway the peddler groaned. His eyes rolled in his head. A white froth bubbled on his lips.

"Noorlythin, the evil! Noorlythin, who lived in the olden days, when all Senorech worshipped him with blood sacrifices. Even today, on the altar in the Temple of Krebb, the dark stains are still there!"

The McCanahan turned away to stare upward at the great metal machine that bulked monstrous in the dim light. It was formed of black steel and silvery chrome. Its tubes and power relays were inset under thin glass globulen so that it resembled a gigantic, transparent-backed spider. High above its arching shell, reaching upward into the dimness of the tower itself, were half a hundred floating, glowing balls that danced and spun in the wind eddies.

Stretching on either side of the central hall were wide corridors, their walls lined by glass bubbles that projected outward like bulging eyes.

The McCanahan moved toward the near corridor, his eyes caught by a scene within one of the glassine bubbles. Flaith followed him, afraid to be alone.

They halted before a curving prism, discovering it to be a dioramic window that seemed to peer into the heart of a distant planet. Flaith whispered, "It's the planet Sfar! I'd know those cold-faced men anywhere!"

Frozen, tiny faces stared back at them from a great, white city, set like a jewel on the shore of a wide, blue sea. The little figures were caught in a locked moment of time, attending to their duties. Some moved with weapons, some drove sleek monocars.

"There's something about them," Kael muttered, scowling. "They're so perfect! They make every move count as if it would be their last. Each of them is long and lean, with bright, keen eyes that never miss a thing!"

Flaith put a hand on the glassine bubble, leaning closer, staring down at the magnified scene. "It's funny, but—"

Her slant eyes slid sideways at the McCanahan, amusement swimming in them. "I've noticed something that I thought *you'd* see, Kael McCanahan!"

His eyes studied the girl in front of him as she cocked her head at him. Even in her tattered garments, through which the McCanahan caught disturbing glimpse of white, rounded flesh, the red-haired Flaith was a tantalizing morsel of womanhood. He put out a long arm and drew her in against him.

"Och, now what would I have been missing that you, with your cat's eyes, have seen?"

She shrugged elaborately. "If you haven't missed them, I won't tell—"

"Shades of Bridget na Gablach! Their women!"

"They have no women! No man of Senorech has ever seen a Sfarran girl. Rumor says that they shelter them because of their loveliness. But if this a diorama of the Sfarran planet, and there are no women, then—"

Kael grunted. "You and your crazy theories! Look, woman! See for yourself. There are women there. There must be women!"

But though they hunted along all that corridor, staring at the Sfarran world and its diverse shapes and colors, its desert storms and wind-tossed seas, its magnificent white cities that looked like milky jewels, they found no woman.

For two hours they hunted, until the McCanahan discovered that by moving a red lever he could make the scenes within the bubbles come to life. The tiny men moved, as if released from a frozen tomb. They walked and piloted their vessels, and went about their tasks. Yet even so, no woman appeared.

"It's some sort of televisic communicator," the McCanahan muttered. "That's spacecasting across a billion billion miles of space."

"They have no hospitals, either," said Flaith in a troubled voice.

"Now what will you be meaning by that?"

THE redhead smiled wryly. "Even in this advanced day and age on Senorech, Kael my darling, women still go to hospitals to have their babies!"

The McCanahan scowled. "And if there are no hospitals, they'll have their brats at home, won't they?"

"Brats, indeed!" flared Flaith, whirling, chin high.

"Peace, peace," grinned Kael. "It's only teasing I was. But I begin to see your drift, mavourneen. No women, no hospitals, no children. Then the Sfarri are not human. Or maybe it's because they're ovopoid. Maybe they're sexless, like an amoeba, or maybe they fertilize themselves and lay an egg to hatch a little Sfarran."

"There are no little Sfarri. All are grown men. Every last one."

McCanahan brooded with his lower lip thrust out. "No little ones. No coibche to bind a man and a woman in holy matehood. No women, even, to comfort a man when he's sad with loneliness. Then they aren't human, with no heart in their chests to beat a little faster at the kiss from a woman's lips. And if they have no hearts, they must be—

"Robots!"

The McCanahan walked in his excitement, taking long steps that drew him past the metal machine with its glass-encased tubes and wirings. "Robots! No wonder they're perfect! No wonder it is that none has ever been caught by a Terran battle fleet for questioning! Being robots, they destroy themselves before capture. And being robots, too, they fight with the same mechanized, incredible fury that's smashed a dozen war fleets between Achernar and Sol."

The McCanahan was warming to his subject. "We fought the Sfarri across a score of galaxies, ever since my grandfather Rhoderick—bless his memory!—first crossed atomic disintegration beams with their cruisers. They've pushed us back, away from the Rim planets. Everywhere our paths have met, there's been bloody war. Bloody? Ha! There's been no blood spilled on their side. Just cogs and wheels and wire!"

Flaith tossed back a lock of reddish gold hair from before her eyes. "You killed them in Clonn Fell. You slew them when you touched your harp strings! The sound did it."

"The harp of Brith Tsinan. Aie! It had the silver string that I took from my father's wrist attached to it. Do you remember how I broke the other, when I threw the harp on the road from Akkalan? Where is the harp, Flaith?"

The old peddler came shuffling forward from the doorway, dropping his shoulder to loosen the strap that held the black sack to his back. From the sack the bright silver harp tumbled into the McCanahan's eager fingers.

He lifted the harp and set it to his shoulder. His hands played across the strings, and the wild sharp peal of the strings swept up and through the tower.

In answer to the high, keening notes, a tube in the great metal machine spannged shrilly. The tinkle of broken glass was loud in the sudden silence as Kael dropped his fingers from the quivering harp strings.

Lunol, the peddler, cried out harshly, his face a wet mass of sweating fear. Flaith screamed high and shrill. Her bare arm lifted and pointed.

The McCanahan whirled, and his harp fell from numb fingers.

Bright and blazing, like the core of a giant sun, a whirling mass of fiery matter whirled and quivered, pulsing before the great machine. Its incandescence was blinding, brilliant. They could read the fury in the flame of its sentient heart. They needed no voice to tell them.

Noorlythin!

The sunburst of brilliance lifted, shuddering. It foamed and grew, incandescent in the sheer brilliance of the white fire that burst and bloomed within it.

A thin stream of fire reached out, touched Lunol and laved him in its blinding whiteness.

And Lunol shrank in upon himself, grew smaller, almost tiny within the bubble of brilliance that held him. He grew, then. Expanded suddenly. And where Lunol and the hungry white fire had been was just blackened smoke, drifting across the yellow floor.

Flaith turned her face in against Kael's chest. Her fingers bit their nails convulsively into his flesh. Her body shook so badly that its trembling moved the McCanahan as he stood on firmly planted legs.

Another pencil of fire stabbed out.

Stabbed out, and—

Halted!

In midair it halted, spreading across an invisible wall of nothingness that was erected before the McCanahan and the girl he held.

There was puzzlement in the pulsing of the thing, in the blind, angry dartings of the pencil-beam of flame. It moved to the floor, and quested upward to the ceiling. It darted from wall to wall, seeking to penetrate the barrier that sheltered its victims.

And now the amazement was gone. The white fire burned lower, as if afraid.

In sheer anger, that made it blaze so brightly that Kael cried out and lifted a hand to hide his face, the thing stabbed again. And again, hungrily, raging with insane fury.

The Doyen shelter you! Only the Doyen could stand against the power of my will!

McCanahan could feel the anger fall away before the fear that ate at the thing. Almost, he could hear its thoughts. Perhaps it wanted him to hear his thoughts.

They can save you for a little while. But they cannot shelter you forever. Not from Noorlythin-the-Doyen can they save you forever! I shall work my will on you yet, man of Terra! You will crawl on bloody stumps for legs, waving handless arms for mercy! Begging me with tongueless mouth for the boon of death!

It came to McCanahan that the thing spoke out of the grip of its own, paralyzing terror. It mouthed threats to bolster its own esteem.

Kael put his mind to the task and forced a laugh between his lips. He made his laugh mocking, challenging.

"You'll never kill me, Noorlythin! I am servant to the Doyen. Such as the Doyen protect those whom they select to serve them!"

The thing that was Noorlythin pulsated like a stream of cobwebs caught in a mad wind. It lifted and shook, swirled and bellied.

And then, suddenly, it was quiet. It hung a foot above the yellow tile, barely moving. And the inertia of the thing was more frightening than all its blinding brilliance.

The Doyen play the game according to its rules. They will not let me harm you with my Doyen powers. Only by other gifts can I let the life from your body, Terran! So be it!

CHAPTER FIVE

AND the thing was gone, blanking instantly from sight with nothing left behind to show its presence but a bit of black dust stirring restlessly on the tiling as a breeze came in off the desert and moved down the long corridor.

"Poor Lunol," whispered Flaith. "Oh, the poor old man!"

The McCanahan lifted his harp and stared dumbly at its glittering surface of polished silver. "The harpstring from my father's wrist broke the tube in the machine. It summoned up Noorlythin from—from wherever he was hidden."

"How can you use that knowledge?" wondered Flaith.

Kael shook his head. "I don't know yet. But I will. Somehow, I'll find out the truth." He lifted his head and peered about the great tower. "And where better to begin than here?"

They ate dried meat plucked from Flaith's girdle-pouch, chewing on hard black bread. And then they slept, with Flaith cuddled against the McCanahan's length, with his own head pillowed on an arm, both of them stretched at the foot of the great metal machine.

It was the McCanahan who stirred first, rising from the soft body of the girl, carefully so as not to disturb her. He wandered about the tower, studying the strange machines that glistened at him from the shadows. A man would need a dozen lifetimes to understand these things, he told himself. He would find no help from them.

He tried to fight the pall of bitter despair that lay across his shoulders. He was the servant of the gods of space, caught up by them to hunt out and punish another god.

Laughter touched his lips; but the bitterness in it stung like acid.

How does one fight a god? How does one go about killing a thing that is made only of white, radiant energy? A thing that by a mere touch of the blazing brightness that comprises it, can blast him and all his kind to a black dust that shifts restlessly across a floor, flung by an errant breeze!

His fists were clenched until the knotted muscles of his forearms ached. "I can't do it," he told the machines. "I'm only a man. I can't fight against a god!"

Deep within him, he knew that someone had to make this fight, that someone from one of the thousands of Terran worlds had to face Noorlythin, had to stand up to him and his awesome power, or the human race itself would go down, crushed and torn and flung into nothingness, as a sand castle went down before the relentless roll of the ocean.

When that happened, the Sfarri and the Senn would expand, would lift their faery castles and their monstrous, monolithic palaces, where now Terran buildings stood. And those of the Senn would have their pick of the women of Earth.

Of women like—

Flaith!

He turned to find her stretched on her back, her eyes regarding him wistfully. A shred of her gypsy costume was caught over one shoulder, falling away from the push of her nearly bared breasts. The thin stuff at her waist hugged round hips and full upper thighs. The breath caught in the McCanahan's throat as his eyes ran over her.

She was a woman to steal the breath of a man from his lungs, and send his senses running in a saraband. She was the dream of every lonely spaceman at his battle station, of every thul-prospector hanging to a wandering asteroid with fingers and a suction clamp. With her red hair frothing over the witchery of her cream-skinned shoulders, she was Deirdre herself, the perfect woman.

Something of his tangled senses came to Flaith and she laughed, with the throaty womanness of her pleased at the worship in his eyes.

In the middle of her laughter, a shadow came and lay on the yellow flooring between them.

A Sfarran officer stood tall and lean in the open doorway of the tower, a glittering Thorn blaster in his right hand.

THE officer regarded them coldly. It came to Kael as he stood dumbly returning that hard glance, that he had never seen a Sfarran smile.

"You will come with me at once."

He stood sideways to the green marble doors, giving them room to pass him. Flaith scrambled to her feet; eying the gesture with which the officer moved his blaster. The McCanahan bent and lifted his harp and thrust it into the black sack that had once belonged to dead Lunol the peddler.

Then he was walking with Flaith out the pylon gateway of the tower, across the hot sands toward the black hull of a sleek Sfarran cruiser.

He was midway through the hatch when he paused, staring.

There were Sfarran men and officers inside the ship, but they were slumped over queerly, in distorted postures and attitudes. He had seen the Sfarri like that in Clonn Fell, when he had plucked at the strings of his harp. But here he had not struck those strings!

Last night he had played for Flaith and Lunol. And when he had played, a tube in the great, glistening tower machine had cracked into a thousand different fragments.

That breaking tube might have summoned up Noorlythin from whatever hell he dwelt.

"Move in, Earther," said the officer behind him.

Kael went with Flaith, at the officer's orders, to an upholstered bench set against a paneled wall. The officer brooded at them, and they could read the raw hate that lay deep in his black eyes.

The officer said, "You ought to be rayed down here, to save the High Mor the agony of listening to your pleas for mercy. But yours is a grave offense. An offense no man or woman has ever committed before. It calls for grave punishment."

Flaith's hand trembled in Kael's big fist.

The officer said, "The High Mor commissioned me to bring you to him. I would be derelict in my duty were I to do otherwise. And I, Captain Herms Borkus, intend to commit no such infraction."

The black eyes studied them. There was curiosity swimming in their depths, mixed with the hot hate, and a grudging respect. He turned away and went forward to the control chamber. Kael could hear the clicking relays picking up the automatic transmission. The ship lifted easily, its null-gravity humming with smooth insistence.

Flaith whispered, "The harp, Kael. You'll kill him as you killed the others!"

But Kael only gestured at the Sfarri that lay in the strange and distorted attitudes, or sprawled on the floor. And even as he gestured, the first of these dead Sfarri stirred and sat up, looking about him. Others moved then, silently, turning at once to their duty posts, resuming their tasks as if they had never been interrupted.

"Mother of balangs!" whispered Flaith, her eyes wide and troubled under their long red lashes. "They live!"

The McCanahan was half out of his seat, his mind questing. *They were dead, but now they live. Like machines, turned off and on!* He thought of the cracking tube in the black tower, and the Sfarri that had fallen in the square in Clonn Fell.

Dimly, he began to grasp the power of the harpstring that he had lifted from his father's wrist. It smashed the tubes in the power-boxes that fed the Sfarri their energy. Without that power, they were idle machines.

With the trained mind of the Spacefleet officer, he saw the possibilities of such harpstring, in the form of a vibrator that would spacecast a flow of microwaves from the battlewagons of the fleet. With a series of these vibrations fanning out ahead of them, Solar Combine ships could more than hold their own with the Sfarri. For at the touch of those microwaves, the Sfarri that ran their spaceships would slump in their form of death.

Bitter mockery rose inside the McCanahan as he sat hunched over. He had the knowledge, but what use was it? He was being carried to an extremely painful death in the damp dungeons of the High Mor's palace.

HERMS BORKUS came toward them from the control chamber. He stared from one to the other. At last he said, "How did you do it? In Clonn Fell, we found our officers and men lying as if dead. As this ship neared the Tower of Noorlythin, my men slumped over unconscious."

Kael shrugged. "I've a powerful evil eye, friend. I cast it at those I don't like and—well, you saw the result."

Borkus said coldly, "You talk foolishly. There is no such thing as the evil eye. What is the answer?"

"Oh, now look!" began Kael, when the thought struck him. *Borkus is a Sfarran, yet he did not succumb to the lack of power!* Kael turned the words on his tongue, and said, "I was talking sense, captain. In my family, as far back as the time of Niall of the Nine Hostages himself, one of the McCanahans has always possessed the evil eye. It's a daft thing, and I'm not understanding it myself, any too well, but it's the only explanation I can give."

Borkus looked at Flaith, but his eyes did not linger on her beauty, and showed no more emotion than a dog would show staring at a building. From Flaith, his eyes swung to Kael who could read the thought that was gripping the officer. *He's wondering if he can strike at me through her.* But that was the way of a man who lacked confidence in his own abilities, and Kael knew that this man before him had powers he had not yet used.

The Sfarran captain shrugged and moved away. He threw back over his shoulder, "The High Mor will know how to deal with you. After all, it is his duty, not mine."

For five hours, Flaith and the McCanahan huddled together on the upholstered bench in the Sfarran ship. With each passing moment, the bleakness in the soul of the McCanahan grew darker and more empty.

The ship landed on the palace grounds, shuddering slightly as it dropped onto the metallic tanbark. A moment after its vanes were clamped, Flaith and the McCanahan were crossing the landing field, moving down a stone ramp that led to the dungeons.

A burly man, with black hair matted over his naked chest, clanked a ring of keys at their approach. He preceded them along the torchlit corridor until he paused at an empty cell.

The cell was unlocked, and the McCanahan thrust inside. And then a sobbing Flaith was dragged away from him, in the grip of one of the burly man's hairy paws.

Kael McCanahan was a spaceman, and spacemen are generally, without quite being aware of it, excellent philosophers. He tested the bars of the cell, found them to be formed of moly-steel, and went over to the cot, where he lay on his back, staring at the blank ceiling. Within five minutes he was asleep.

He woke to the touch of a soft hand on his chest, to find a woman bent above him, her limpid brown eyes soft with pity. A tumble of yellow hair framed her oval face.

"I bring you food and drink, lord. You will need your strength for what lies ahead."

Kael laughed harshly. "Better to be weak and near death when the High Mor begins his tortures."

She moved closer. She was fragrant with some Senn perfume, and the little she wore—a red silk thing twisted about her loins, with a slave girl's golden chains about her throat—showed her body to be exquisite, even in the half-light of the cell. The McCanahan read the pity in her eyes, and began to take interest.

"Sometimes, those live the longest who have no false pride," she told him.

"You give me hope. Were you sent to do that?"

There was reproach in her eyes, and she started to draw away. The McCanahan caught her slim wrist and held her.

"Who sent you with your tempting offers?"

She pouted at him. "No man sent me. I am Slyss, the slave girl from Aakkan." She rubbed her wrist when he released her, unconsciously posing for his eyes.

The McCanahan said, "Tell me more!"

But she shrugged a white shoulder and went to stand by the cell bars while he ate. When he was done, she took his tray and wooden bowl and mug, and walked off with them, unlocking the cell door with a key that hung from her wrist, attached to a thick metal manacle.

Her hips wriggled as she went, and she threw a glance at him over her shoulder. Her voice was music as she caroled a farewell.

She left the McCanahan with a fever of impatience in him. He strode back and forth in his cell. His hands tested the moly-steel bars a hundred times. He told himself that the

Senn did not love the Sfarri overmuch, that the Senn, being descended from animal ancestors, had no common ground with a race of robot men. He asked himself where in this pile of giant masonry Herms Borkus had hidden Flaith. If he could get away, if he could use this yellow-haired slave girl to unbar these cell doors for him, he would find Flaith and flee.

Flee?

Where on all Senorech was there sanctuary for Kael McCanahan?

The slave girl told him when next she brought his food. This time, he was awake and restless, and her soft, quick tread was like music to his ears.

SHE came close to him, with only the width of the little tray between his chest and her breasts that stirred gently to her quickened breathing. Her brown eyes were full of gentle pity as they studied his haggard face and sunken eyes.

"Lord, you were never meant for prison bars! If only you would trust me, I know a way that leads from the palace."

"Trust you, Slyss? I'd love you for a chance at freedom."

Again she preened, smiling as he wolfed the food. "Only for that?"

His eyes studied her. She was a lovely thing, slim and gently rounded. Beside the flame-haired Flaith she was a cooling breeze, but he knew many men who would have walked through the fires of Nanakar for an hour in her arms.

"Not only for that," he told her. "You're a sight to send a man's blood to pounding in his veins. You don't look like a slave girl. You're much too beautiful."

Her laughter was soft, pleased. She came and sat beside him, so that her hip and thigh were warm on his. She carried perfume in the yellow hair that dripped on her shoulders. It was rare perfume, and the McCanahan thought, that if her mistress knew about it, that creamy back would be striped with red whipwelts.

"There are men of the Senn who hate the Sfarri," she whispered close to his ear. "Rumors have come to them that you possess some strange weapon, some magic means of killing the hated Sfarri."

The McCanahan swallowed the cheap wine that had been chilled in a coil of refrigerated steel. He nodded. "I know a way."

It was on his lips to say more when his sidewise glance surprised a momentary gleam in the gentle brown eyes. He needed no psychiatrist to read that triumph for him, even though it was quickly veiled behind her curving lashes. *Now why should a slave girl of the palace know that feeling because of what I said?* he asked himself.

The McCanahan put his arm about the girl, drew her in against him. With his lips buried in the yellow mass of her hair, he whispered, "It ought to be worth a lot to the Senn to get that knowledge! With such a weapon they need never fear the Sfarri again. They could cast them out! Even seek alliance with the Solar Combine!"

It was his last words that tensed the muscles across her soft back. Instantly, the muscles were relaxed, and she melted closer against him, her soft lips moving across his face to find his lips.

The McCanahan kissed her. Why not? But he was warned, and only a fool disregards a warning. And Kael McCanahan, as he drank from the scented lips of Slyss the slave girl, was even then congratulating himself that no McCanahan was ever a cursed gossoon.

He let her go after a while. She was a pleasant little thing, but she was no Flaith. He said, "Suppose I agree to trade my weapon for freedom from the High Mor? How do I know the Senn can guarantee my liberty?"

"I have the keys," she whispered. "Tonight I will come for you, to lead you through the dungeons, to the vaults below the dungeons, where the sea seeps in through solid rocks. No Sfarran ever walks down there. It is a dead, damp place. But the Senn go there to hide from the Sfarri. It is the one safe place on all Senorech. Slyss will take you there."

He lingered over her lips, close by the unlocked cell door, to bind their bargain. But when she was gone, he took to pacing his cell, his brows drawn together. She wants more than the body of Kael McCanahan, that one, he told himself. The weapon I possess, and me! Or am I playing the buffoon in thinking she was fond of me? He went back over their meetings and discovered to his chagrin that each of her moves seemed calculated. Like a Sfarran! Cold, careful! Even her kisses lacked the fire such a woman should bring to them!

As the sun sank below the hills above Akkalam, the McCanahan rested. He was fresh when Slyss came to him on her bare feet, her key grating silently into the cell lock. "Slib, the jailer, lies drugged with wine," she told him. "He won't stop us."

She went quickly along the cell corridor ahead of him. At an intersection in the rock walls she slipped to the right, into dark shadows. He heard the rough grate of metal, and a section of the floor was rising and falling, as a balanced slab of rock fell back to expose a number of hand hewn stone ledges that served as steps.

Slyss went first. The McCanahan came after her, and at her whispered bidding, tilted the stone slab back into place. An instant before it fell, as his eyes were still above the floor level, he saw a man standing in the cell corridor, grinning at him.

The McCanahan almost cried out to Slyss.

The man in the cell corridor was burly, with black hair matted over his chest. He jangled a ring of keys at his side. It was Slib, the jailer, and his little eyes were clear and evil.

No man who lay drugged with wine ever boasted eyes like that! The only thing that troubled Kael was whether Slyss knew the jailer was awake and watching. If she knew, then he was being led into a trap, like a steer to the axing. If she did not know, then she was taking herself unwittingly into that same trap.

The McCanahan kicked off his buskins and walked with bare feet after the girl, along the cool damp floor of the sea vaults.

In olden days, the primal men of Senorech had made their coves in these vaults to escape the ravening monsters of the dawn era. Here and there, in the light of the torches along the wall, he could see piles of white, bleached bones.

They walked for more minutes before he heard the faint rasp of metal touching rock.

Slyss was whirling, crying out.

From the shadows, men came leaping.

As he plunged sideways, Kael noted that they were hard-faced Senn warriors. There was not a Sfarran among them.

The McCanahan used his fist like a club, bringing its balled weight down in a full arm stroke, hitting the nearest man at the side of his neck, and driving him sideways into his companions. Before the man's falling club touched the floor, Kael held it, bringing it upward in a ceiling-wise blow into the middle of the next man's belly.

Kael McCanahan had fought in the port taverns of Marsopolis and Dunverick. He had traded fists with Deneban dockwallopers and Karrvan stevedores. He knew every trick in the creeds of a dozen fighting races.

He used them all in the sea vaults below Akkalam. He used the club like a sword, driving it hard into a Senn's face. He hit backwards with it. He used an overhand, downward stroke, that drove the inches-long spikes that studded its knob, deep into a man's braincase.

It is no easy matter for ten men to cage one man. Not in dimly lighted pits, with that one man an explosive cyclone of fists and bashing club. Ten men keep getting in the way of each other. And Kael McCanahan was there to make each mistake a costly one.

He cut his opponents down to five in those first few minutes. Then he was at the wall, ripping loose the olisene-drenched torch, hurling it in their faces, to splatter in thick little globs of burning chemicals.

With their screams of pain ringing in the sudden darkness, the McCanahan slid forward into the blacker shadows. Out of sight he ran.

He found a tunnel that sliced at an angle into the main vault. He went along it, his bare feet making no sound.

He discovered another converging corridor and raced along that. Inside ten minutes, he lost himself in the labyrinthine vaults.

He came to a halt in the blackness, lungs gulping at cool air that was faintly spiced with sea salt. He listened, but heard no sound. When his heart ceased to thud so heavily against his ribs, he moved again. But now he went more cautiously, with the club before him like an overlong arm, probing the darkness.

He felt the cool updraft of air, just as his feet went out from under him.

CHAPTER SIX

HE SLID for thirty feet on a wet ramp that dropped him flat on his back on the floor of a huge chamber lighted by radioactive filaments set flush to the stone walls. At the far end of the vast room, two mighty metal doors were hung on great bronze hinges.

On the floor of the room rested a hundred great daises. And on each dais lay a man or a woman.

"A tomb," the McCanahan muttered. "I've found one of the Senn burial chambers."

As he crawled to his feet and stared, he knew that this was no tomb. The bodies were flushed with life, and clad in the uniforms and trappings of a hundred different people. The McCanahan rubbed a bruised shoulder and went to walk among the daises.

A shepherd boy with a ragged sheepskin across his loins and over one shoulder, lay beside a trimly garbed officer of the Palace Guard. Beyond them, a silk-swathed dancing girl lay beside a heavily muscled halgor-driver, with the brown of the desert sun still on his forehead.

The McCanahan touched an arm. It was warm. It yielded beneath his fingers. He tried to rouse the man, without success.

A face in the third row over from the main aisle tugged at some chord of memory. He slipped between the daises, to stare down into the cold, haughty face of Captain Herms Borkus of the Fleet.

"Now would I had the wisdom of Bridget herself, the wisest woman in all Ireland," muttered the McCanahan. "Is this a storeroom where the High Mor keeps those he has doomed to some punishment? Is it a place such as the visi-chambers on Vreer and Anafelm, where men and women spend most of their lives dreaming? And if it isn't any of these things, what in the name of the sons of Strongbow is it?"

He walked on, staring down at the faces of those who lay in this trance-like slumber. He saw a face or two he knew from remembered glimpses, in the days when he had walked the court of the High Mor as the son of the Terran Ambassador.

And then the McCanahan froze, and the blood in his veins moved with sluggish torpor.

Ahead of him, on the two largest daises of all, lay the twin bodies of the High Mor.

There was no mistake. He had seen that thin-lipped face too often where it leered down at Solar Command uniforms from the ruboid throne of Akkalam. The eyes were staring now, lifeless, but he remembered the scorn and the supreme contempt that had been in their depths.

The McCanahan was a baffled man.

He walked around the coffers, and his lips opened to speak, but no sound came out. "It's dreaming I am, with the little people flooding my brain with fancies from a fevered mind! The High Mor, twins—no, triplets!—for he must sit even now on the throne, dreaming up tortures for my body."

The creak of a door-hinge sent him to the floor.

He stared at the opening door, and smothered a curse in his throat when he saw the slave girl, Slyss of Aakan, glide into the room. She was alone. She went to an empty pier and lay upon her back.

And now the hair at the base of the McCanahan's neck stood straight up, for something was rising from all along her body. A something that was white and bright and dazzling, and from where he lay, Kael could feel the utter coldness of the thing.

"Noorlythin!" his numbed brain told him, and he hid his eyes.

He heard a faint tinkling, such a sound as he had heard once before, when he floated between the stars among the Doyen. He looked, and the swirling white radiance that was Noorlythin was settling down on one of the bodies of the High Mor, and the High Mor was sitting up, chafing at wrists and fingers, swinging his legs to the floor.

In the ancient legends of Terra, there was mention of an Arabic ruler, one Haroun al Raschid, who went in disguise among his people, that he might learn their thoughts and their way of living. It came to the McCanahan as he lay here that Noorlythin was such a one, but he used no simple disguises. He took the body of a man, or the body of a woman, and possessed it.

Kael retched silently, remembering the caresses he had given the slave girl. That thing had been inside her, controlling the pity in her eyes, the poses of her body. It had been Noorlythin who had led him into the vaults below the castle, for some reason he did not yet know. It had been Herms Borkus, seeking the secret of his harp. He knew now why the smashing of the tube in the great machine had not shut off his lack of motive power, as it had the robot-like bodies of the Sfarran crew.

"By all the sand on Mars," the McCanahan gritted between his teeth, "I have a secret worth a thousand suns in my hand. But how can I best use it?"

The High Mor was at the huge doors now. He went out without a backward, glance, and the doors slid shut behind him.

KAEL came to his feet. He looked around him at the faces of the men and women who lay awaiting the coming of the Doyen. He knew what he had to do, and his face twisted in repugnance. Without these bodies, Noorlythin was trapped in the body of the High Mor; he was the High Mor, and no other. If these bodies were destroyed, smashed beyond recognition, Noorlythin could never use them, perhaps to appear again before the McCanahan in the guise of an officer or beautiful woman.

Kael gripped his club more firmly and walked slowly down the long rows of coffers. At each dais, he paused a little while and did what had to be done. Once he stripped a man and donned the uniform of the Senn Fleet, acquiring the rank of major.

He left Slyss until the last.

But when he stood there, looking down into that smooth face, eyeing the yellow hair that tumbled around the creamy shoulders, he could not nerve himself to the task at hand.

"I'll let her be. At least I know her as a cradle for Noorlythin. I'll be on my guard."

With a sword at his side and an addy-gun holstered to his service belt, the McCanahan dropped the club. He went to the doors and swung them open, and walked out into a long corridor hewn from living stone.

For nearly an hour he followed that corridor, travelling steadily upwards. He emerged into a palace guardroom whose rack-hung walls were filled with handguns and swords, with keen-edged axes and cloaks with the dragon of the Senn emblazoned on collar and breast.

And in the guard room, he found the High Mor waiting for him.

"It is better this way," said the High Mor. "Just the two of us, face to face. I thought it might be better, as Slyss, to lure you into a Senn trap, and then to pretend a rescue by my Sfarran guards just as they were about to torture you. I thought I might claim your allegiance that way."

The McCanahan showed his teeth. "And after you'd wormed the truth of my secret weapon out of me, you'd hang me to a rack with the metal hooks biting into my naked back, and pull on my legs until the hooks came out. After that—"

The High Mor waved a hand.

"There is no need of torture between us, Terran. Oh, at first I wanted your life. Your father stumbled on a Senn scientist who discovered that a certain microwave shattered a peculiar type glass much used by the Sfarri, due to sonic disturbances created in the atmosphere.

"Since the Sfarri are a race of robots, created by the Doyen so long ago that were I to tell you the number of years involved they would be meaningless to you, they are necessarily energized by machines. In those machines a klyptric tube, made of that glass, forms an antennae that picks up and transmits the power generated by the machine. It broadcasts it in wave-lengths attuned to the internal structure of the Sfarri."

"You tell me nothing new," Kael grated. "Most of that I learned myself from putting one and two and three together."

The High Mor threw back his jeweled cloak and rested a thigh on the edge of a gaming table. His eyes glittered brightly.

He said, "You are no fool, Terran, I do not underestimate you, believe me. I tell you this to explain why I felt it necessary to kill your father."

"And Captain Edmunds! And Cassy Garsson! And all the men who were in the *Eclipse* when your Sfarrans rayed her into a smoking ruin just outside the planetal orbit of Senorech!"

The High Mor gestured. His graceful white hands waved apology. "For all that, I am sorry. I made a mistake. Now I offer what I can to atone for my errors.

"Join me. Wear my dragon! To you, I promise such power as no man has ever dreamed. The wants of a Napoleon, or a Bral Kan of Procyon! Not even Gartillin Vo of Deneb, or Cygnis Hannon will outshine you in the splendor of your triumphs!

"Do you think I want to spend my time in this?" and here the High Mor gestured at his body. "I want to go back to the Temple of Sharrador where once I dwelt for many ages, worshipped and adored."

The McCanahan grinned. "You know I recognize you as Noorlythin?"

"You were in the chamber where I keep the bodies I use. I felt your presence."

Kael stared his surprise.

"I knew you watched," the High Mor went on. "I could have spoken to you there. But it is better to meet you this way, face to face, away from those reminders that I am not as you. In a humanoid body, I may speak with you, as man to man.

"Only this way can I hope to convince you that I offer you more than you can ever gain without me. I am no man. I am a god! A god of primal space! I have lived for eon piled upon eon, hunting and seeking through the stars, studying the worlds I found. On some I lived for ages, on others I dwelt, for only a little while. All those worlds, Kael McCanahan, I offer you!

"Be an emperor, Terran! Rule every planet in all space. The greatest jewels of Strae'eth or Vrann can by yours, to wear on your person or to be hung in ropes of diamonds about the neck of any woman in all space! Lead my battle fleets! On distant Sfar, my technicians shall make you a hundred billion Sfarrans to serve under your banner. They shall make the greatest warships that ply the starlanes, each one encrusted with your name!"

The McCanahan shivered. It was a prospect that shook a man loose from his moorings.

To rule the stars! To sit on a throne and gaze out at the peoples of the universe bowed before him. To have the faery women of Cygni and Flormaseron in a harem, waiting his pleasure.

It was a thought that would have appealed to nine men in ten. Kael McCanahan called himself a fool, but he turned his visions aside. "I want no conquests. I want no jewels. The only woman I want is Flaith. Where is she?"

THE High Mor sighed, "In a tower, well-guarded. No harm has come to her. No harm will come. I am no sadist to harm a woman. Not when what I seek is possessed by a man. Tell me, Terran. What is your price?"

"Peace! Friendship with Terra and the men of Terra. Let the Solar Combine send its traders to Senorech. Peace between the peoples of the stars."

The High Mor laughed. "I too, seek peace. A peace that will end with my dragon banner floating above the towers of New Washington, Terra. With your precious Solar Combine run by the Sfarri. I offer you a place in that peace, Kael McCanahan. A high place. The highest place of all! I am a god! I have no need of earthly things. You do.

"Give me your answer, Terran!"

For a moment, the temptation was there. But in that same moment, the McCanahan remembered the blasted *Eclipse*, and the dead Father he loved, and Captain Edmunds, straight and lean in his white Fleet uniform. A memory came to him of Cassy Garson and the kisses she had given him in a drifting galley on the Tigranian Sea. The High Mor was not human. He knew nothing of the loves and lusts, the fears and terrors of human beings. He was as far removed from the Senn and Terrans as man is from the ant.

"I answer—no! You'd blacken Earth with your rays and leave empty ruins. You'd take everything in space! And me—what of me?"

The High Mor smiled. "You would rule the universe!"

But Kael McCanahan shook his head stubbornly. "I cannot believe that. If I once tell you—"

Beware, Terran!

The Doyen thought warned him just in time.

The High Mor brought his hand out from under his cloak and he held a black-metal stinger in his fingers. It spat a stream of violent fire at the McCanahan.

Kael dove sideways. The tip of his finger sliced through the violet fire and it stung with the agony of seared nerve-ends. If full effect of that blast had touched him he would be writhing helplessly on the floor, his body one gigantic mass of pain.

He had seen the stinger turned on unregenerate killers. It softened them in a hurry.

His shoulder hit the edge of the table where the High Mor sat. The table upended, and the High Mor fell to the floor with him.

Kael put a hand to the throat of the other man and his fingers tightened and squeezed. It was like choking a bar of steel. The High Mor forced a laugh through his lips, and his body twisted like an uncoiling spring and forced the McCanahan from him.

"The Doyen warned you. I caught the thought they put in your brain! Well, let them play their game. They can only interfere with me when I use my Doyen powers to destroy you. I have other gifts to use!"

A fist dove at his face, but the McCanahan was a master at rough and tumble fighting. He slipped it and bored in. His fists drummed into the High Mor's belly, lifted and threw him back to rebound off the far wall.

A dozen weapons came tumbling down on the ruler of Senorech. A cloak swathed his flailing arms.

Kael stepped back, waiting.

That was where he made his mistake. For the High Mor slid to the floor in a crumpled heap, and the thing that was Noorlythin glowed and pulsed and moved its frosted tendrils, free of its fallen body.

As Noorlythin moved its tendrils, the floor fell away beneath the booted heels of the McCanahan. The walls of the guardroom went out of existence, and Kael was falling, falling.

Gird yourself, Terran! You go into sub-space where no other living thing can enter! Not even another Doyen to shield you from my wrath! For each Doyen has in him the seeds of material creation, and what one Doyen materializes, no other Doyen can disturb!

And the high, mocking laughter followed him down and down, into the eternal blackness where he fell.

CHAPTER SEVEN

A HOT sun blanketed his naked body. It blazed from a molten sky and cooked him where he lay on warm red rocks. Kael McCanahan lifted his head and stared at the searing desolation before him. Sand and rock, and the shale of evaporated seas, stretching like the finger of Time to infinity itself, outward to that blazing blue bowl of sky where the golden sun hung high, pouring down its heat.

He came to his feet and swayed with the pain that the heat was putting in his muscles.

Come to me! Come! Come!

He put trembling hands to his head, and again that sweet call sounded, with the siren lure of all the lost treasures of all space. He stumbled forward, hearing the summons in his brain, in every fiber of his being.

Come to my riches! Lift up your hands to the jewel that gives man everything he wants! Touch me! I am yours!

He was running across the hot sands that bit his naked feet with hot teeth, and over the sharp rocks that cut into his flesh until he bled. Dimly, he knew that nothing could help him now. That here he was cut off from everything that was sane.

This mad world was a creation of Noorlythin. His was the wild brain that dreamed the sands and the rocks and the awful desolation. His dream, that sun that cooked while it shone.

Sobbing, he ran. He fell to his knees, and he crawled.

With bleeding fingers he clawed at the rocks, making himself rise and run again.

It seemed to the man that had once been Kael McCanahan that he was running around a planet. The pain was part of him now. His muscles jerked in agony at every step, yet always he forced himself to run faster, faster, gulping down the hot desert air. That siren call was strong in his ears.

Run, Terran. Run to me!

He ran on and on, and now he saw the others, men like himself, running on bleeding feet, crawling when those feet were worn to cracked stumps. And before each of those men, or before Kael McCanahan's own eyes, gleamed—

The eye of Lirflane!

A globe of a red jewel it was, the eye. Imprisoned in its faceted surface were the dreams of a billion people. The man that looked on it saw the happiness he sought, and he fought to join himself to it, that his own dreams would add to the total of all the others. And on the dreams and on the flesh of these men who came to it, drawn by its siren voice and by the eternity of delight it promised, the eye of Lirflane feasted, waxed and swelled.

A man tried to claw at his legs as Kael McCanahan ran past him. Red eyes in a bloated face hurled hate at him, as his hand closed on his ankle.

The McCanahan shook himself free and ran on.

The eye was closer now.

It grew massive, transparent. In its redness, the redness of the hair of flaming Flaith beckoned. Her white body swayed and danced, and her throaty voice summoned him.

The McCanahan's arms shook as he put them out, trying to pull himself forward with handfuls of hot, desert air.

Now the Eye of Lirflane was before him, and all he could see was Flaith moving toward him, her arms wide and beckoning—

One step he moved, and another.

His hand went out, toward the gleaming red side of the monstrous jewel.

Come to me, Kael McCanahan! Come to the peace and the forgetfulness you have earned. Take me in your arms. Drink kisses from my lips!

The McCanahan sobbed.

He shook in torture more vivid than the agony in his feet and muscles.

"Not Flaith!" he cried. "Not Flaith! You—woman of the jewel! Witch woman of Lirflane! Not Flaith!"

He went to his knees, to anchor himself the better to the ground, against the siren call of the mighty Eye.

"No. Got to fight! Get free. Free..."

He fought there on his knees, while men streamed past him, rushing with insane desire into the red heaven of the jewel. Their eyes were mad with the greed or the lust that shook them, for every man saw in the Eye of Lirflane what his own eyes wanted most to see. Their bodies were torn and gaunt from their struggle across the sand and rock desolation.

But they would lose their pain, within the bosom of the red eye.

Kael fought. He fought silently, until the sweat came out on his face in big globes, until it runneled down his chest and thighs. His belly and his back were awash with the salt dampness.

At last he turned, just a little, so that only a corner of the fabulous Eye remained in his vision.

An hour later, he turned again, and now he saw only the barren loneliness of this abandoned world. And as he stared, the sand and the rocks and the sky ran with liquid movement as a painting might run in a bath of chemicals. And the streaming reds and buffs and yellows, the black and the greens and purples flowed together and formed a river, that swept the tortured legs of the McCanahan out from under him.

HE SCREAMED in his agony as the salt water bit into his bleeding wounds. He babbled and twisted, flailing the salt sea with animal desperation. He drowned in this vast emptiness of ocean, with no hand to grasp his or eye to witness his going.

"No," he shouted to the gray leaden sky above him. "I won't die! I'll live! I'll live!"

His arms and his legs moved, and clumsily, he swam. No driftwood floated here. Here a man had to swim to stay alive, until his arms and his legs grew numb with his effort, and he sank.

The McCanahan turned on his back, and the salt water buoyed him up. He floated for endless days, and during endless nights, and the tiny spark of life within him waxed and waned. And out of the eternity of no-time, as he swam and alternately floated, a wing-prowed galley slipped through the foam-crested waves. Its white sail bellied in the ocean wind. It veered and came for him, running easily in the water.

From the rail, a bearded face scowled down at him. A hairy hand threw a rope that he twisted around his middle. He was dragged on deck, to stand dripping with the salt water that seared his wounds.

A rope was whipped around his wet wrists and he was dragged to the slim mast that rose from the deck, before the oarbanks where slaves pulled at smooth-handled oars.

A woman whose flesh was tinted a delicate green came toward him. She walked with quick, supple strides, and the McCanahan noted numbly that her eyes were a feral green, and that her tiny ears were pointed. A whip coiled in her hand.

She showed her tiny teeth in a cruel smile.

"You are the man from Terra! You are the one who turned down all the worlds of space! For that you must be punished!"

And the long lash went snaking out in an arc, slashing into his back, and the sheer agony of the cutting whip slammed his body against the mast. The lash came down and lifted, came down and lifted, and the McCanahan sagged in the ropes that held him.

With the cruelty of her species, the catwoman flogged him. When she was done, she cut him loose and stood over him on the swaying deck that was stained with his blood. Her voice was soft, furry.

"Take him and chain him to an oar! Rivet the manacles on his wrists and ankles! Let him tug an oar for a year! Then perhaps he will obey Him who is ALL!"

He was kicked and shoved across the deck. He tumbled into an empty slot on an oarbench. His wrists and ankles were shackled, the armorer not caring where his metal mallet fell.

For a day he rested, with black bread soaked in wine forced between his teeth. For a day, he knew only the blessedness of not moving. His slumber was dreamless—

In a red dawn, he was wakened by the bite of an overseer's whip across his bloody back. His hands lifted and went to the oar-handle, and his body swayed and returned, and he put his weight with the weight of the men who held the same oar as he.

The galley slipped through the heaving ocean, and the red oars flashed in the sun and the salt spray stung, and only when an errant wind swept across the seas was there any rest for the men who slaved on the benches. Sometimes men died, and were flung overboard. Other men were unshackled and dragged screaming to the foredeck where the catwoman waited, pink tongue licking her lips, the whip curling like a live thing in her hands.

And of all the men who worked the oars in this endless ocean, it was the McCanahan who was chosen most often for her amusement.

Once he almost died under the biting whip, and in that moment of pain and numbness, when his senses seemed about to float from his body, the catwoman leaned close and her furry voice whispered, "Speak your secret to me, man of Terra! Tell me the weapon that slays the Sfarri!"

But the McCanahan only shook his head and his hair, long uncut, tumbled on his bleeding shoulders.

The days were endless on that ocean, and the oars swung and the sail creaked, flapping overhead, and the overseer tramped the runway with endless patience, his voice a sullen growl. The catwoman came to look upon the McCanahan and her slim greenish fingers came forth to stroke his naked back where her lash had marred it. Always her throaty voice whispered to him, speaking of the delights that might be found in her cabin, if only he were not so stubborn.

When her patience was at an end, she motioned to the overseer and he came with armed guards and unchained the McCanahan, and he was led to the mast and roped.

And then, in the middle of a whipsting, the ocean and the ship and the catwoman's whip fell away...

HE LAY on a hard, cold floor. The High Mor stood before him, his hard eyes glittering. Kael was back in the guardroom that he had left—how long ago?

"A year," said the High Mor, reading his thought. "A year and five days! And yet, the barest split second of Time. I sent you out to those worlds of subspace, Kael McCanahan. There you lived, and almost died. You rowed at a real oar. You suffered the cuts of a real whip. Look at yourself!"

The High Mor threw a small metal mirror at him. Dazedly he stared at the grim, hard brown face and the cold blue eyes he saw mirrored on its surface. His flesh was brown, and great muscles swelled under it. The oar had put those muscles there, as the whip put the scars on his ribs and back.

"Only a split second of our time, Terran," said the High Mor. "But a year and five days in the worlds I made! I told you I had gifts! I have made a thousand million worlds for that subspace, in the eons that I have roamed the stars. I am a god!"

Kael shook his head and his long hair flicked his naked arms. If he needed proof of the High Mor's words, his long uncut hair was proof enough.

He thought: Tell him, and let him have his way! How can a man fight a god? The thought washed over him that he fought for all mankind, that the men and women of a thousand planets unknowingly depended on his fight. Women like the flame-tressed Flaith, men like his father and

Captain Edmunds, who did their duty and died for it, all depended on what he did.

He had to think, to go over this logically. What would be the thought processes of a god? A god was no mere mortal, to be judged and weighed by human wants and failings. In it there was no mercy, no thought for anything but itself.

Kael pushed himself away from the floor to stand on long brown legs.

Courage, man of Terra! He shall not trap you so again!

The Doyen voice gave him heart, but the High Mor sneered.

"I heard it, too, Terran! The Doyen cannot help you. Not unless I strive by Doyen means to kill you. I need not do that, Kael McCanahan, need I?"

The McCanahan shook his head like a dumb animal. He would never go back to that subspace where Noorlythin was a god, in truth! To that hell, where a second was a year, where the Doyen themselves could not enter!

"I could put you there again, Terran. I could forget you, let you live out your life for an eternity of seconds that are years! Would you listen to reason then? Would you like to test your will again against that of the Eye of Lirflane? Or feel once more the lash of Vigrette, the catwoman? No, I read in your eyes that you would not!

"Come, then. Tell me how you made the Sfarri die!"

Speak, man of Terra! Tell Noorlythin what he seeks! Only then, as he absorbs the knowledge, can we reach him!

The McCanahan shrugged the great shoulders that were scarred with the lash above the smooth roll of their bulging muscles. His head hung so that his uncut hair shielded his face.

"The harp," he whispered. "On the harp of Brith Tsinan is a silver string. The d-note! I strung it with a silvern wire that I loosed from my father's wrist!"

And as he spoke, he moved.

As liquid as the falling waters in the Veil of Valmoora was the leap of the McCanahan. Full into the High Mor he hurtled, knocking him sideways. And as they went down together—

The Doyen struck!

The very rocks of the palace misted and swirled under that awesome clutching. White fire flared and seared, and where it touched, all matter was destroyed! The walls of the palace shook and quivered. Beams groaned under the sudden stress.

Where the guardroom had been, was empty nothingness!

In a flame that lapped him protectingly as it flared fiercely and strongly at Noorlythin himself, the Doyen carried both men upward. So swift was their transmission through normal space that in one blinding surge of the white flame, the McCanahan found himself between the worlds, in some lost, dark blotch of empty space.

"No Doyen may slay another Doyen!"

That voice rang triumphantly in the abyss.

"There is a way, Noorlythin! That is why we have let you work your will on this man. He hates you with a deadly hate, Noorlythin. Yon put him in your worlds of subspace, and you abandoned him to the creatures of your own creation!"

"Aie! I abandoned him! Were it not for him and his harp, I would reign as a god on every planet in all inhabited space. The Solar Combine would have fallen to my Sfarran battle fleet!"

"You dared not move before you knew the one weapon that might defeat you!"

"Now I know! Now! Now!"

The radiant energy in the thing that was Noorlythin was awful. It beat and flared redly through the whiteness. The McCanahan shuddered as its heat beat out at him, chilling even as it seared.

Courage, Terran! Courage for what lies ahead!

And now the voices shrank and whispered, piping like elfin horns within his head, that none but he could hear.

Through you, we may destroy him! Courage! With your help, he dies—forever!

He knew what he had to do. Of his free will he had to offer himself to Noorlythin! Of his free will, he had to fling himself into the mad embrace of those pulsing tendrils, that had turned Lunol the peddler to black and drifting dust!

He gave you to the Eye of Lirflane! He gave you to the catwoman and her whip!

The McCanahan snarled. "Destroy him, and I save the Solar Combine! I hear you, Doyen. I hear and I obey!"

And Kael McCanahan flung himself headlong, forward into the white whirlwind of force that was Noorlythin.

IN THE Chamber of Living Death, she who had been Slyss of Aakan quivered fitfully. A bubble of froth broke from her red lips. She moaned and stirred. A hand lifted, struggled feebly, fell back to her side, limp and waxen.

Slyss opened brown eyes. She lay silent, staring upward at the ceiling. A sob fought its way upward from her throat.

"Noorlythin is dead! His control over me and the others—gone forever!"

She rolled off the dais and stared around her, at the dead bodies. She shivered. She went to the doors and pulled them open. In the distance, she could hear the frightened roaring of terrified men. She began to run.

Flaith shook the bars of the cell that held her. Her red hair made a living flame about her shoulders.

"What is happening? What is it?" she screamed.

A terrified jailer paused in his heavy run past her cell.

"The palace is falling in! The High Mor is dead. His body has been found!"

Flaith shook the barred door.

"Let me out! Please, please! Give me a chance to save myself!"

The jailer licked his lips. He glanced up and down the corridor, then slid the key into the lock. The door opened under a push from his hand. "If the High Mor is dead," he told the girl, "maybe the Sfarri won't stay here on Senorech! Maybe the Senn can rule themselves, now."

Flaith caught the man by his arm.

"The one I was captured with! Kael McCanahan, the Earther! Where is he?"

"Nobody knows! His cell is empty."

"His harp? Man, where is his harp?"

The jailer shook himself free and started down the corridor. Over his shoulder he called, "Look in the storehouse beyond the cell block. We keep all prisoners' effects in there!"

Terran! Wake to life, Kael McCanahan!

He was dead. He had thrown himself into the fiery maw of the thing that was Noorlythin. Who called him now? Who spoke these lies?

You live, Terran. You served as the catalyst that enabled us to focus our powers against Noorlythin.

Even a high school student knew that a catalyst retained its own identity during the chemical change it brought about between two substances; even such substances as were the Doyen, gods of space.

Kael opened his eyes.

He lay on a floor in the wreckage of the guardroom in the palace of Akkalam. In the distance, but growing closer, he heard the faint strumming of harpstrings. He lay there and listened to the harp, as life flowed stronger into his body.

The strumming came nearer.

The McCanahan stood up and he waited, big and brown, marked with scars.

Flaith stood in the broken doorway, her fingers falling from the harp. Tears had formed twin channels from her red-lashed eyes along her cheeks. When she saw Kael, she did not know him. And then he grinned, and his long hair and scarred brown body were forgotten.

She flung herself at him, and lay against him, trembling.

He told her of the High Mor and what he had been, and of how the Doyen had destroyed him. "We've won, Flaith. He's dead, forever. With the harp—and the vibrators that we'll build to duplicate its pitch—the Solar Combine will move on Sfar. Smash it, and its robot life!"

Laughter bubbled in her throat as she looked up at him. "They'll reward you, Kael. Make you somebody big on Terra!"

The McCanahan grinned and hugged her.

"An admiral at least! How would you like to be wed to an admiral, Flaith mavourneen?"

Her answer rocked him, in the hunger of her mouth on his.

THE END

If you've enjoyed this book, you will not want to miss these terrific titles…

ARMCHAIR SCI-FI & HORROR DOUBLE NOVELS, $12.95 each

D-11 **PERIL OF THE STARMEN** by Kris Neville
THE STRANGE INVASION by Murray Leinster

D-12 **THE STAR LORD** by Boyd Ellanby
CAPTIVES OF THE FLAME by Samuel R. Delany

D-13 **MEN OF THE MORNING STAR** by Edmond Hamilton
PLANET FOR PLUNDER by Hal Clement and Sam Merwin, Jr.

D-14 **ICE CITY OF THE GORGON** by Chester S. Geier and Richard Shaver
WHEN THE WORLD TOTTERED by Lester del Rey

D-15 **WORLDS WITHOUT END** by Clifford D. Simak
THE LAVENDER VINE OF DEATH by Don Wilcox

D-16 **SHADOW ON THE MOON** by Joe Gibson
ARMAGEDDON EARTH by Geoff St. Reynard

D-17 **THE GIRL WHO LOVED DEATH** by Paul W. Fairman
SLAVE PLANET by Laurence M. Janifer

D-18 **SECOND CHANCE** by J. F. Bone
MISSION TO A DISTANT STAR by Frank Belknap Long

D-19 **THE SYNDIC** by C. M. Kornbluth
FLIGHT TO FOREVER by Poul Anderson

D-20 **SOMEWHERE I'LL FIND YOU** by Milton Lesser
THE TIME ARMADA by Fox B. Holden

ARMCHAIR SCIENCE FICTION CLASSICS, $12.95 each

C-4 **CORPUS EARTHLING**
by Louis Charbonneau

C-5 **THE TIME DISSOLVER**
by Jerry Sohl

C-6 **WEST OF THE SUN**
by Edgar Pangborn

ARMCHAIR SCI-FI & HORROR GEMS SERIES, $12.95 each

G-1 **SCIENCE FICTION GEMS, Vol. One**
Isaac Asimov and others

G-2 **HORROR GEMS, Vol. One**
Carl Jacobi and others